D1453893

THE **WITCH** OF **GRAY'S POINT**

LORESTALKER - Book 3

J.P. BARNETT

THE WITCH OF GRAY'S POINT
Lorestalker – 3
Copyright © 2019 by J.P. Barnett

All rights reserved. No part of this book may be used or reproduced in any manner whatsoever, without written permission, except in the case of brief quotations embedded in articles and reviews. For more information, please contact publisher at Publisher@EvolvedPub.com.

FIRST EDITION SOFTCOVER
ISBN: 1622530845
ISBN-13: 978-1-62253-084-7

Editor: Mike Robinson
Cover Artist: Richard Tran
Interior Designer: Lane Diamond

EVOLVED PUBLISHING™
www.EvolvedPub.com
Butler, Wisconsin, USA

The Witch of Gray's Point is a work of fiction. All names, characters, places, and incidents are the product of the author's imagination, or are used fictitiously. Any resemblance to actual events or persons, living or dead, is entirely coincidental.

Printed in Book Antiqua font.

Praise for the "Lorestalker" Series

THE BEAST OF ROSE VALLEY:

"...a marvelous romp into the little-known world of cryptozoology... plot is clever and irresistible, and his book is a sheer pleasure to read. Horror, thriller and mystery fans alike will find much to their liking in this intriguing story about the unknown. ...most highly recommended."

~ *Jack Magnus for Readers' Favorite (5 STARS)*

~~~

"Intrigue, curiosity, surprises, and the depth of the plot will keep you on the edge of your sea... As the first book in the Lorestalker series, *The Beast of Rose Valley* certainly sets a high bar for those to follow."

~ *K.J. Simmill for Readers' Favorite (5 STARS)*

~~~

"Barnett is a fluent storyteller and I found myself gripped to the last page."

~ *Lit Amri for Readers' Favorite (5 STARS)*

THE KRAKEN OF CAPE MADRE:

"Along the way, the real power of the horror novel kicks in more and more, and what might seem like a slow burner soon becomes an inferno of action, terror and frightening realities revealed... an excellent addition to the horror genre: a read not to be missed."

~ *K.C. Finn for Readers' Favorite (5 STARS)*

~~~

"Fans of monsters and folklore are in for yet another treat... His fast-paced storytelling and the mystery and suspense of his monster keep readers intrigued and wanting to know more."

~ *Alicia Smock, Roll Out Reviews*

BOOKS BY J.P. BARNETT

The LORESTALKER Series
The Beast of Rose Valley
The Kraken of Cape Madre
The Witch of Gray's Point

...and more to come.
(Books 4-6 are contracted and in the planning stages.)

PROLOGUE

The others whispered in the darkness, but Ana kept mostly to herself, nestling her baby against her bosom and praying the journey would soon be over. An old, battery-operated radio crooned out the twangy tones of American country music from the floorboard of the van. She'd heard the song, but she couldn't understand the lyrics. Without a watch, she could only guess as to how long she'd been sitting like this. Hours, surely, but many more lay ahead.

With her free hand, she clutched tightly to the strap of her canteen, helpfully provided to her by the driver of the van. The water would be crucial to her survival. Each of them had one, but the pattern on hers uniquely swirled with purple and gray camouflage. She'd probably already drank too much.

Her baby squirmed in her arms. Thankfully, as if sensing the danger himself, he'd hardly made a sound the entire trip. Still, Ana heard the murmurings in the dark. The rest of the refugees referred to her baby as *desafortunado*, but he gave her the strength to escape. He was far from unlucky.

The van jostled as it turned off the pavement onto rougher terrain. The whispering stopped, each of them waiting, worrying about what could happen next. Ana held her breath, trying to hear anything outside the thin metal walls around her, but she could make out nothing except the metallic tings of gravel striking the undercarriage.

There were soft gasps when the van came to a sudden, screeching stop. Like Ana, they all knew that they couldn't possibly have arrived at their destination yet.

Within moments, the double doors swung open. A beam of light burst across the darkness, blinding Ana. The light searched the faces, one by one. Ana's heart stopped when the light fell on her.

"*Tú. Ven,*" said the shadowed man on the other end of the flashlight.

Ana looked to those next to her, desperate to believe that he'd spoken to them instead, but all eyes were on her. When she didn't immediately move to exit the van, the man grabbed her upper arm. Not hard, but forcefully enough that she moved without putting up a fight.

Meekly, she protested that they surely could not have arrived already. The man didn't seem to care. Once Ana's feet squarely hit the gravel, he retrieved her canteen and dropped it on the ground next to her. After slamming the van doors shut, he pointed up the road to the faint lights of a house sitting alone in the desert.

"*Ve allí.*"

"*No,*" she begged. "*Éste no fue el acuerdo.*"

"*Lo sé,*" he admitted, casting his eyes downward. "*Lo siento.*"

With his half-hearted apology, he quickly rounded the van, jumped into the driver's seat, and pulled away. Ana slammed her free hand against the doors and screamed before it surged out of her reach. Her baby, for the first time since they had crossed the border, cried.

As the taillights disappeared into the darkness, Ana scanned the horizon, hoping to find any semblance of civilization aside from the house at the end of the gravel road. She found nothing. Only the foreboding shadows of scrub trees and cacti barely visible under the light of a crescent moon. She pulled her baby closer to her chest, trying to decide whether she should walk into the darkness or towards the house.

Something moved in the corner of her eye. Near one of the small trees sat a dog—or a coyote—on its haunches, regarding her with a calm but unsettling stare. She turned towards it, taking in its size. Its form was bigger than she expected, surely larger than any coyote. But it wasn't its size that stopped Ana's breath; it was its strange, human-like face, flat and white, full of depth and understanding no animal could possess.

She took a step forward and screamed at the animal, but it did not falter. Her baby howled now, surely sensing her unease. The dog cocked its oddly-shaped head at the sound of the baby, then stood up. Not on all fours, as Ana expected, but on two strong, furry legs with knees that bent backwards.

It started towards her, and she ran.

Scrambling down the road, she was certain that anything under that house's roof would be better than this abomination from hell. A kind of garbled crack sounded behind her, like a bone breaking underwater. Glancing back, she saw the creature was on all fours now, its limbs more canine even as its face remained... wrong. Ana shrieked and stumbled down to one knee, stopping just short of smashing her baby into the ground.

Up in an instant, she rushed forward. The house sat only a few feet away. She could see the wooden steps; could feel the warm glow of the lights on her face even as she felt the dog gaining on her, nipping at her heels. She whispered a prayer and stretched her legs as far as they would go, advancing towards safety with every hurried step.

Then—it was gone.

She didn't see it disappear, but could tell it was no longer there. Stopping at the bottom of the steps, she turned to make sure. She jumped as a near-silent owl barreled towards her face, letting out a piercing screech. As she cradled her baby tighter, it crested the peak of the roof, and disappeared into the desert night.

The gravel road stretched back towards the highway, eerily desolate. Ana tried to catch her breath, her heart beating against the soft skin of her baby. Tears streamed down her cheeks. Her chest filled with dread at the prospect of whoever lived on the other side of this house's front door. She had no choice, though. She needed shelter from the terrors of the desert.

Mustering her resolve, Ana slowly ascended the steps towards an empty porch. An old, beat-up swing hung silent and frozen in the still air. The window in the door had no coverings, giving her an unfettered view into a cozy-but-rustic cabin peppered with olive and mustard furniture. The mounted head of a buck stared at her from above the fireplace.

Shushing her baby, Ana raised a free hand to knock on the door, but before her knuckles met the hard wood, the door slid open with a creak. A man stood in the doorway, his elongated frame swallowing the light behind him, and bathing Ana in shadow.

She craned her neck, regarding him with dark brown eyes. Though she couldn't make out all of his features, she could see a thin, graying mustache and old, kind eyes. His lips curled up into a welcoming smile as he widened his arms.

"*Ana Marie! Bienvenida. Estoy tan contento de que hayas llegado.*"

His voice sounded familiar, though she didn't recognize his silhouette. Still, she felt safe, as if this man could protect her from the horrors of the world. She stepped into his arms and he embraced her like family, careful to give the baby room to breathe.

He stroked the back of her head. "It's okay, dear. Everything will be fine."

She barely knew English, only understanding the word *okay*. But the tone of his voice felt genuine. He backed away from the hug and stepped aside.

"*Ven. Rápida.* It's not safe out at this hour."

Reluctant, Ana carried her baby across the threshold of the mysterious house, and into a new life.

CHAPTER 1

Campus seemed quieter than usual, abandoned by students holing up in their dorm rooms trying to cram a semester's worth of material in a few days. Miriam liked it better this way.

Though there were few trees to speak of on the outskirts of West Texas, she still enjoyed the stern, scholastic beauty of the concrete and brick. Usually, though, drunk co-eds and childish pranks marred any such sanctity. Dobie Tech boasted the dubious distinction of being a "party school."

She almost hated to leave campus when it was this quiet, but she had a road trip before her. Miriam didn't have her own transportation, so when she needed to go anywhere by car, she had no choice but to turn to Macy Donner, her best friend and proud owner of a beat-up Sentra that, while not much to look at, certainly got the job done.

The Sentra now sat on the curb, hazard lights flashing while Miriam loaded up for the trip. Macy rushed past her and popped open the trunk.

"What if we get a case?" Macy asked, standing aside so that Miriam could heft up her bags.

"We dealt with the kraken over two months ago," Miriam replied. "And we haven't gotten a single call. Cryptids don't just pop up every day."

Macy shrugged. "I dunno. They seem to follow you."

Miriam offered a faint smirk. It certainly felt that way sometimes, with two unbelievable encounters under her belt in just a couple of years. As thrilling as the hunt was, though, Miriam found herself enjoying the downtime, focusing on school and planning out her future. She'd get back to tracking monsters eventually, of course—it's what she was made for—but everyone deserved a breather.

"At least tell me where you're going," Macy said. "In case I need to come get you."

"Nope," Miriam said. She dropped her backpack in and closed the trunk. "It's my super-secret study place. I need the quiet."

"Yeah, but I hate when you go there. You don't ever answer your texts."

"No service. That's the beauty of it."

Macy pouted, a move she somehow pulled off without seeming infantile. "Fine. Keep your secrets."

Miriam had fallen hopelessly behind in school after slaying the kraken in Cape Madre. She'd spent weeks studying the carcass, and her professors didn't seem to want to count that towards her grade even though she made a valiant effort to convince them otherwise. Still, her exploits impressed some of them enough to throw her a few bones in the way of extra time on her projects, and some unscheduled office hours. Success wasn't completely out of reach yet, but Miriam desperately wanted to get her head back above water. She didn't like flirting with failure.

"I'll check in," Miriam relented. "Okay? I'll call at least once. I promise. It's only four days."

Macy nodded and followed Miriam as she rounded the car to the driver's side. Dropping down into her seat, she looked up at Macy. "Tell Tanner good luck on his first final."

"I'll tell him," Macy said. "If he'll let me get close to him. He says I'm a distraction."

One of many who would likely describe Macy that way. Miriam closed the door, started the ignition, and rolled down the window. Macy stooped down to look inside. "Take care of my baby. She's the only car I've got."

"She's the only car I've got, too, so don't worry."

Macy laughed in her effortless way. "All right. Well good luck then, I guess. See you Tuesday?"

"Yep. Tuesday."

Macy stood and backed away. The Sentra protested as Miriam hit the gas, but quickly started down the path. She glanced in the rear-view mirror where Macy stood in the road waving. She waved back.

As she put Dobie Tech's sprawling campus behind her, Miriam shifted into solo mode. She'd learned to adequately approximate social interactions much better in recent months, but she still craved complete and utter aloneness. These study trips invigorated her; helped her navigate normal life. She envisioned herself curled up on the old bed with a textbook in one hand and, though the weather seldom called for it, a warm mug of hot chocolate in the other.

Her secret destination lay in the deserts of West Texas, surrounded by scrub bushes and trees barely scraping by to survive. Her father's abandoned ranch, where scorpions and rattlesnakes and coyotes stalked the shadows. She relished having no communication with the outside world, though that carried its own risks.

Of course, he had no idea that she visited the ranch so often, and would certainly forbid it. Since the death of her brother, Miriam and her father had become hopelessly estranged, and Skylar Brooks had gone to extreme measures to strip Miriam of everything he'd ever given her. That surely included access to the ranch, but the spare key still hid in the same place, and Miriam used it without guilt. She felt that it was the least the bastard could do for her.

As far as she knew, her father hadn't been to the ranch in almost ten years. He'd bought it to investigate reports of skinwalkers, which, even at twelve years old, Miriam thought was ridiculous. She could believe in animals that science had never stumbled upon, but shapeshifters? Biology just didn't support that. And a skinwalker wasn't an animal anyway, if the Native American myths were to be believed.

As she merged onto the highway, the wind whipped through the window, stinging her face and tousling her hair. She smiled. In a few hours, she'd have to focus on biology textbooks, but for now she enjoyed the hum of the road and the blue expanse of the sky, empty but for a few scattered clouds.

Minutes melted into hours, Miriam's serenity growing with each mile. It almost surprised her when she came upon the turn-off as quickly as she did. By then, the sun was waning, basking the entire ranch in a wondrous shade of purple and orange. The Sentra's balding tires objected to the bumps, and the gravel sounded like it might shoot through the floorboard, but Miriam managed to make it up the driveway. As she drew closer, however, her bliss came crashing down: in her normal parking space sat a garish yellow Jeep.

Miriam swallowed hard, gritting her teeth. She threw the old car in reverse and, facing the highway once more, gunned it, the tires making an awful racket as they struggled for traction. In the rear-view mirror, she saw someone step onto the old wooden porch—a person that she'd never met, but whose face she'd seen on her father's website. A person her father had hired to replace his lost children. She didn't even know the guy on the porch, and she already hated him. He represented so much of what was wrong in her life. For two years, she'd managed to avoid contact with her father, and now she'd almost driven right into a confrontation with him.

Hopefully he didn't see her. With any luck, he would write her off as a lost tourist who'd turned down the wrong path. The man on the porch didn't move, a perplexed look on his face as he watched her drive away.

Miriam took a deep breath. It would be embarrassing to explain why she'd decided to head back to campus, but any awkwardness there far outweighed the agony of having to deal with the painful memories of her childhood and of her dead brother.

She could see the highway just ahead.

Before she could make it through the stone pillars flanking the exit, though, another yellow Jeep turned into the driveway, blocking her escape. Miriam stood on the brake and froze as her eyes met the driver's. His small, alert eyes still judged her as they always had, and he still had that stupid handlebar mustache.

There was no way out. All the ignored calls. All the pleas filtered through Tanner. She couldn't avoid it any longer, even though she didn't feel ready to work through the issues between her and the man sitting in that Jeep. Miriam would happily confront any vicious predator in the wild, but she had a knack for avoiding emotional pain, and her plans had called for her to ignore this forever.

Nevertheless, Miriam had inadvertently wandered into the Brooks family reunion from hell.

CHAPTER 2

Gabe scratched at his dark beard, studying the taillights of the old, worn-down Sentra pulling away from him. Probably only a confused tourist. With so few roads across the interstate, wrong turns were fairly common. He'd only been at the ranch for a few days, but it'd already happened three times. Poor *chica* probably didn't know how to get anywhere without her precious phone telling her where to go.

When the boss-man turned into the driveway and cut off the Sentra, Gabe laughed. "Hey Brynn," he hollered through the door. "Wanna go have some fun with a lost tourist?"

A girl of above-average height squeezed past Gabe and glanced down the driveway. With her hair too short to support a proper ponytail, a blonde strand escaped and brushed against her cheek. She pushed it up over her ear. "Don't be an ass, Gabe. Probably just needs directions."

"Directions to where? Go west. Go east. There's only two choices."

Brynn rolled her eyes, but Gabe ignored her and bounded down the steps towards the standoff between the tiny Sentra and the boss-man's comparatively huge Jeep. By the time he got there, the two drivers had exited their vehicles and stood silently facing one another. The tourist wore faded jeans and a plain colored t-shirt. She looked fit, capable, and a lot less lost than Gabe expected.

Skylar Brooks seemed spooked in a way that Gabe hadn't seen through the handful of expeditions they'd gone on together. Generally, Gabe could count on his boss to be cool-headed and in-control, though sometimes a bit boorish.

"Everything okay, boss-man?" Gabe asked.

Skylar's eyes shifted away from the tourist. "Everything's fine, Gabe. I'd like you to meet someone."

She turned around, frowning, her expression stern. Her light brown eyes almost matched her mousy hair. Her shoulders were wide and strong, but balanced out her thin, but pear-shaped figure. The confidence in her stance, and the anger in her eyes, intrigued him. This girl was more than a tourist. In fact, she looked eerily familiar, though Gabe knew he'd never met her.

Skylar made the introduction. "Gabe Castillo. This is my daughter, Miriam."

Oh damn. That's right. Gabe had seen her on television. So this was the mighty slayer of the kraken? She hardly looked capable of the task, but he supposed with the proper training maybe she could have pulled it off. Lucky for her, she happened to be in Cape Madre when the most significant cryptid discovery in a century surfaced in the Gulf of Mexico.

Gabe took a few steps toward her and offered his hand. "Hey. How's it goin'?"

"Been better," she said with a sigh and sideways glance, before firmly shaking his hand.

"So, Miriam," Skylar said as he walked up beside her. "Will you be staying with us for a bit?"

"No," she snapped. "I've gotta get back to school. Finals coming up."

Gabe watched the two of them, carefully noting an inaudible conversation conveyed through their eyes, vitriol from Miriam and something more indescribable from Skylar. Gabe didn't like where this headed. The goal was to investigate the skinwalkers. Not whether his employer deserved a father of the year award.

Skylar clicked his tongue and turned back to the Jeep. Before climbing up, he regarded Miriam. "Ah. A shame. With all the recent skinwalker sightings out here, I thought you might be interested in lending your... expertise."

Gabe couldn't help but notice the massive amount of emotional baggage dripping off that last word. But hey, the girl had killed a giant octopus. Anyone who could do that could surely assist in tracking down something as enigmatic as... well, whatever they might wind up having to track down.

"Recent?" she asked.

Skylar hauled himself up on the running board and peered over the door at his daughter. "Why don't you come up to the house? We'll fill you in. If you don't wanna stay, that's fine. Just give it a few minutes."

Without waiting for a response, he dropped fully into the Jeep, fired up the engine, and drove through the scrub brush around Miriam and her car. She slouched down and issued an audible sigh.

"Tell him I said thanks, but no thanks," she said.

Gabe flashed a smile. "I'll tell him, but I think you should really consider it. We got full on pandemonium out here right now."

"He's always convinced there's something, but he never finds anything. Can't you see he's just a con-artist?"

"He killed that beast thing up in Rose Valley," Gabe responded.

"No he didn't. He hid behind his Jeep like a little kid." Miriam fumed. "I killed that thing."

Gabe considered her response. His boss could be bombastic, prideful, and sometimes stretched the facts in his favor. Could it be true that she pulled the trigger that brought it down?

Maybe. Gabe could see it.

"Look, I wasn't there," he offered. "But, seriously. I think this time might be different."

"And why is that?" she asked.

"Because I've seen'em. With my own eyes. And my mom saw'em, too. They're out here."

The anger in Miriam's eyes faded away just a little, her mouth twisting up thoughtfully. She'd have no reason to believe him, Gabe realized, but he could only speak the truth. Whatever messed up relationship she had with her father, the fact remained that she surely loved this game as much as he. As much as Skylar or Brynn. And Miriam had at least one legitimate kill under her belt. Maybe two.

"Come on," he urged. "What do you say? I'll stay with ya. Make sure you don't have to spend any time alone with him."

Miriam rolled her eyes. "Fine. Get in."

***

Crammed around the kitchen table, Gabe sized up the situation. Skylar had never really talked much about Miriam, though Gabe vaguely knew about Cornelius' death at the hands of an unbelievable science experiment. But given current information,

Gabe questioned whether he could trust anything Skylar had told him. He'd spent more time with his boss than this new girl, but, somehow, she still seemed considerably more trustworthy.

Gabe jockeyed to make sure he sat by Miriam on the creaky wooden bench, leaving Brynn and Skylar across the table. He intended to fulfill his promise of keeping Miriam separated from her father.

Brynn offered a slender hand across the table and trained her intense hazel eyes on Miriam. "I'm Brynn Kerrison."

Taking Brynn's hand, Miriam mumbled, "The new me?"

Gabe chuckled. No one else at the table laughed.

"What about the other one?" Miriam asked. "Don't you have another team member?"

Skylar looked entirely too pleased with her question. Miriam had messed up. Her question implied that she'd spent some time internet-stalking the team. Surely she knew better than to flatter Skylar's vanity. Even Gabe knew that much, and he'd only been on the job for a year.

Gabe quickly jumped in, trying to diffuse whatever vile comment threatened to unroll from Skylar's tongue. "K-Dawg. Er. Kent, I mean. He had a final or something like that. Something nerdy."

"It's no matter," Skylar said. "Let's get down to business."

"Did you see that gas station down the road on your way in?" Gabe asked Miriam.

"Uh. Yeah. Looked closed."

"It's not," Brynn interjected. "It's just gone downhill since the owner's wife died."

"To skinwalkers?" Miriam asked.

"No. Heart attack. Unrelated."

Skylar seemed curiously quiet, his eyes trained on Miriam with an awkward intensity.

Gabe jumped back in. "After his wife died, though, he was working in the store. Doing stocking and stuff, I guess, he says. And he saw her."

"His wife?" Miriam asked, somewhat incredulously.

"Yep."

Skylar finally spoke. "He says that his wife stared him down through the front window. Then she smiled at him. When he moved towards her, she melted away."

"So he's mourning," Miriam replied. "Hallucinating. Wishing. Doesn't mean he saw a skinwalker."

"Yeah, yeah, yeah," Gabe said. "But when he went outside, there was a rattlesnake there. Right where his wife was standing."

Brynn finished the thought. "He said his wife just crumpled down to the ground and then there's a rattlesnake right there? Shapeshifting, maybe?"

Miriam seemed dubious, and Gabe couldn't really blame her.

"Surely you've got more than that to go on. Are you that desperate for a score?" Miriam's question was clearly aimed at Skylar.

Skylar ruffled himself, as he tended to do when he got annoyed. "Of course not. It's just the first of many in recent months."

Miriam turned back towards Gabe. "What about the rattlesnake?"

"Slithered away. He chased it around the corner of his station, but when he got there, nothing."

"Nothing?" Miriam asked. "Even if we're going to pretend that an animal can change its shape, surely we can all agree that it can't disappear entirely."

"Okay," Brynn said. "Let's talk about the second report then."

"Hope it's better than this, or I'm outta here."

Brynn continued, "A guy was rolling through here about a week ago in his Dodge Ram. He saw a dog on the side of the road, but as he got closer, something seemed off about it. He said it had a human face. And it was big. Like, way bigger than any coyote out here."

Gabe joined in. "Right. And when he passed it, it followed him, and in his rearview, he saw it take off after him and before he could even react, it jumped into the bed of his truck, even though he was going highway speeds."

Skylar stood up from the bench and moved to the kitchen where a messenger bag sat on the formica countertop. He rifled through it, while Brynn picked up the story.

"He said it tried to get in the back window, and when it couldn't, it started digging at the bed of his truck. Eventually, the guy just brake-checked the thing, slamming it into the cab. That dazed it a little, he said, but then it jumped back out on the road and ran off."

Skylar returned and threw a handful of photos on the table that slid toward Miriam. Gabe moved to stop them from falling on the floor, but she beat him to it, scooping up the stack and cycling through them one by one.

Gabe leaned over so he could see each one. "That one's a view from inside the cab. You can see the back windshield shattered. And it looks like maybe some blood."

"Did you get a sample?" she asked.

"Nah. He washed his truck before we tracked him down. At least he took pictures, though."

She switched to the next one, highlighting the damage done to the bed of the truck. The picture showed dents and tears in the steel. The one after that just showed a stretch of highway.

"That's where he said he was when he saw it. He went back to take pictures the next day."

Miriam squinted and pointed to the corner of the picture. "Isn't that here?"

Gabe focused in on the blob of darker color in the distance. It was so far off and so faint that he could hardly make it out. Certainly, he couldn't confidently say that it represented a house at all, much less the one they sat in.

"Umm. How can you possibly tell?"

She ran her finger along the horizon, stopping on random cacti and scrub brushes. She finished her journey on the giant outcropping in the distance. Not quite big enough to qualify as a mountain, the locals called it Gray's Point, and its distinctly high elevation made it the most significant feature of the barren landscape.

"You can tell," she said. "From the landmarks. Each tree. Cactus. They all look different."

Still standing, Skylar's horseshoe mustache turned up in what Gabe took to be a slight grin, before disappearing. He crossed his arms over his chest, and said, "Miriam spent a lot of time here as a girl."

She looked up briefly at her dad before focusing back on the pictures. "Not a whole lot. I was twelve. Just a few weeks, right?"

"Well. Long enough, it seems."

Brynn held out a hand, silently asking to see the photo in question. Miriam obliged and handed it over.

After studying it, Brynn said, "So. This happened here? Like just out on the highway? Creepy."

"That's why we're here," Skylar replied. "So, the closer the better. We need to come up with a plan, but it's getting late. I think we should turn in for the night."

Miriam sat the stack of photos on the table. Gabe caught her briefly glancing at the door. The time had come for her to make her decision. Would she stay, or would she go? Maybe just because he secretly liked the drama, Gabe hoped for the former.

Skylar seemed to relish the silence, slowly walking to the kitchen and pulling a bottle of water from the refrigerator. He made his way back to the table and offered it to Miriam.

"So, Miriam. Interested in an expedition? For old time's sake?"

Miriam's face looked pale and conflicted. She took the water and busied herself with drinking a big portion of it.

When she finally lowered the bottle and looked at him, Gabe tried to silently convey that he'd continue to run interference for her.

"It's late," she finally said. "I can't exactly drive back to Dobie tonight. We'll see how I feel about all this in the morning."

"Excellent," Skylar said, slower than a normal person might, as if hoping to infuse the word with menace.

"I'll sleep on the couch," Gabe offered. "You can have my room."

"That's gross, Gabe," Brynn teased. "At least change the sheets first."

"Yeah. Of course."

Gabe stood to start the task, and Miriam stood with him. Clearly, she had no interest in leaving his side with Skylar still awake.

"G'night everyone," Gabe mumbled as he shuffled towards his former bedroom. He stopped at a closet in the hallway to retrieve fresh sheets.

When they got to the room, Miriam closed the door. "You guys aren't telling me everything."

Gabe began stripping the sheets. "Why do you say that?"

"For one, dad said *many*," she replied with her back leaning against the closed door. "He doesn't exaggerate his enumerations unless he's trying to impress someone."

"How do you know he's not?" Gabe said, shaking a pillow out of its case. "Trying to impress someone, I mean."

"Who? You? Brynn? You guys are just lackeys to him. And me? I'm even less."

"Huh. Maybe, I guess. Wouldn't be my interpretation, though."

She rolled her eyes with a clear intention to avoid the implication. "Secondly, you said you saw'em. That your mom saw'em. I want to hear that story."

He hadn't known her long, but Gabe supposed that he should've known that she wouldn't give up easily on that nugget of information. He sat down on the stripped bed. Miriam didn't move.

"Not recently," he said quietly.

"When, then?"

"When I was a kid. A little kid."

"Where?"

"Here," he stated.

"Like somewhere in West Texas?"

"No," Gabe shook his head. "Like here. In this house."

"What? How?"

Realizing that he'd been staring at the floor, Gabe raised his eyes to meet hers.

"This is where I grew up. My *tío* sold it to Skylar nine years ago."

CHAPTER 3

Miriam stayed glued to the door, trapping herself between her father in the kitchen and this stranger sitting on her bed. Her insatiable curiosity quelled the urge to run back to Dobie and nestle into the safety of her dorm room. She had more questions than she could organize in her head, which paralyzed her into silence. Gabe stared at her, waiting for a response. His hulking frame slouched down. He looked more vulnerable than she'd thought him capable of. When the silence became awkward, he looked down at his hands and played with his fingers.

Eventually, he broke the silence. "The first time I saw one, I was a kid. Maybe seven or eight. I was playing outside and there was a jackrabbit. It was just kinda staring at me, and being a kid, I just barreled right over to it. But it didn't run away. What kind of rabbit doesn't run away from a kid?"

He paused as if waiting for an answer, but Miriam didn't give him one.

"Anyway, I got to it and reached out and then it sorta just..." Gabe paused, and swirled his hands around. "Clouded up? That's not exactly right. But suddenly, it was a rattlesnake."

"Did it bite you?"

Gabe let out a light chuckle and raised up his right finger. "Yeah. Got me good."

Miriam moved forward and studied the scars on his finger. Clearly he'd been bitten by a snake at some point, but that didn't lend any credence to the existence of a legendary creature.

"What about your mom?" she asked. "You said she saw one, too?"

"Yeah. Well, that's what my *tío* told me anyway."

"Did you ever ask her?"

When he didn't answer right away, Miriam knew she'd said the wrong thing. It was only a matter of time before she said something insensitive, though, so better to get it out of the way early. The fact that she cared at all annoyed her. She'd already invested too much emotion, and that meant she wouldn't be running back to school any time soon.

When Gabe didn't offer a quick answer, she stumbled over her words. "Nevermind. Sorry. I..."

"No, it's fine. She, um, died."

"Childbirth?"

"Naw. I was born in Mexico."

Miriam noticed his more correct pronunciation of the country, eschewing the hard X sound that the Americans liked to force onto it. It sounded more exotic his way.

Gabe continued, "She risked everything to get me here. To my *tío*. And then she died after we got here. Got sick."

Miriam wanted to probe into the specifics of the death, but the memory of Macy's patient empathy nagged at the edges of her brain. "That's rough. I'm sorry."

"Thanks," he said quietly. "Anyway, he says that she was running from one the night she arrived. A big one. Like a coyote, but bigger. It turned into an owl, he says, and she barely escaped it. Or that's her telling of it, anyway. He didn't see it, but he believed."

"That's why dad bought this place, isn't it? Because of your uncle's stories?"

"Yeah. We needed the money, and Skylar came around asking questions about the skinwalkers, so, you know, *tío* did what he had to."

The whole thing seemed confusing and wildly coincidental. Gabe grew up in the very house that her dad would eventually buy, and then ended up working for him? Miriam didn't often look for conspiracies, but this situation felt like it had all the makings of one.

She sat on the bed next to him, hardly noticing that she'd let her guard down. "And now you're back? How? Did dad find you at college?"

Gabe laughed mirthfully. "No. No, no. I never went to college. Or school, really. I mean, I was homeschooled. I'm not a dummy. But, you know, um... it's been easier for me to stay away from scrutiny."

Miriam took his meaning. "So, how then?"

"I don't really know. Skylar just showed up one day at the shop. Where I worked. Recruited me to help with some expeditions. It seemed like a good fit, especially when I realized he meant to hunt things exactly like that bunny I saw as a kid."

"Kinda strange that you ended up back here so soon after he hired you, isn't it?"

He nodded his head. "Yeah. I dunno, Mimi. It's a good job, ya know? Better than what I had. And he didn't ask any questions that I didn't want to have to answer."

Miriam felt blood rushing to her cheeks as she processed the nickname. "Did you just call me Mimi?"

"Oh yeah. I... it's short for Miriam, right?"

A whirlwind of emotions blew through her. No one had called her Mimi in years. Her mother had called her that. Miriam didn't really know if she could remember actually being called Mimi, but she'd watched and rewatched old videos of herself as a baby, with her mom always nearby, cooing that nickname.

Miriam tried to control the anger when she replied, "Don't call me Mimi ever again."

He held up his hands, flashing her a teasing smile. "Fine, *chica*. Miriam. I meant Miriam."

She held his gaze for a few seconds, then allowed herself to relax. As a peace offering for her over-reaction, Miriam said, "Sheets. Let me help."

She stood up and tried to compose herself, crossing to the other side of the bed. Gabe stood and tossed half of the fitted sheet her way.

As they worked, Gabe asked, "So what's the deal with your dad?"

Miriam stretched the elastic band around the bottom corner and moved to the top of the bed. "We had a falling out."

"Over your bro?" he asked unabashedly.

"Something like that. It's complicated."

"Family always is."

Eager to change the subject, Miriam asked, "What about your uncle? Where's he?"

"He saved all the money from the ranch when he sold it. Used it to get himself into a retirement home. It's not that nice, but I don't got enough money to help yet. Maybe soon. I'm saving up."

"So he's older?"

"Yeah," Gabe said with a smile. "I don't remember him ever being young. He was an old man when I got here."

They'd gotten off course. Only the potential threat of a shapeshifting demon stalking the deserts mattered, and she felt perplexed to have so easily veered off into personal questions. As they tucked in the top sheet, the conversation fell into silence, with Miriam trying to concoct a scheme to properly hunt this thing. Though she'd muddled through two such encounters, she still struggled to form a cohesive and actionable plan. The last time she'd tried, Tanner almost got eaten by a giant octopus.

"Pillows are over there," Gabe said, pointing to a built-in desk in the corner.

She took the two standard-sized pillows and tossed one to Gabe. He caught it with one hand and tucked it under his chin so he could guide it into the pillowcase. Miriam fetched the other case from the bed and followed suit.

Once finished, Gabe patted the bed. "There ya go. All set. You got bags?"

With all the commotion and drama, Miriam never unloaded the car. "Yeah. I've got a couple. I'll go get'em."

"Let me," he said. "Skylar may still be up."

As much as Miriam hated relinquishing her independence to a man she'd just met, she also detested the idea of having to exchange even two words with her father. The day had stretched on long past her normal bedtime, and the exhaustion scratched at her eyes. To confront her dad, she'd need all her wits, and she wouldn't be able to muster much more tonight.

"The keys are in the ignition. Bags are in the trunk."

Gabe nodded and spun towards the door. Once there, he turned back with a silly grin painted on his face. "Be right back, Mimi."

He skirted through the door before she could respond. She sat in the silence. Instead of fuming as she had before, Miriam curiously caught herself smiling.

***

She rarely chose this room on her super-secret study visits. Smaller than the rest, it pressed in on her, and she didn't like how the one window faced empty desert. The other rooms all boasted a view of Gray's Point, its craggy silhouette always a source of inspiration and awe. This room would have to do, though, if she chose to stay at all.

Miriam focused on her breathing. She needed to center herself. She needed to decide how deep she wanted to go with this messed up situation.

She liked Gabe so far. He seemed genuine, far from the monster she'd painted in her head. But he'd only be able to run interference for so long. She and Skylar wouldn't be able to get by on pleasantries, business, and nasty looks forever. And, of course, she had to consider the possibility that they might succeed. If they actually found a skinwalker, things would only get worse. The attention. The press. It would include them both, and Miriam felt no compulsion to share success with her father.

As she unwound her mind, a gentle knock echoed through the room. At first, she thought Gabe had returned with her luggage—respectful of him to knock—but as she stood, she immediately realized that the sound couldn't have come from that direction.

Another knock drew her attention to the window.

She pulled the paisley curtains aside and jumped back as she stared into those familiar light brown eyes.

Her heart stopped. Confusion and terror warred in her. The woman on the other side of the window shared Miriam's eyes. Her hair. Her strong shoulders. The passive expression chilled her, leaving her with a distinct feeling that she now stared at a dead version of herself.

She screamed at the apparition. It remained unshaken.

Pushing through the overwhelming sense of horror, Miriam pulled up on the window while the doppelgänger outside calmly watched her. She couldn't be sure if the other one stared into her soul or simply reflected it.

Miriam pulled up again, but the window wouldn't budge. For a moment she considered breaking the glass, but thought better of it, instead opting to bust out of the room. With no sign of Skylar or Brynn, Miriam rushed out to the porch and down the steps. Gabe popped up and hit his head on the trunk of the Sentra, eliciting what Miriam vaguely recognized as Spanish expletives.

With only the briefest thought about her lack of weaponry, Miriam rounded the corner, ready to face an imitation of herself.

Nothing there.

She stopped and listened, trying to find a sound over the blood rushing through her ears. She inched slowly towards the window, and glancing through the parted curtains. Her heart thumped in her chest. She felt almost certain that she'd see herself sitting on that old bed. The room sat empty... but for Skylar standing in the doorway and looking at her through the window.

She spun to look for anything slinking off into the distance, but caught no movement. The moon bathed the desert in a faint white glow, giving Miriam enough light to account for every shadow on the horizon. Had she imagined it? Could the face in the window have been only her reflection? Surely she wouldn't be so foolish as to mistake a reflection for a flesh and blood human, albeit one that looked exactly like her.

A hand touched her shoulder. Instinct kicked in and she grabbed the wrist and twisted it, yanking the figure before her.

Gabe looked at her with a wide-eyed grimace. "Damn. That hurts!"

Miriam didn't let go. Not immediately. She couldn't trust anyone, and although the man in front of her looked like Gabe Castillo, it could be someone else—something else. Something that had looked like Miriam Brooks minutes before.

Gabe writhed his arm to try to get a more comfortable angle. "Mimi, seriously. Let go."

Miriam released her grip, and Gabe immediately nursed his wrist in his good hand. Surely, a skinwalker wouldn't have Gabe's memories, and only the two of them would know about her newly minted nickname; a nickname she still wasn't sold on.

"What happened? What's going on?" Gabe asked.

"I saw something. Out my window." Miriam kept scanning the landscape.

"Yeah? One of them?"

"One of me."

Before Gabe could react, Skylar and Brynn crept around the corner of the house.

Skylar's beady eyes focused in on Miriam, burning uncomfortably into her psyche. "What the hell is going on?"

He wore plaid pajamas, comically old-fashioned for a man who tended to wear khaki safari attire. It conjured memories of Miriam's childhood. Of Christmas mornings and late-night stories. She couldn't remember the last time she'd seen her father dressed this way. The family had moved away from such frivolities years before Cornelius died.

Gabe shot a sympathetic look towards Miriam, which she took as a question. If she didn't talk, he would, and she needed to control this narrative. "I thought maybe I saw something out my window."

Skylar blinked. "Saw something? What did you see?"

"Not sure," she said, still looking for movement. "Probably nothing. Maybe just a coyote or something."

She didn't know why she did it. If she hadn't just scared herself into seeing ghosts, then she most likely saw the exact creature they'd come to hunt. She could have admitted to it. They could have taken flashlights and recording equipment to comb the desert well into the night. But something kept her cautious and guarded. For now, at least, Miriam wanted to keep this sighting to herself.

The desert night brought a cool breeze. Miriam saw Brynn shivering, as the girl ran her eyes over the horizon, hugging herself for warmth, her long legs crossed. Skylar watched Brynn intently.

Miriam let the silence hang, with no attempts to embellish her story. The best lies were simple and believable. And, certainly, a coyote seemed likelier than a doppelganger.

Brynn looked at Skylar. "I don't see anything."

Skylar nodded. "Gabe. Go get the cameras. Set them up here. Get them recording."

"It's late, boss, and I gotta help Miriam—"

"Tonight," Skylar interrupted.

Gabe skulked off without any further protest, leaving Miriam alone with her father and Brynn—the new and improved Miriam. Taller. Stronger. Prettier. While Gabe seemed willing to admit the shortcomings of his employer, Brynn had thus far shown no such inclination.

"Get some sleep, Miriam," Skylar instructed. He turned away and stalked off, Brynn following dutifully behind.

Miriam felt the rebirth of that part of her, the part too much like her father. Sure, the working conditions were poor, but something strange was out there, waiting to be found.

Another beast.

Another kraken.

Another hunt.

CHAPTER 4

Brynn locked the door to her room and pulled the cover off the bed to wrap around her shoulders. Though hot during the day, she found the nights insufferably cold.

The tension of the new girl showing up had seared into Brynn's soul. She hated the feeling, knowing that the emotions of two people simmered so furiously that there would be no escaping an inevitable explosion. She'd seen it too many times. Felt the repercussions too many times.

Confident of her privacy, Brynn tested the floorboards one by one, trying to find the loose one she'd stumbled across earlier. Miriam's scream had interrupted her the first time just as she'd laid eyes on the prize, and the promise of new information stoked Brynn into action. If she could solve this mystery, then maybe the new girl would scuttle off so that things could return to normal.

It only took a few boards before she felt the jiggle under her foot. She sank to the floor, draped in her blanket, and used her fingernails to pry up the board. Once removed, she looked down at an aging notebook in a plastic bag. As far as she knew, no one else knew of its existence. She'd tell Skylar in time, but for now she wanted the information for herself.

Gingerly, she removed the notebook from the bag and studied the plain, leather cover. She flipped it to the back and found nothing of interest. The elastic band holding the cover together had become brittle with age and stuck to the cover. By the time she slid it off, she knew that it would never hold the book together the same way again.

She opened the cover, studying the handwritten scrawl inside. She read the first few lines before realizing that the words were in Spanish. Years of studying the language made reading it second nature to her.

***

Hector says he is my father's brother, and something about him seems familiar. He was quick to invite me into his home, providing me with everything I need to take care of my little boy. He hasn't asked for anything in return yet, but I worry that he wants something from me that I'm not willing to give.

He disappears at night. Goes somewhere that I haven't yet had the courage to follow. When I ask about it, he gets angry and admonishes me for prying into matters that I shouldn't involve myself in. Wherever he goes, he must sleep, for he seems to have boundless energy. More than I would expect for a man of his age.

Little Gabriel knows none of this, of course, cooing and crying each day in his new home. If he misses Mexico, he shows no signs of it, though I suppose I would expect nothing less from such a small baby.

I wish father were alive. Not that I would have a hope of contacting him now. He never spoke of a brother, but circumstances as they were, he rarely talked of his family at all. I don't have the means to leave this place, nor the strength to fight my host should it come to that.

Even if I had the resources, the desert isn't safe. Something waits for us out there. Something vicious and cold, blending with the other animals of the desert. I can hardly believe what I saw the night we arrived, but I think Hector knows something of it. He doesn't seem as afraid as he should.

Though cautious, I can do nothing but continue this existence. Perhaps I will find a way out eventually, but even if I don't, this life is far better than the one I left behind in Mexico. And far safer than the desert outside these walls.

***

Gabe's mother? It had to be. Brynn knew of Gabe's childhood in this home, but had been given the impression that his mother, Ana, died shortly after his arrival. Thumbing through the notebook, Brynn lost count of the entries. To write this much would have required months. But very little so far pertained to the real goal of discovering more about the shapeshifting creatures she sought.

She shuddered to think of how this might up-end Gabe's view of his childhood. Brynn had always loved hearing stories of Gabe's youth, so carefree and loving. A far cry from her own. She'd been drawn to him by his gleeful stories of exploring the desert with his uncle. They had made her want to share in his exuberance, to shelter herself in his surety. After a lifetime of feeling unsafe, Gabe's arms offered her a security that she'd never known.

But that chapter had ended almost before it started. She owed him nothing now.

A yawn crept up from her chest as she tried to focus on the second page. She read the first line three times before closing the journal and giving up. She'd find time to study these words in the future, but for now she needed to keep it secret. If this notebook contained key information, then Brynn needed it to present to Skylar. She could almost feel the warmth of his approval washing over her.

Miriam had walked away from a great man, disappointing and destroying him at the same time. Brynn wouldn't make that mistake. She'd make him proud, and together, they'd build an empire. Skylar promised her that level of success in his recruitment speech, and, until it was achieved, she intended to pursue that dream with every ounce of her strength.

Brynn climbed into bed and wrapped herself tightly into the blankets. She tried to ignore the silence and the insecurities that waited in the shadows. Eventually, her mind grew fuzzy and wandered, conjuring images of monsters in the dark, and of monsters from her childhood.

Then, as always, the nightmares came.

CHAPTER 5

Morning arrived quickly. The old, broken-down couch poked and prodded Gabe regardless of his sleeping position, so he eventually just relented to the assault and started his day. He'd made it longer than he thought. The sun peeked through the blinds and bathed the living area in a dingy orange glow. From the sounds of it, though, he was the first to wake.

It felt strange being back in this old house. He glanced around the living room until his eyes landed on the built-in bookshelves in the corner. His uncle's wingback chair still sat there; where his *tío* could most often be found, lounging deep into the cushions with a book. Sometimes two. Gabe could still remember climbing up in his uncle's lap and trying to decipher the words and pictures on those pages. Though he had a hard time recalling the specifics, he remembered heroic tales and dark curses.

Over the years, Gabe lost interest in the stories his uncle read in that chair. The bookshelves looked bare now. The few books on the shelves all came from Skylar's cryptozoology library, not from the fairy tales and lore of Gabe's youth.

Groggy, he got to his feet, grabbed a few things from his bag and stumbled into the bathroom to get ready for the day. As he brushed his teeth and stared into his almost-black eyes, he pondered the skinwalkers. He hadn't gotten a chance to talk to

Miriam after setting up the equipment, so he didn't fully know what she meant when she said she'd seen herself. The lights could play tricks. Maybe she only saw her reflection. He'd never heard of a skinwalker mimicking the person watching it.

He enjoyed his new life with Skylar for the most part, though their first expedition had proved fruitless. The whole idea that there might have been living pterodactyls in Papua New Guinea was silly to begin with. But Gabe was still new to it all. He didn't know where to even start. They had no leads to go on, and combing through the scrub brush didn't sound like a particularly good time. How would they even know if they found it? Every snake or coyote or bird could be one, after all.

Refreshed, Gabe opted to skip the shower and save it for the end of the day, when he'd surely be covered in dirt. He changed out of his yester-clothes into some new ones. He expected to have a private room, so he hadn't bothered bringing pajamas.

He decided the first order of business would be to review the video from overnight. Quietly sneaking onto the porch, he crept down the creaky wooden stairs and made his way around the house. The cameras all sat undisturbed. In the morning light, he scanned the ground for any signs of footprints but found none that he wouldn't attribute to the four of them.

Kneeling beside the small box on the tripod, Gabe retrieved a USB cable out of a compartment and plugged it into his cell phone. Within a few moments, he had a visual representation of everything it'd captured. Mostly, the graph sat low against the x-axis, but there were a couple of peaks that indicated movement. He clicked the first one.

On the screen, a jackrabbit scavenged in the distance, its wiry frame standing out in bright green against the backdrop. Maybe a skinwalker, he supposed, but it only went about normal rabbit business for the duration. He tapped back to the graph, scanned for the next peak, and then stopped when he heard a rap on the glass behind him.

Miriam stood on the other side of the window, her hair tangled and messy. She looked at him with sunken, bloodshot eyes. She'd clearly gotten even less sleep than he. She pointed at his phone and her eyes widened, silently asking whether he'd found anything. He shook his head, then motioned for her to open the window.

He watched as she tried, her biceps flexing. She looked strong. Gabe admired that, though he'd never thought of it as a desirable quality in a woman before. She shook her head and gave a mock frown to indicate her failure. Gabe made a mental note to fix the window soon.

He tried to stretch the cable further to show the screen to her, but it wouldn't reach. He considered moving the entire setup before she knocked on the window again, scrunched up her mouth, and held up one index finger, asking for him to wait. In a flash, she closed the curtains. Taking that as a sign that she'd be out shortly, Gabe sat his phone on the ground next to the tripod.

While he waited, he wandered and studied the landscape. The dirt. The house. Everything looked to be in order, but then he noticed something. A tuft of brown grass growing at the base of the corner looked trampled. He tried to remember whether he'd seen any of them walk that direction, but came up blank.

Probably nothing, but he inched towards it and peeked around to the back of the house.

Something caught his eye. Something big and unexpected and fixed into the ground, gnarled wood surrounding the base. His heart pounding, Gabe frantically turned in every direction, suddenly aware of how exposed he felt in the flat open land. He swallowed hard, accepted that he could see nothing watching him, and moved towards the strange totem.

Everything about it seemed wrong. By its color, the wood appeared sickly, and the way it twisted on itself felt unnatural. At the top hung a dirty skull, its cavernous sockets staring straight into his soul.

Skylar had insisted they learn about the anatomy of animals, but Gabe didn't recognize this. It looked vaguely canine in its shape, but onyx antlers curled out of the temples. Large teeth threatened from the elongated snout, and the cranium seemed abnormally wide, more rounded than he'd expect from any animal... except maybe a human.

Though he found it disturbing, something about it felt familiar. His mind scrambled to place the feeling, reaching for any semblance of a memory that might explain it.

"What is that?" Miriam's voice came from behind, more curious than fearful.

"I don't know," he stammered. "I just found it."

Every bone in Gabe's body told him to get away from this thing, but Miriam snatched it out of the ground in one smooth gesture and headed back towards the front of the house.

She glanced back over her shoulder as Gabe stood in stunned silence. "Come on. Let's study it."

***

"That can't be real," Brynn said, her nose only inches from the strange skull on the table.

"It's real bone," Miriam replied. "But I think you're right that it's not natural. Someone stitched this together."

Miriam ran her fingers along barely-visible seams. Gabe hung back, not so far away that he looked cowardly, but far enough that he felt safe. It seemed ridiculous to be so shaken by an inanimate object, but warning bells echoed in his head as he started to dredge up barely-formed memories. He couldn't quite remember all the details, but he'd seen something like this before. Maybe as a child—in one of his uncle's books—but he couldn't deny the terror that came with it.

Skylar leaned against the island in the kitchen and silently watched Miriam and Brynn work. Gabe tried to decide whether Skylar derived pleasure from seeing his new protégé square off against his old one. If Gabe were keeping score, he'd hand the match to Miriam so far.

"Okay," Brynn said as she stood back up. "So let's say that someone made this. Why did they put it in our backyard?"

"Did you guys scout the place when you got here?" Miriam asked. "Are you sure it showed up just now?"

"Of course we did," Brynn responded. "We're not amateurs."

Miriam didn't say anything, but Gabe thought he saw the makings of a witty comeback in her eyes. Maybe Brynn wasn't an amateur, but he still felt like one.

Gabe swallowed hard before piping in. "I think I've seen it before. Or something like it."

The room fell silent as three pairs of eyes all focused in on him.

"When I was a kid, I think. I can't remember exactly. But it just feels really familiar."

"Like in a book?" Miriam asked.

"Maybe," Gabe said. "Or it could have been in real life. Maybe in a cave or something? Somewhere indoors."

Brynn narrowed her eyes. "Are there caves around here?"

"Not many," Miriam answered. "But I think there might be a couple at the base of Gray's Point."

"We should check them out, then," Brynn suggested.

Skylar suddenly took a step away from the kitchen island and slammed his boots on the wooden floor. The action seemed purposeful, but Gabe couldn't discern the reason. Intimidation? Anger?

"This is a red herring," Skylar said. "Obviously it's constructed to confuse us."

"But who would do that?" Brynn asked.

Skylar smoothed out his mustache and walked over to the table. He didn't look at the totem stretching across the tabletop, though. Instead, he ran his eyes over all three of them, measuring and judging.

"Who indeed?" he responded. "An animal didn't do this, so it can't be the skinwalkers themselves."

"I dunno, boss," Gabe interjected. "We know they can mimic humans."

Miriam retreated from the table, closer to Gabe and farther from her father. "I don't buy that. I think maybe they can appear that way, but that doesn't make them smart enough to fuse bone together."

"Right," Skylar said. "I think we can all agree on that. So, the question goes back to who would do this, and I think the answer is obvious."

Gabe disagreed. The answer didn't seem obvious to him at all. They were miles from civilization, with no neighbors. No law enforcement. No visitors. The very act of getting to the house without a car would be long and difficult. Having slept in the living room, Gabe felt confident that he would have heard the approach of a vehicle.

"Who could possibly do this without us knowing, though?" Gabe asked.

"It would be difficult, huh?" Skylar smirked as if he knew some special secret that he wouldn't be sharing with the rest of them. "I guess you think it's funny to derail our investigation with this?"

What the hell? Was Skylar implying that Gabe planted this thing? He felt the heat rising in his cheeks, as part of him instantly bristled for a fight.

"Are you kidding me?" Gabe yelled more than asked. "Why the hell would I do this? And what investigation are you even talking about? We've been here for days and done basically nothing."

Skylar focused on Miriam. "You then? Trying to make a fool of me?"

Gabe glanced towards Miriam, unsure of how she'd react to the accusation. Her moistened eyes burned with anger. She clenched her fists at her side, inflated herself with a deep breath, and seemed to become heavier, grinding her feet against the old wooden floors. Gabe worried that she might attack, so he stepped in front of her, taking up her field of view.

"Hey, Mimi. Let's, uh, step outside maybe." He threw a glance towards Skylar, now with Brynn at his side. "Let your dad rethink this."

Miriam's teeth stayed clenched. "Don't... call... me... that."

"Yeah, yeah. I'm sorry," Gabe said, placing his hands on her upper arms. "Let's just take five."

Miriam's arms exploded outward, instantly pushing Gabe's hands away with determined force. She shoved him out of the way, not hard enough to knock him down, but enough that he almost lost his balance. She took two steps towards Skylar, looked like she was about to say something, then just shook her head. In a flash she banged through the front door and onto the porch. The sounds of the screen door slamming reverberated through the stunned silence of the room.

Gabe didn't know what to do. His instincts told him to follow her, but judging by the pain left by the palms of her hands against his chest, he worried that he might not be welcome. Gabe shared a look with Brynn, who seemed as shocked as he. Skylar on the other hand...

Skylar seemed perfectly fine.

CHAPTER 6

The tires hit the pavement before Miriam could think clearly enough to realize that she'd left her stuff back in the house. She didn't care. The frustration and anger overwhelmed her, robbing her of rational thought and leading her mind to dark places. How could she have been so stupid as to think that she could rebuild some sort of relationship with that man?

A few miles up the road, she saw the tiny gas station in the distance. The one that looked rundown. The one whose owner saw his wife come back as a skinwalker. Something nagged at Miriam to stop, but she dismissed it. She wouldn't be dragged into this investigation. Not when it would only bring pain. Yet the Sentra's low-fuel light begged for attention, and she wouldn't find gas for a long time. Pay-at-the-pump. That was it. No small talk with the proprietor.

She slowed down, pulled up next to the pump, and killed the engine. She rested her head on the steering wheel between her hands and took a few deep breaths. Only then did she remember that she'd need her books. Her clothes. Her wallet. She couldn't just run back to Dobie with her tail between her legs.

Miriam popped out of the front seat and stood in front of the pump. No wallet meant no credit cards. She cursed under her breath, pushed the button to indicate that she'd pay inside, and locked the handle in place. She always kept a couple twenties tucked into the back of her cell phone case, and thankfully, she always had that on her person.

For all the good it would do her out in the desert.

She walked to the back of the car and pulled her phone out to study the screen. Miriam's heart jumped at a text from Macy. Did she have service at this rundown station? One vertical bar. It might not last, but she clicked on Macy's name and hoped for the best.

The first ring started and faltered, its tone breaking up. The second sounded clearer. On the third, Macy's tinny voice shot into Miriam's ear.

"Hi, Mir. Didn't expect you to check in so soon."

"He's here," Miriam uttered into the phone.

"Umm... ok. Who's he?"

Miriam didn't want to say it. She didn't feel comfortable calling him Skylar and she couldn't bring herself to call him *dad*. Not right now.

Miriam repeated herself again, more emphatically this time, hissing, "Him."

The silence on the line caused her to pull the phone from her ear to make sure she hadn't lost the connection, but the call time ticked on. Eventually, she heard whispering, and increased ambient noise as Macy switched the call to speakerphone.

"How?" Macy asked. "Is he stalking you?"

Macy didn't know about the ranch, of course. But Tanner did, and Miriam had little doubt that he now sat beside his girlfriend, waiting with bated breath to hear about this whole story.

"My study place is a ranch my dad owns."

The pump clicked off. Though she'd heard horror stories of cell phones near gasoline, she casually went about buttoning up the gas tank.

Tanner's voice echoed into her ear. "What? The skinwalker place?"

"Yeah. Apparently, he's rekindled his interest."

Macy again: "That sucks, Mir. Just come home. I'll help you study."

"Yeah. I should. But I gotta go back. I left my stuff there."

Tanner said, "Wait. If he's there, that means something's going on, right?"

Miriam swallowed hard, reticent to think about the stories she'd heard from Brynn and Gabe. She couldn't trust herself to stay mad if she spent too much time pondering the possibilities. She couldn't resist the urge to find the truth. Maybe she could do it with the strength of Macy and Tanner behind her, but she possessed the only car the three of them had.

"There've been sightings," Miriam finally said. "A few encounters."

"That's what he said last time, and we didn't find anything."

Miriam's mind conjured the stories that Gabe had shared with her. Something about his sincerity lent the stories more credence than they deserved. Somehow, Gabe was the key to everything. Though she couldn't quite understand yet, the link Gabe shared with this place had to mean something. Something important.

Miriam responded, "He's got a new guy. Gabe. I think he might know something."

"You know," Tanner said. "Skylar's not that bad. You just gotta look past the exterior."

Tanner had resumed a relationship with Skylar shortly after the incident with the kraken in Cape Madre, unable to resist the avalanche of calls from his uncle. Miriam's hackles raised at Tanner's subtle attempt to intercede into her relationship with her father. Was it because he wanted her to find a skinwalker, or because Skylar had pulled the wool back over Tanner's eyes? She couldn't be sure, and that made Tanner hard to trust on the issue.

"I'm gonna go get my stuff," Miriam said. "And then I'm coming back to Dobie. If he finds something out here, then good for him. It's not worth it to stay."

The line fell silent without a response from Tanner. She imagined a silent conversation on the other end, as Tanner and Macy came to some conclusion on what to say. Neither of them fully understood, and they had reasons to want her to stay. After all, they both had a stake in a budding monster hunting business that still coasted on the buzz of the kraken. It wouldn't last forever without more forward momentum – the kind of momentum that finding a skinwalker might get them.

"Drive safe, Mir," Macy said.

Miriam replied, "I will. See you soon."

She hung up before any goodbyes, then flipped her phone over to dig out the emergency cash. With forty bucks in hand, Miriam shuffled into the small convenience store across the parking lot.

The inside of the store smelled musty and old. A quick scan of the shelves revealed non-perishable goods that might have been there for the better part of a decade. The soda cooler hummed and rattled, as if straining, while the counter sat empty. She preferred to get some change, rather than leave both twenties on the counter.

Assuming the attendant might be in the bathroom, Miriam slowly walked the three aisles, trying to ignore the massive amount of dust collecting on every item. Only the candy bars up front seemed to be fresh.

Before long, she'd memorized every item in stock, and found herself studying pictures and news articles lining the walls. A few detailed the mundane goings-on of the small community dotting the perimeter of Gray's Point, but her eyes quickly homed in on the more interesting headlines.

The ones about the skinwalkers.

They stretched back into a previous century, decades before Miriam's birth. Originally a Navajo story, she'd always been curious as to how skinwalkers managed to make their way to the West Texas desert. Perhaps they came with the Apache. Some of the articles mentioned the Native American ties, with even a few admitting that it all started with evil shaman capable of wearing the pelts of dead animals to shift into any animal of their desire. Mostly, though, it only spoke of skinwalkers as misunderstood—and dangerous—animals.

She came across an account of a woman purportedly killed by one of the creatures. They called her Jane Doe. Her naked, mutilated body had turned up when a hiker discovered it in a cave at the base of Gray's Point. No one ever came forward to identify her.

"They're real."

Miriam spun into a crouch, only to relax at the sight of an older man now standing behind the counter. How had she not heard him come in? He regarded her with drooping brown eyes, but she couldn't tell if they drooped from age or sadness.

"Seen one?" she asked, already suspecting the answer.

"You with that research team up the road?"

"No."

Her answer came quickly. She didn't consider it a lie, though it certainly obscured the finer points of the truth.

He grunted. "No? What brings you out here, then?"

Miriam thumbed towards the parking lot. "Gas."

He glanced out the window at her car, then down at the meter on the counter. "$26.32."

Miriam moved towards him and presented the cash, waiting patiently as he slowly punched the amount into the register and counted the change out from the drawer. She dropped the coins into an unlabeled jar full of others and crammed the bills into the front pocket of her jeans.

He stopped her before she exited. "That's not an answer."

She looked at him quizzically.

"You didn't drive out here for gas. Passing through?"

"You didn't answer my question, either."

The corners of his mouth turned up. "Maybe I've seen one. Hard to say."

Miriam ignored the urge to ask for more information. The bell above the door tingled and she turned, only to find herself looking up at Gabe's worried face. Rage filled her.

"Excuse me," Miriam said, motioning her intent toward the exit.

Gabe didn't move. "You ok?"

Before Miriam could answer, the old man behind the counter said, "Thought you weren't with them."

"I'm not," she huffed, pushing past Gabe and out into the parking lot.

She saw only one of the yellow Jeeps, which gave her hope that Gabe had come alone. She heard his steps behind her as she rushed to the car, which only caused her to hurry.

"Wait!" Gabe shouted. "I brought your stuff."

Miriam stopped, before slowly turning around. Gabe fished the keys to the Jeep from his pocket and held them out for her. "No strings. What happened back there, that was messed up."

She marched just close enough to grab the keys, pushed the button to pop the back, and began to fish out her bags. Gabe reached over her to grab the biggest, and though her first instinct was to turn away his help, she let him take it.

"Your dad can be a jerk."

"Tell me about it."

"But there's something out here."

She started towards the car with Gabe in tow, looking over her shoulder to respond, "I know. I saw it. But it's not worth it."

"What if we could look for it without him? Just you and me?"

Miriam lowered her bags into the trunk of the Sentra, trying not to give away anything with her expression. A part of her that she could barely register jumped with excitement at the prospect. A head to head competition with the ignominious Skylar Brooks. A race to find one of the oldest and most elusive cryptids in North America.

"I can't pay you," she said, closing the trunk and finally meeting his gaze.

"That's ok."

"And if we find it, you can't afford to be in the spotlight."

"I have that problem either way."

Miriam considered the situation. "I don't want to be responsible for that. For keeping you under the radar. I have a habit of attracting attention."

"Stop worrying about things you can't control. That's my problem."

Maybe, but she couldn't bear the thought of what might happen if too many people started asking too many questions. And, she couldn't exactly bring on another member of the team without weigh-in from Macy and Tanner.

"This isn't a job," she offered. "Just a temporary partnership."

"Understood."

She realized she didn't need to think about it anymore. She'd already committed to it on intuition and hope, the way that she made far too many of her decisions. Instead of fretting about it anymore, her mind instead started working out the logistics.

"Where are we going to stay?"

"There's nothing for miles," he said. "But I've got some stuff in the Jeep. Tents. Lanterns."

She hadn't been camping in a long while, but on the rare occasion during her childhood when she got a vacation instead of a monster-hunt, camping always tended to be the go-to option. She could remember wanting something more exotic, but Skylar seemed to think that camping provided both a vacation and a learning experience.

"Two tents?" she asked.

"Yeah. Of course."

"And sleeping bags? It gets cold out here."

"Brynn and I planned all this out for weeks. I've got everything we need. I promise."

Miriam narrowed her eyes, trying to read any deception on his face. She found none. Only the same kind eyes and inexplicable, fast-earned loyalty. She wondered what Gabe would be capable of, wary of a partner that she couldn't predict. Surely, Tanner would be a safer choice. Maybe she could drive back to Dobie and pick him up, but she knew that if she did, it would kill a lot of time and tempt her into giving up the hunt.

"He won't like this."

Gabe shrugged. "No. I'll probably lose my job."

"He'll come to take his stuff back."

"We'll stay one step ahead. Find this thing before he finds us."

Miriam gazed out over the nondescript flatland and tried to imagine how they would evade detection in an area with so few hiding places. She appreciated Gabe's optimism and confidence, but it would only be a matter of time before Skylar found them and stripped them of everything they needed to survive.

"I don't know if this is a good idea," she said, unintentionally voicing the concern in her head.

Gabe smiled and offered a handshake. Warily, she shook his hand as he replied, "Yeah. Me neither."

CHAPTER 7

Brynn sank into the leather wing-backed chair, careful to keep her eyes on the strange totem stretched across the table. Her heart rattled in her chest, adrenaline coursing through her veins. She could handle the misshapen skull, but the intensity of the fight she'd just witnessed threatened to bring on a panic attack. It'd been a while since she'd had one, and she didn't want to invite another, so she tried to numb herself as Skylar paced back and forth on the creaky wooden floor. No, pacing provided too gentle a description. Each thunderous step reverberated the chair.

A part of her wanted to ask why he went out of his way to breed paranoia and misgivings in their group, but she worried about the repercussions that would have. Instead, she chose to believe that he had a purpose.

Skylar blustered. "When Gabe gets back, we'll get started. No more waiting for things to happen."

Brynn did not expect Gabe would return. She could already sense the admiration forming between him and Miriam. The real question thus became whether the two of them would quietly disappear or stay to make trouble. She didn't know Miriam well, but Gabe tended towards rash action, especially when his heart got involved.

He had a big heart. Too big for Brynn to handle.

Skylar finally stopped his pounding footsteps to study the skull. "So if none of us made this, then someone's toying with us. Trying to make a mockery of our mission."

Brynn spoke meekly from her corner. "You don't think the skinwalkers are capable of this?"

"Of course not," Skylar said. "They're just mindless animals. With some extraordinary abilities, sure, but not capable of this level of thought."

She considered disengaging and leaving him with his ideas, but she'd too often been rewarded by offering up alternate theories. "Maybe they aren't. Maybe they fall closer in line with the Navajo tradition. Maybe they're people. Shaman with uncanny abilities."

"Witches?" Skylar said, making no intention to hide his disdain for the suggestion. "We do not live in a world of magic, Brynn. Whatever these things are, we will be able to explain them with science."

A quote from Arthur C. Clarke flashed through Brynn's mind, forcing the idea that perhaps the skinwalkers employed a science that she could not yet conceive of. She repeated the quote out loud, not directed at Skylar, but more of a reminder to herself. "Any sufficiently advanced technology is indistinguishable from magic."

If Skylar heard her, he didn't react. Instead, he moved to the open door and stared out towards the highway. "Dammit. Where is he?"

Brynn sank back into her chair, eager to retreat. *Get it together, Brynn.* She wouldn't let Skylar see her like this; weak, pathetic, and withdrawn. He would never reward weakness. With great effort, she forced herself to stand, pushing away the panic and reasserting her tall and regal facade. Skylar needed her right now. It's what he'd hired her for. It was her job to run the expeditions. To take care of the logistics. To keep Skylar on track and provide guidance when the paths grew dark. He'd said as much in her interview.

"It might be a while," she suggested. "Or he might not even come back. I think he might be into your daughter."

Skylar spun, eyebrow arched. Was it so unbelievable to him that someone might be attracted to his daughter?

"He'll come back," Skylar protested. "He would never betray me like that."

Unlikely, but Brynn knew better than to disagree twice. "Well, he might have to drive a while to catch up with her. Let's just start now."

Sometimes, she wondered whether Skylar meant to do any hands-on research at all. He seemed eager to get out and talk to every person they could find in the shadow of Gray's Point, but he'd thus far dragged his feet on the actual hunt. He did well with people, gathering stories and evidence, but when it came to mounting the expeditions, it fell to her to lead the charge into the unknown, no matter how much she wished she didn't have to.

While Skylar went back to the doorway to stare into the distance, she gathered the gear they'd unloaded into the cabin. At the very least, they would walk through the countryside and look for anything out of the ordinary. She was particularly keen to check out the base of Gray's Point. Its hulking footprint promised caves and other natural hiding spots for all manner of animals.

She threw some cameras in a backpack, then hurried off to her room to gather more supplies.

Furtively, she glanced behind her and listened to see if Skylar moved about. Confident that he remained obsessed with Gabe's return, she pried up the plank and scooped up the journal. She wanted to spend more time thumbing through it, but with things moving as they were it was hard to find the time or the space. Hopeful for a chance in the future, she slipped it into one of the pockets running along the side of her bag.

Back in the living room, Skylar had retired to the kitchen, sipping on a bottle of water. She tried in vain to read the emotions on his face.

"Ready to go?"

Skylar's small eyes focused in on her, and he nodded, chugging the rest of his water and leaving the empty bottle on the counter.

On the porch, Skylar asked, "What if he comes back? We should leave a note."

The question appeared to be rhetorical as he disappeared back through the door. Brynn felt so certain that Gabe didn't mean to return that it hadn't even occurred to her to leave a note. Or maybe, a note presented just one more delay tactic in the arsenal of Skylar's avoidance techniques.

Down the steps, she hung a left and moved towards the Jeep. Something looked off. Wrong. Her eyes narrowed as she surveyed the scene, and she dropped her bag when she finally saw it. The Jeep sat lower than it should have, the two tires that she could see deflated entirely to the ground. How the hell could this happen?

She rushed around the front-end to verify what she already suspected. Two more flat tires. This couldn't be a coincidence or an unlucky encounter with a bed of nails. Not these tires.

The heat in her cheeks surged. Someone was out here. She spun in hopes of finding some clue to the culprit, but her view filled only with empty desert and the old, wooden cabin.

Could Gabe have done this? He could be rash, but he wouldn't leave them stranded like this. He wouldn't do that to her, especially. After their... time together, he'd been distant for a while, sure, but the misgivings had resolved into cordiality at least. He wasn't spiteful. Or vindictive. Was he?

She studied the horizon again, this time hoping to see a track, or a disturbed shrub, or a hazy figure in the distance—anything or anyone that she could hang the blame on other than Gabe.

When she found nothing, she rushed back to the house to tell Skylar, unsure of how she was going to frame it, or who she was going to blame.

When she reached the porch, a *thud* echoed from inside the house. She was through the door before she could process the noise, but it all came into stark focus when she saw Skylar stretched out and unconscious on the floor.

***

Brynn skimmed his eyes with a flashlight, looking for any signs of a concussion. Skylar held an icepack to the back of his head, occasionally muttering expletive-laced phrases that she mostly ignored. His pupils reacted as expected, so they didn't have an urgent need to get to a hospital. Not that they had a working vehicle, anyway.

"What happened?" she asked gently, now for the second time. He'd been too dazed to answer her first inquiry.

Eliminate the threats, then check the wounded. Skylar had drilled that into her head during training. It was one of his biggest mantras. She'd already spent too much time tending to him when she should have been looking for the perpetrator.

While he formed his thoughts, she took the time to finally inspect the perimeter of the house. She'd been just outside the front door, so any intruder would surely have come through the back.

Yet the rear door remained closed, locked and secured.

A window, then? She started trying each one, quickly finding that most of them sat unlocked. With no screens between the glass and the outside air, any one of the windows could have been the entry or exit point.

From her backpack, she pulled out her pistol and checked the ammo and safety. She hated guns, truth be told, but Skylar had insisted that she train relentlessly, and she considered herself a pretty decent shot. Someone had slashed their tires and attacked Skylar, and she needed to be ready for that someone to reappear. When required to carry a gun, Brynn preferred to wear a holster, but for now she slipped it into the waistband at the crook of her back. The cold metal sent shivers up her spine.

When Skylar didn't answer her question again, she knelt in front of him and rested her hand on his. "We'll figure this out. We'll find out who did this to you."

She couldn't find anything wrong with him other than a bump on the head, but the more time that went by in silence, the more she worried that they would need a hospital, after all. He just wasn't acting like himself. They had a satellite phone in the Jeep, but it was the only one they had. If Gabe had gone far enough, perhaps his cell phone had service. It seemed worth a try.

As she crossed the room back to the front door, Skylar whispered quietly, "Don't leave."

Brynn turned and regarded him, seeing for the first time the fear in his eyes. It unnerved her. "I'll be right back. I'm getting the satellite phone so I can call Gabe and tell him to get back. I think we might need to get you to a doctor."

Grunting, Skylar pushed himself up from the floor and onto his feet, wobbling a little. "I'll come with you. We need to stay together."

Together, they made their way to the Jeep where Brynn popped the back open to reveal their equipment. Only when she could account for everything did she realize that she'd half-expected it to all be taken. With all this stuff, they stood a chance. They could hold out for a while, and with a few more hours for Skylar to recover, they could walk the few miles to the convenience store to get help. Their situation wasn't dire yet.

Pushing gun cases, video equipment, and other assorted weapons out of the way, Brynn pulled the heavy satellite phone to the back of the cargo area and unzipped the top. She flicked the switch to power it on, thankful that she'd remembered to charge it before they'd left Rose Valley. Receiver in hand, she scrolled through her cell phone until she found Gabe's number, then keyed it into the panel in front of her.

The call setup took a while, giving her time to pay more attention to Skylar's behavior. He stood facing away from her, anxiously watching her back.

"Want a weapon?" she asked.

He glanced briefly at her. "No. Not right now. I think it's gone."

The first clue as to the assailant. *It.* Not he or she. Or they. Brynn felt the cold prickles of the unknown run down her skin, finally faced with not just stories or promises, but the actual threat of a creature she couldn't fathom.

She decided to ask her question again. "What happened?"

Skylar again glanced at her, then looked down to the satellite phone panel and nodded at the green light indicating that the call had started. Brynn put the handset to her ear. It rang once. Twice. Three times without a response. On the fourth, she heard Gabe's cheerful voice offering the opportunity to get a call back with a proper message.

She waited patiently for the beep. "Gabe. This is Brynn. Something's going on here. Someone slashed our tires. Attacked Skylar. We need you back ASAP."

Hanging up the phone, she flicked off the panel and zipped the bag. She wanted to take it inside and make sure it stayed charged. Receiving calls on this old hunk of junk tended to be dicey, so she held little hope that she'd get a call back. Hopefully Gabe would return soon, and together they could fortify themselves against whatever stalked them.

"They're watching us," Skylar said as Brynn closed the hatch on the Jeep.

Hoisting the strap of the bag over her left shoulder, Brynn started towards the house. "Then we better get inside."

On the walk, she tried to find any evidence that they were being stalked, but could find nothing. She didn't even have the intuitive nagging that she'd sometimes felt when being watched. In any other circumstance, she would have accused Skylar of succumbing to paranoia.

Inside, she placed the satellite phone on the floor next to the wing-backed chair she'd sat in earlier, pulling the charging cable out and plugging it into the wall. When she stood back up, she found Skylar locking every window and door, frantically moving from one to the next. Though before she'd attributed his relative silence to the injury, now his stoic refusal to describe his encounter started to frighten her.

She pitched in, starting in the bedrooms, checking each lock. Scanning each closet. Peeking under every bed and behind every shower curtain. If something had been inside with them, it might still be here, and she wanted to ensure all potential hiding places were clear.

Only when she felt satisfied in her search did she return to the living room, where she found Skylar, still alert and melted into the couch cushions. Brynn had little doubt now that Skylar had encountered a skinwalker, but she was having a difficult time believing that an animal—no matter how fantastical—would be smart enough to slash tires and rely on blunt force trauma. If they were predators, they would have attacked more viciously.

Standing across from Skylar with her arms across her chest, she asked, "Was it a skinwalker? That did this to you?"

"No," he said with shaky uncertainty. "Maybe."

"Tell me."

He shook his head. "It was like nothing. Just a shadowy form of something. A person, maybe? I don't... I can't... this isn't what I expected."

"What did it hit you with?"

"That," Skylar said, thumbing behind himself to the table. The totem sat undisturbed. She found it hard to believe that this thing would have taken the totem, clubbed Skylar with it, then carefully placed it back on the table.

"The totem?" she asked.

He only nodded, prompting Brynn to cross behind him to study its placement on the table. Nothing on the front indicated any damage, so she gingerly turned it over and gasped. The back of the inhuman skull now sported a circular indentation, the bone cracked inward. Brynn had memorized every facet of this thing. She knew it had been whole when Miriam brought it in from outside.

Brynn's life was one she had chosen, ecstatic to apprentice under such a widely known cryptozoologist, but nothing had prepared her for this. She expected animals. Maybe even science experiments. But all of this sidled up far too closely to the supernatural. Witches and magic. Perhaps even demons.

Shaken, Brynn took a deep breath, pulled the pistol from her waistband and, once again, checked her ammo.

CHAPTER 8

Gabe brought up the rear, a position that he didn't entirely hate. He tried to keep his eyes on the horizon, scanning the desert around them, but occasionally he caught himself admiring the curve of her hips. He felt a little guilty for enjoying the view, but, to be fair, he did try to walk side-by-side with her. She insisted that they take up a more practical formation. He didn't entirely believe that this protected them, but it seemed important to her, and Gabe didn't care enough to protest.

Or rather, perhaps he cared too much to protest.

He shimmied his shoulder to try and move the pressure of the backpack strap. They'd brought a lot of stuff, and though he hit the gym with some regularity, none of the exercises prepared him for prolonged cardio. Most of the equipment had been designed for weight, but the copious amounts of bottled water they'd picked up at the convenience store negated any benefit of the superior engineering of their gear. He didn't complain, though, primarily because Miriam hadn't even adjusted the weight on her backpack yet, handling the burden with ease.

Every step took them closer to Gray's Point. And every step somehow made it seem equally far away. As the only shelter in view, Miriam decided that it was their best hope for finding any evidence related to the skinwalkers. Gabe tended to agree, though he entertained the possibility that they hid under cars, or porches, or even in tunnels dug under the dirt. A creature that could change its shape could fit into an awful lot of places.

"Have you ever been all the way out there?" he asked, hoping to pass the time with some small talk.

He saw her ponytail shake from side to side before she answered. "No. I don't know why we never did, though. I'm starting to think his first expedition was a farce."

"How many did he drag you on?"

"Dunno. Lost count. Until Rose Valley, though, we never found anything that couldn't be explained by paranoid citizens or misidentified animals."

Gabe wanted to ask more about Rose Valley. To find out how Miriam brought down the beast, but he could tell from their earlier conversation that it wasn't something she'd be comfortable talking about. Instead, he focused on their current mission.

"What's the plan if we actually find one of these things?"

A shrug this time. "Seems unlikely that we'll be able to capture one, and given the longevity of the reports, there must be a breeding population. I think we'll have to kill one."

"And carry it all the way back?" he asked, trying not to sound too exasperated by the thought.

"Guess so."

Gabe's first instinct had been to bring along the Jeep, but this land belonged to somebody, and finding a way inside the fence proved to be more challenging than they'd expected. Miriam seemed uncomfortable with the idea, anyway, confident that moving along in a huge yellow beacon would attract unwanted attention.

She was probably right. He didn't know how long it would take before Brynn or Skylar realized he wouldn't be coming back, and that small advantage necessitated getting a head start.

"Tell me about the kraken," Gabe said.

"It was big," she replied, slowing almost imperceptibly. "Now it's dead."

"Was it scary? Fighting it?"

Another shrug. "I guess. Didn't have time to be scared."

"Come on, Mimi. Surely, you're not that modest."

She stopped and turned to face him. Her light brown eyes reflected the sun, and he almost thought he could see fire burning there, but her lips told a different story, slightly turned up in the corners, or, at the very least, neutral and without malice. The nickname seemed to be losing its effect.

"I didn't seek out that thing," she protested. "It took Tanner. I took him back."

He smiled. "Yeah, but be honest. It at least made you feel like a badass, right?"

"It put some things in perspective, I guess," she said, cocking her head with a smirk. "It let me know that I can do this."

"Well, I think you're a badass," Gabe replied, locking onto her eyes with sincerity.

The smirk vanished, as her eyes clouded over. "Come on. I don't want to be rooting through caves in the dark."

She spun quickly and continued her march, leaving Gabe no choice but to follow. Tough nut to crack, this one. Usually, he could rely on his charm to at least get him in the door, but Miriam seemed to be having none of it. Flirting came second nature to him, and he didn't quite know what to do with a woman who wouldn't accept his advances, at least playfully if not seriously.

"You got friends back home?" he asked, hoping she'd be willing to continue the conversation.

"Yeah. Though, I don't suppose I have a home exactly. Just school."

"College sounds horrible. No thank you."

"Nothing more pure in life than learning new things," she said, swiping a hand through the air and motioning to the horizon. "It's what we do. It's not about monsters. It's about explaining the unexplained."

Gabe supposed they each had their reasons. Skylar provided him an escape hatch from a dead-end job, and if that meant hunting monsters or learning, he'd take either one.

In the distance, Gray's Point still loomed, but for the first time, he could believe that they drew closer to it. He could see the ragged sides now, each red-dusted crag shooting up at awkward angles. The peak plateaued out over the desert, casting an eerie shadow that displayed in full grandeur the size of the formation. He looked up, wondering if any path led to the top.

"We should climb it," he said.

Miriam's head craned upward. "Maybe. If we don't find anything at the bottom."

"We don't have any rock-climbing gear, though," Gabe said. "Also, I've never been rock climbing."

She turned her head and shot him a teasing glance. "Guess we'll have to improvise."

***

The base of Gray's Point would take days to fully explore, especially if they poked their heads between every rock. Miriam moved along slowly, occasionally bending down to study the ground, or a branch of scrub brush. Occasionally, she'd point out tracks of rattlesnakes, lizards, or coyotes. Gabe couldn't help but wonder if each one of them could be a skinwalker instead.

Suddenly, she stopped and held up a finger to indicate for Gabe to remain quiet. She remained still for an excruciating amount of time before saying, "Do you hear that?"

Gabe strained to listen, but heard nothing except the gentle breeze and the low, nondescript hums of civilization in the distance. He shrugged.

"The humming," she said.

"Just people. Living life."

She shook her head. "No. We're too far to be able to hear any of that."

For the first time since they'd left the Jeep, Miriam slid her backpack from her shoulders and lowered it to the ground. She knelt, leaned down, and pressed her ear against the dirt. Not knowing whether he'd actually be able to make sense of what he heard, her insistence on the action shamed Gabe into following suit. The reddish-brown dirt felt cool on his ear, despite the sun beating down.

After listening for a few seconds, she twisted around and sat on the ground, her knees pulled up to her chest while she leaned back on her hands. "I don't hear it now."

He hadn't noticed the sound disappearing, but now that she drew attention to it, only the breeze remained, gently rustling the sparse foliage around them. He dropped his own pack to the ground and sat down across from her.

"Might just be infrastructure," she said. "Water or gas pipes maybe."

Gabe didn't have a reply. He didn't even know enough to guess that. Instead, he fetched a bottle of water out of his pack and tossed it to Miriam. She caught it with ease and mumbled a thanks before shifting to a cross-legged position to free up her hands. He followed suit with his own bottle.

Somehow, sitting on the ground made the heat seem more bearable. They'd both slathered on sunblock. Gabe didn't worry too much about his own skin, but Miriam's pale complexion surely bore more risk. If she worried about a sunburn, she didn't show it. In fact, she hardly seemed put out at all, despite the rosiness of her cheeks.

"We can move over to the shade," he offered, pointing to an outcropping nearby.

"I'm good."

"Does this work?" he asked. "Just randomly walking around and looking at stuff?"

"Sometimes. It's all we've got to go on right now."

"I'd feel a lot better if we found this thing in the daylight."

She laughed. "Scared of the dark, Castillo?"

"I mean, if what you saw is real... I don't want to see another me."

Her jovial expression faded away. "Me neither. But I'll be ready this time."

She paused to take a swallow of water. Good thing she was ready, because Gabe felt a strong desire to retreat to the Jeep. He felt safer than he would have if it had just been Brynn and Skylar with him, though.

Despite being reserved and timid, Miriam managed to project confidence. He wouldn't have expected it, given his experiences with Skylar.

"Tell me about Brynn," she said, after emptying half her bottle.

Inside, emotions swirled. He fought back images of Brynn cradled in his arms. For the briefest of moments, the desert air carried the scent of her shampoo.

He tried to sound neutral. "Driven. She works hard. Respects your dad."

"What's her motivation?"

Gabe thought about it, unsure of the answer. He couldn't pretend to know everything about Brynn's past, with their time together often devolving into physical intimacy without too much deep conversation. The only thing he could be certain of: she was fundamentally broken inside. Still he yearned to fix her, and was disappointed in himself for having given up his chance. Even his big heart could only take so much.

"Rough childhood, I think," he finally said. "Her mom cycled through a lot of men. Not all of them were good guys."

Miriam arched an eyebrow and studied his face. He hoped she wouldn't see anything other than what he chose to tell her.

It felt like a punch in the gut when she asked: "How long were you two together?"

He ran his hand over his beard, attempting to hide more of his face before he answered. "Not long. A couple of months."

Miriam took her time finishing off what was left of her water, then stood up in a flash. She dusted her hands against her jeans, hefted her backpack over her shoulders. Her face remained impassive and impossible to read.

She looked down and offered a hand. "Come on. Let's see what we can find."

He took her surprisingly soft hand and hoisted himself up. On his feet, standing tall, he felt a little better, taking back the confidence she stole from him with his height. She locked her brown eyes onto his. For a moment he thought she meant to say something, but then her head whipped towards the shadows running along the stony ground near the base of Gray's Point.

She broke away from him and sprinted. "Did you see that?"

He followed, searching for any sign of life between her and the mountain, only to come up empty. She stopped near a wad of brush growing out of a crevice and knelt to the ground. Before he caught up, she pulled out her cell phone and snapped a picture.

"What is..." he said, trailing off as he got close enough to see it for himself.

He beheld a footprint in the sand, wavy around the edges. Not large. Maybe a men's size eight or nine, with a rounded heel. Just when he wanted to attribute it to a human, though, his eyes moved to the toes, causing his heart to thump against his ribs.

It looked as if the front of the foot ended in a cloven hoof. Tense, Gabe just circled, terrified to turn his back on whatever had left the print.

"Did you see what left this?" he whispered for fear of being heard.

"Yeah," she replied breathlessly. "I think so. It was crouched down. And dark. It had horns."

"Like a deer?"

"No. Like a... goat, maybe?"

That tracked with the hooves, but didn't explain the rest of the foot being so decidedly human. By the time he realized his need for a weapon, Miriam had already begun to dig through his pack. She presented him a pistol, then turned her back to him so that he could retrieve hers.

He searched for it for a few seconds before finally pulling it out and handing it to her. She wrapped her hand around it with practiced ease and held it tightly at her side.

"It couldn't have gone far," she said, inching along the perimeter.

He took a step backwards, careful to keep his back to her so that he could see whatever she couldn't. Something scuttled in the distance, not hiding behind anything, but somehow still hard to see. As if the sun itself refused to cast its rays on it.

"There!" he shouted.

Miriam spun, spreading her legs before raising her gun and firing. The *pop* from the gun deafened him, but he thought he heard a screech in the distance. He lost sight of the creature. Had Miriam tracked it that quickly?

"D-Did you hit it?" he asked.

She shook her head. "I don't think so."

Another screech pierced into Gabe's skull, this time too clear to be explained away by a gunshot. Before he could find its source, Miriam ratcheted her arms towards the sky and fired again, knocking a shadowy bird from the sky. It spiraled downward in slow motion. Gabe tried to place its shape.

He followed when Miriam moved slowly towards its landing spot, ready with his own gun, though he suspected he'd never get a shot off before she would. In this moment, the entire world felt surreal, as if he'd shifted into an alternate dimension. His head spun, and his stomach roiled with the possibility of what they were about to find.

When he caught up, Miriam knelt over the carcass, then looked up at him with eyes full of confusion. He didn't see the shadowy terror anymore. The light-bending texture of its visage was gone. Its talons twitched, its eyes vacant. It didn't make sense. They'd both seen something more.

He tried to make sense of it. To find an explanation that fit with the story his eyes had told him when Miriam pulled the trigger. In the silence, however, the truth seemed obvious and unavoidable.

On the outside, at least, it was only a hawk.

CHAPTER 9

She preferred a scalpel. Her father spared no expense on his pocketknives, but they lacked the precision required for a proper dissection. Splayed out on the flattest stone she could find, the bird looked surprisingly normal, far from the shadowy phantasm she'd shot. The adrenaline kept her at high alert, studying each organ and looking for anything out of the ordinary.

Gabe paced frantically nearby, exuding enough nervous energy for them both. Occasionally he would stop and mutter something rhetorical, but Miriam managed to mostly ignore it so that she could focus on her task. He seemed a good enough guy, but clearly the rigors of hunting monsters presented more of a challenge than he could handle.

Her nose itched, but she ignored that too, not wanting to spread more blood on her. Her latex-covered hands dripped from it, but she hardly noticed the carcass' unique death stench. She pushed intestines out of the way and verified her clean shot, staring through the bullet hole at the bare stone just beyond the exit wound. Further digging revealed the bird's tiny heart, no longer beating with life. By all accounts, everything looked normal as far as she could tell, though it'd been a while since she'd dissected a bird.

Gabe stopped again and stood over her. "We can't stay out here, now. It's not safe."

Miriam made a slit up the bird's throat, pulling apart each half to study its esophagus, on her way to the skull and brain. She stopped when Gabe's shadow didn't disappear. "Of course we aren't safe. This isn't a safe line of work."

She barely choked out the last sentence before memories of Cornelius popped into her head. All the proof that she'd ever need about the danger of her profession.

Gabe's chest heaved up and down. Sweat beaded his brow. He was supposed to have received training. He should have been able to handle this. She couldn't afford to be taking care of a coward while also protecting them from this thing. Or the others like it. She still couldn't decide whether this bird had once been the dark creature in the bush, or if that goat-like apparition still stalked them. Either way, she felt certain there would be more, and it'd be much harder to see them in the dark.

Frustrated, she said, "Did you think this would be easy? That you could just use your charm to slay monsters?"

She regretted it the moment it came out of her mouth, but she also couldn't stomach the thought of apologizing. She looked back down to the bird before registering Gabe's reaction, but she did note the almost immediate disappearance of his shadow looming over her.

With a clear path to the skull, Miriam inserted two of her bloody fingers into the base and exerted just enough pressure to pry it apart. It made a sickening *pop*. Using the knife, she carefully removed the brain. She held it up as if the sun might illuminate something meaningful, but deep down she knew that she didn't know enough about brains to detect anything abnormal. Whatever unholy characteristics this thing possessed lurked deeper down, in its DNA. Unfortunately, she had no way to test the blood yet.

"Can you get me some vials and evidence bags?" she asked. "And put on some gloves."

Gabe immediately rounded to his backpack and knelt to dig through it. Miriam waited patiently for him to find what she needed, then motioned for him to kneel beside her. She didn't know which parts of the bird she'd need, but she started by dropping the brain into one of the larger vials, which Gabe chose for her. He capped it off and set it down beside him before presenting her with another.

With no way to siphon blood out, she used the knife to scoop up as much as she could and drain it into the vial. A few more scoops, then she nodded for Gabe to close that one up as well.

She could tell that he was biting his tongue. He hadn't been this quiet the entire time she'd known him.

"I know it's weird," she said. "The first time you see something that shouldn't exist."

Not exactly an apology, but she hoped he'd take her meaning all the same. Also, not entirely truthful. It had never seemed weird to her, but she'd learned enough to see the fear in others. He didn't answer right away, but continued to cooperate as she worked to preserve more of the carcass.

"Yeah," he finally replied. "Sorry I don't know what to do or how to help."

Satisfied that she'd gotten all that she needed from the bird, Miriam rose to her feet and slipped off the gloves. The bulk of the blood stayed with the latex, but she still felt dirty. Compromised. In desperate need of a shower.

"I don't need help," she said.

She noticed the slightest wince as he also stood and cast his eyes downward. Is that what he wanted? A girl who needed his help? The thought of being that kind of woman turned her stomach. He wouldn't find that with her. Ever.

When he didn't respond, she continued, "I just need you here. I'll tell you everything you need to do. I'll protect you. Us. I won't let one of those things get you."

"Maybe we should just head back," he said.

She failed to suppress an indifferent shrug. "One of these things was at the house, too. It's not any safer there."

"But we'd have Skylar and Brynn."

"Trust me," she responded. "My father's not going to save you from anything."

She retrieved a small trash bag and filled it with her inside-out gloves. Gabe followed suit. Next, she fetched a bottle of water and handed it to Gabe, with as reassuring of a smile as she could muster. "You can help me wash my hands."

Miriam grabbed a handful of sand and held out her hands in a cup-shape to accept some of the water. Once Gabe turned the sand into a gritty mud, she used it to scrape her knuckles, her fingers, her wrists, up to her elbows. If she could have made a mud-bath for her whole body, she would have. Gabe assisted with more water so that she could get most of the mud off of her, which left her feeling a little cleaner than when she started.

"I'd prefer to find a cave," she announced, packing away the specimens. "Harder to protect a tent. With a cave, we only have to protect the entrance."

"Unless they're in the cave with us," Gabe said with a sour expression.

"We'll just make sure they aren't. We've got a few hours before sunset. We've got time. If we find it now, then we'll have a base of operations."

Without waiting for confirmation, Miriam took off looking for the shelter she sought. Gabe followed. The eerie quiet from him unsettled her, filling her with guilt. Her cheeks felt hot, not from the sun, but deeper. She felt bad for snapping at him, worried that she might have ruined their working relationship.

She tried to focus. Why should she care what this random guy thought of her? He didn't even know what he was doing. The question bounced around her head as she walked, but she came up with no answer. All she knew was that she'd started to regret this expedition.

Preoccupied, she didn't notice the hole in the dirt in front of her. By the time she noticed it, a *pop* reverberated up her leg, past her knee and into her hip, sending shivers of pain through every nerve ending in her leg. She tried to stay on her feet, but her ankle would have none of it.

Miriam went down. Hard.

***

She stood on one foot with an arm draped around Gabe's shoulders. The pain hadn't abated, but she insisted they find shelter before he spend any more time fussing over her. She'd be fine. It wasn't broken. Just sprained.

She glanced down at the bad ankle and took in the sickly purplish knot already swelling. She'd have to abandon her shoe soon.

Okay, so *badly* sprained.

Both of them now peered into what felt like an endless abyss. She'd hoped for more options, but so far, this cave provided the only shelter. Carved into the side of Gray's Point that currently hid from the sun, it looked ominously cavernous, but she suspected that it didn't go back as far as it looked. They could keep going. They hadn't made it all the way around yet. She could handle it, especially with Gabe dragging her along.

"What do you think?" she asked, trying to make Gabe feel as included as possible, knowing deep down that she'd choose the cave of her liking.

Miriam felt his shrug.

"Not sure we have a choice," he said.

She slung her backpack to the ground at her feet, fetched an LED flashlight and forced the two of them to take a step into the mouth of the cave.

"Let's check it out," she pressed.

Their first step over the threshold sent shivers up her spine, recalling her spelunking in Rose Valley. They'd found key evidence in that cave, but also her brother's murderer. Every time she thought she'd dealt with the trauma, it came creeping back. Perhaps it always would.

It didn't take long for her to confirm her suspicions about the cave. The walls quickly curved in and met in the back, providing less than ten feet of usable ground space. Enough to sleep in. Easy to protect. Empty, she saw no signs of animals using it for shelter. She liked it.

"I'll set up some lanterns," Gabe offered. "Lay out supplies."

Miriam made a show of looking him in the eye and smiling as best she could, hoping for reciprocation.

Hard to tell, but his countenance seemed maybe a little softer since she'd hurt his feelings. At any rate, he quickly went to work.

With hours of daylight left, she hated to hunker down for the night. There was more to do, and every second they wasted brought the surety that Skylar would find them. Maybe that wouldn't be so bad. Maybe just this once, she could stomach losing something for the chance to extricate herself from this situation and get back to the sanctity of her dorm room. The comfort of Macy's friendship. The strength of Tanner's presence. But now the choices in front of her were few. She could only do what Gabe would let her.

She supported herself against the mouth of the cave while Gabe worked. He started with a sleeping bag, then helped her over. He lowered her down slowly and gently, then crouched beside her. She winced as she tried to situate her ankle to minimize the pain.

"What do we say?" he asked, a silly grin on his face.

Embarrassingly, it took her a few seconds to realize what he meant. He started gingerly working on removing her shoe while she processed.

"Thank you," she finally mumbled.

He scuttled off, leaving Miriam thankful that he hadn't followed up with a snide remark about it not being that hard. Her ankle looked bad. Certainly the worst sprain she'd ever gotten. She wanted to believe that the swelling would break by morning, but she knew it wouldn't. Something scary and potentially dangerous waited for them outside of that cave, and she couldn't calculate a path forward that didn't involve her facing those horrors alone.

She took a deep breath. "You're going to have to go for help."

Gabe flicked on their second LED lantern and stood back up. He looked menacingly tall standing over her, his massive shadow plastered over the cave wall. She cleared her throat, preparing to make her case. With a busted ankle, words provided her only weapon.

"No way," he said emphatically. "I'll carry you back. Tomorrow. When we have the whole day."

Gabe was strong. She couldn't help but notice his biceps, and the strong lines of his back. His thick, muscular thighs. Maybe he could carry her for a little while. But not for miles.

"You can't. I'm too heavy. It's too far."

He chuckled. "You *are* surprisingly dense."

"You better be referring to my mass," she said.

He cocked his head and shot her a teasing smile. "Sure. Let's go with that. How often do you work out?"

"Not as often as I used to. He made us workout at least once a day. Sometimes twice if nothing else was going on. Just a few days a week, now."

"Well, it's impressive," he said.

"Thanks, I guess. You clearly spend some time with weights, yourself."

He flexed one of his biceps and patted it. "Oh this? All comes naturally."

Miriam laughed, a brief reprieve from the pain. He responded by striking a few more poses, trying to look like a weightlifter and instead looking a little more like a ballerina.

A manly ballerina, though, if such a thing existed.

When the laughing died down, she worked hard to bring the conversation back to the matter at hand. "Seriously, though, Gabe."

"Mimi. I can't leave you like this. Trapped in a cave. What if one of them comes for you?"

"Then I'll kill it."

He protested, "What if you miss? What if it gets to you? You can't run like this."

"I need drugs that we don't have," she begged. "And crutches. Probably a boot."

He didn't answer right away, instead turning back to set up more lanterns. Then, in a move that Miriam considered quite clever, he unrolled one of their tents over the mouth of the cave and went about trying to find a way to attach it to the rock. It wouldn't stop a vicious predator from bursting through, but it might give them a little more time to react.

"Gabe, look at me," she gently commanded.

When he slowly turned to meet her gaze, she saw it for the first time. The fear. Why hadn't she seen it before? He didn't want to face what he might find alone in the desert. Not without her. But they had no choice. No other way.

She meant to give a speech to convince him once and for all, but instead she leaned over and pulled the other sleeping bag towards herself. She unrolled it and placed it next to her, a little closer than she wanted, but with her limited mobility it was the best that she could muster. Gabe stood and watched, as if her command to look at her meant he couldn't turn away until she released him.

Though she didn't manage to get it completely unfurled, she felt confident in her show of comfort. She reached over and patted the empty sleeping bag, and, surprised by the vulnerability in her voice, said, "Tomorrow. You can go for help tomorrow."

CHAPTER 10

Brynn watched as Skylar slept restlessly on the couch, sometimes snoring and sometimes not, depending on which way he tossed. She'd tried to keep him awake, but since she felt certain that he didn't have a concussion, she finally gave in and let him drift away. The sun's hot rays still pierced through the curtains, but even when they were replaced by moonbeams, Brynn felt confident she wouldn't be able to sleep.

The winged-back chair provided comfort and refuge, strategically positioned for maximum visibility. To her right sat the back door. Across from her, the front. Breaking through the windows would create an unmistakable racket, and she counted on that to alert her. Nearby, she kept a pistol and a crowbar. She would take no chances if the intruder returned.

Enough time had passed that the adrenaline no longer urged her into action, so she settled down now with the journal from Gabe's mother. Reading it in plain sight of Skylar carried certain risks, but given his injury and his insistence on sleeping, she doubted that he'd notice.

She chose a random page, switching her mind to Spanish as she read.

***

Hector introduced me to some friends today. They came to the house in suits and left me with a handful of pamphlets, but they're all in English and I can't really understand what they say. The men both spoke in my native tongue, though, and led me on a winding conversation about the nature of the universe and the sacrifices we must all make for the greater good. Hector sat by in silence, but I could see him watching my face with great interest.

I assumed at first that they meant to talk to me about the Lord, but they didn't specifically talk about religion. They focused instead on nature and balance, and the complex relationship between humans and the earth. Perhaps that is a religion all by itself.

Since my arrival, I haven't been to mass. Hector says it's not safe for me to show myself in public. Though I say my prayers and try to maintain my faith, I've seen little indication that Hector is Catholic. I can only conclude that he's a member of this new religion, worshiping the elements or some such nonsense. I'm grateful for his shelter, but I cannot forsake my God for superstition.

Gabriel is thriving in his new home, growing stronger every day. Hector is a great uncle, always striving to teach my child from the countless books on his shelves. He's smart, with great wisdom. I can only hope that Gabriel can say the same when he grows to be an adult.

I wonder sometimes how I'll explain it to him. But I have a while yet before he'll ask. Until then, I will continue to do the best I can as a mother, and hope that I can give him the life that I never had.

***

Moisture formed in Brynn's eyes. She batted it away with the back of her hand, hoping that the action would also stave off thoughts of her own mother. And her fathers. So many fathers. She couldn't even remember the real one anymore. Just the others. Their foul breath and unpredictable temperaments. They mingled together in her memories to form one insurmountable adversary that haunted her at every turn.

Gabe's mother loved him so much. She tried so hard. Brynn envied that. Her own mother had offered her very little. Starting at the age of twelve, Brynn had been taking care of herself. Washing her own clothes. Making her own food. And avoiding the adults in the house. Some days, she drew strength from her past. Used it as her source of power, and congratulated herself on clawing her way out.

Not today.

Lost in thought, she didn't notice Skylar stirring across from her. He'd fully sat up by the time she noticed, studying her with those shrewd eyes.

"What's that?" he asked.

She looked down to the journal, tried to compose herself. "Um. My diary."

His eyes narrowed. Having a pen would make this look more legit. He'd notice she couldn't possibly be writing anything down.

Brynn shuffled it off her lap and leaned over to stuff it into her bag on the floor. She sat back up with a forced laugh, hoping to convey embarrassment. "I like to read what I've written sometimes. It helps me become better."

The silence stretched on as he seemed to judge the worth of her explanation. She pondered the meaning of his solemn expression, relieved when he finally said, "Good. That's good. We should all work to make ourselves better."

She exhaled the breath she'd been holding. "Want some coffee? Let me make you some."

"That would be lovely," Skylar replied. "I'll take first shift tonight. I don't want us to both be asleep at the same time."

"Makes sense," she said, moving to the kitchen and fetching bottles of water from the refrigerator. They'd learned on the first night not to use the water from the tap. No one cared for dirt-flavored coffee.

While she worked, Skylar moved to her chair. The breath caught in her chest as he inched towards her bag, but he reached past it to pick up the crowbar she'd leaned against the wall. He flexed his hand around the shaft and swatted the air, practicing blows against an invisible adversary. Brynn found it easy to forget that he'd had decades of experience with a weapon.

As he swung, he said, "I think you may be right."

"Oh?"

"I don't think Gabe's coming back."

She leaned against the bar and stared into empty cups while the coffee brewed. "He... gets distracted. Easily, I think."

"Not the best quality for a cryptozoologist."

"Why'd you hire him, then?" she asked, genuinely curious.

Skylar put the crowbar back against the wall and moved to a window to peek outside. "When I bought this place, he and his uncle were having a tough time. Hector didn't want to sell."

The bubbling of the brewer stopped, and Brynn went about making two cups of coffee. She knew just how he liked it, though he'd never officially made that part of her job.

"I needed a safe base of operations here," he continued. "So I finally convinced him not with money, but with a promise. To look after Gabe. Hector was old already, struggling to get by. Gabe was just a kid."

Surprised by this revelation, Brynn almost dropped the cup of coffee as she carried it to him, but recovered in time. A scalding drop burned her thumb's knuckle. Embarrassed, she made no move to nurse it.

"Thank you," he said, taking the cup. "I couldn't take on a ward. Not when I had my three to deal with and a constant schedule of expeditions. But I could help in other ways. From afar, I made sure he was taken care of. Made sure he could find work. He's a good kid."

She knew some of Gabe's plight, but didn't know anything of this secret arrangement. Did Gabe even know? She made a mental note to ask him if she ever saw him again.

"He might still come back," she offered, half-heartedly.

Skylar just quietly drank his coffee, so Brynn followed suit. They sipped in silence until they heard the faint sound of screeching hinges, followed by the soft rattling of the front door's handle.

Then—a heavy knock. Brynn's breath caught in her throat. Could it be Gabe? Had he come back?

Skylar reacted quicker, pacing over to the door, clearly trying to get a view through the curtain without getting so close as to give away his own position. By the time Brynn drew near enough to see for herself, the window showed only the light of the sun. No head. No shadow.

"Gabe?" Skylar asked through the door.

No response. Brynn fetched her pistol and the crowbar, returning to Skylar's side and offering him the latter. He took it in his right hand, used his left to turn the lock, then to open the door. Brynn thought her heart might jump out of her chest as he unveiled the porch in full. Nothing. No one.

Skylar cocked his head. Brynn followed his gaze to see a rabbit calmly sitting at the threshold, chewing on grass. Not a jackrabbit, but a white bunny. An animal that didn't roam these deserts. And tame at that, judging by its insistence on holding its ground.

Skylar frowned. "What the hell?"

Before Brynn could answer, she heard the back door jiggle, followed by another knock. This one did not come with the hope of Gabe. Only the terror of something sinister. She moved quickly this time, raising the gun to the window of the back door, ready to shoot through it if she had to.

When she saw it, every muscle in her body froze. She should have pulled the trigger. Wanted to. But couldn't. Through the small window she saw the skull of a deer, but its neck gave way to very human shoulders. Its hollow eyes bore into her soul, despite the curtain between them.

By the time she regained her bearings, it'd dashed away from the door, causing her to finally fire too late. The bullet crashed through the window and whizzed over empty desert. The clang of Skylar's crowbar drew her attention back to the front door, where the same deer-man reeled from a hit to the side of the head.

How did it get there so *fast*?

No door between them now, Brynn saw the human shoulders and human frame... but things were wrong. Off. One spindly arm tapered into a skeletal hand. Its legs seemed thicker than they should have been, holding its balance even with the force of the blow.

Expertly, Skylar drew back and took a second shot at the thing's breast, then a third at its knees. Each blow elicited strange grunting noises, familiar and exotic. Brynn pulled up her gun but couldn't get a clean shot. Not with Skylar standing in the way.

"Move!" she yelled.

Skylar looked towards her, then pivoted to his right. The deer-man stopped and stared at her, but she wouldn't be so easily frozen this time. She took a quick breath and squeezed the trigger.

The deer-man melted. Or evaporated. She couldn't tell. Her eyes wouldn't let her process it. She hadn't hit him, though. She felt certain of that.

Glass shattered nearby, from down the hall. She spun, aim still rigid, but nothing emerged from the bedrooms.

Silence.

She pushed down her breathing, trying to quiet her own body enough to listen for what might be coming for them. Skylar slammed the front door, locked it, and retreated to her side. His own breath seemed even louder than hers.

Together, they waited.

Skylar suddenly pointed, "There."

She ran her eyes down his arm and saw a rattlesnake slithering out from Miriam's bedroom. A simple snake hardly scared her, but she wondered whether it might become something else.

Another window broke nearby. Though she'd done well so far, Brynn couldn't suppress a scream this time. Glass from the front door tinkled across the ground, the skeletal hand of the deer-man reaching through to unlock the door.

"No!" she screamed, spinning and firing a wild shot. She missed the arm, failing to stop it from completing its task. The handle turned just as more of the broken glass of the backdoor fell to the ground behind her. Her world spun.

"You take the back. I'll take the front!" Skylar cried, bounding forward with his crowbar and more courage than she would have ever thought possible from him.

Brynn lunged towards the back door, leaving Skylar to defend the front. She threw her weight against the door, using the butt of her gun to club the grasping hand. Unlike the other, this one looked like a normal human hand, but the skull of a goat stared back at her through the window. Each blow caused the hand to retreat before trying again.

She only vaguely registered Skylar across from her, squaring off with the deer-man. No door stood between the two of them, and no matter how many hits Skylar seemed to sneak in, it didn't deter the intruder from punishing Skylar's every blow with one of its own.

They needed to work together. Whatever these things wanted, Brynn felt certain that splitting her and Skylar up was exactly part of their plan. He'd wanted to attribute their behavior to animals earlier, but there could be no doubt they possessed more intellect than a goat, or a deer, or a rattlesnake. This assault implied planning and forethought.

Skylar lost his footing, dropping to one knee. He fought bravely, but he was losing the fight. Brynn mustered her resolve and pulled the gun up, aiming it right between the goat's venom-yellow slit-eyes. It bleated and grabbed for the muzzle just as she pulled the trigger, pushing her aim off into the distance. It lunged towards her, pushing more broken glass to the floor as its head slammed into her nose.

Black spots erupted across her vision.

She fired again, unable to tell where her shot went this time, and then heard the goat's hand scramble through the window to turn the door handle. She'd lost. It came for her now. The pain in her face prevented her from moving in time, and the door slammed into her, knocking her to the ground. She lost her grip on the gun and it clattered to the floor. By the time her vision returned, the goat-man had moved past.

Propped up on her elbows and trying to ignore the blood and pain, Brynn watched Skylar collapse to the ground. The deer slammed one of its huge feet into his head. The *thunk* reverberated the wooden planks beneath her, and she knew he couldn't possibly have retained consciousness. She needed to find the gun. She needed...

"Help!" she screamed, loudly. She didn't think anyone would hear, but maybe it would scare away these otherworldly monstrosities.

Crouched over Skylar, the goat-man turned his head and studied her. He bleated, grabbed Skylar's ankles and stood. The deer-man followed suit, hooking Skylar's armpits. The two easily lifted him up. What were they doing? Where were they taking him?

Brynn scrambled for the gun, eyes bleary with blood and tears. The sobs poured out of her, her labored breath catching in her chest. Where the hell was her gun? It had to be close.

There! The gunmetal glinted just enough for her to see it in the darkened hallway. Somehow it had skidded away, past the now-coiled rattlesnake, its tail rattling.

A stupid snake would not stop her. She pushed herself up, jolted down the hallway, and kicked at the snake. It lunged, widening its mouth and exposing its fangs, but it struck too late, biting at air as it hurtled away. She grabbed for the gun, moved back to the living room and readied to fire on the abominations destroying her world.

They were gone.

So was Skylar.

The living room sat eerily silent, glass everywhere. The smell of fresh coffee strangely juxtaposed the wet, rank smell of the skinwalkers. Only then did she notice that the snake's rattle no longer echoed down the hallway.

"No," she blubbered to herself. Tears streamed down her face, mixing with the blood from her nose, trickling into her mouth. She barely noticed the foul taste.

She needed to leave. To find the police. To get as far away from this place as she could. But the Jeep's shredded tires made escape impossible.

She collapsed into the wing-backed chair, too exhausted to worry about whether the snake was still nearby. Behind her, the satellite phone remained plugged into the wall.

Brynn regretted everything now. Joining up with Skylar. Thinking she could pursue such a dangerous career. She didn't have the mettle. The strength. She'd stubbornly refused to see it before, but it was true. She was worthless.

Sobbing, she reached over and slid the satellite phone towards her. She would call the police. They would come and take her away from all of this. They would give her the out that she so desperately needed.

They might even find Skylar. But she doubted it. He was gone and she could only save herself.

CHAPTER 11

"So, I put my elbow up and I jumped as high as could," Gabe said, gesticulating wildly from the middle of the cave. He recreated the action, hopping into the air with his elbow pointing upward. Tears of laughter welled in Miriam's eyes. "Well, the ceiling was much lower. And I hit it and knocked a hole in it. Plaster came crashing down. But I won the bet."

"Which was a grilled cheese sandwich, you said?" Miriam asked.

He nodded and smiled a big, welcoming smile. "Best grilled cheese sandwich I ever ate. He taught me how to make'em, too. I'll make you one some time."

She crinkled up her nose. "I don't like grilled cheeses. They're so boring and bland."

"What?!"

He clutched his heart and faked a heart attack, crumpling onto the sleeping bag next to her. Unsure of what to do with such antics, Miriam just stared at him. After a few seconds, he opened one eye, saw she was looking at him, then quickly closed it. The laughter having died down, she found herself alone with her discomfort again.

Awkwardly, Gabe eventually opened his eyes and sat up. "Anyway. Juan's crazy."

With no more light seeping through the makeshift curtain at the cave mouth, the lanterns cast amorphous shadows along the walls. Darkness had crept up on them, and for the first time since the sun went down, Miriam felt the claustrophobia closing in.

Eager to keep talking a little while longer, she surprised herself by sensibly continuing the conversation. "Do you still talk to him?"

Gabe looked remorseful. "Nah. Not really. He works a lot. I'm never around."

"You could write him a letter."

Gabe laughed. "A letter? What is this, 1945?"

Miriam felt the blood rush to her cheeks. She just wanted to help. This was exactly why she didn't engage in social conversation. It never went the way she wanted, and she always ended up feeling more embarrassed than happy. The larger part of her just wanted to get on with the hunt, get back to school, and back to the perfectly-curated life that she'd made for herself. She didn't like the new and foreign feeling that nagged her into wanting to stay in Gabe's good graces.

She tried to force a sympathetic giggle, but it came out strangled, more like a hiccup. More self-conscious than ever, she said, "We should get some sleep."

"We should sleep in shifts, yeah?"

Miriam appreciated the question, choosing to take it as him yielding to her experience. "Makes sense. Two hours? I'll take the first and third, so you can get more sleep before your walk."

He rolled onto the hard dirt so he could unzip his sleeping bag, then rolled his pack over to use as a pillow. He slid in and tossed a bit to get comfy, eventually settling on his back.

"Maybe your ankle will be better tomorrow," he said. "Maybe you'll be able to come with me."

Miriam glanced at her ankle and tried not to wince at the purplish mass of flesh it had become. "Yeah. Maybe."

Not a chance.

Miriam asked, "Should we turn off some of the lanterns so you can sleep?"

"Nah. I'm good, *chica*," he said, closing his eyes. "I want you to be able to see so you can protect my ass from those things."

She scooted back against the cave wall, checking to make sure she could still reach her pistol. Two hours. It seemed like a long time, but the throbbing in her leg would've made it hard to sleep anyway. The ibuprofen only helped a little.

With hours having passed since they encountered the hawk-thing, the fear of what might lurk in the desert had abated a little bit, but as silence settled in and Gabe drifted off to sleep, the shadows started to take on a life of their own, undulating and morphing, pushing Miriam back into high alert. She studied each one carefully, but only found tricks of the light.

A calm breeze billowed the tent-curtain, but Gabe's handiwork stayed strong. If something came for them, it would have to tear down the canvas first, and that would give her time to react.

As the time passed, she considered the science behind it all. How could these things change their shape? A lot of animals changed color, and some could even regrow limbs, but to completely morph would require some sort of change at the atomic level. Like ice into water, or rock into molten lava. The energy required for that sort of shift would be huge. It just didn't make any sense. The idea had no analog in modern science. But, she also couldn't ignore what she'd seen.

She'd tried to ignore the ramifications of them being able to take on the shape of people. It meant she couldn't really trust anyone. It was certainly possible, too, that the Gabe she'd met at the convenience store and taken into the desert might not really be him at all. But he had the Jeep. And the memories. It had to be him. She had nothing to worry about.

Still, sitting in the dim light of a cave as the desert wind knocked at the door, Miriam felt the paranoia start to envelop her.

***

She glanced at the cheap, over-sized watch on her wrist. The designers likely intended the relic for a boy's wrist, but Miriam liked it because the batteries lasted forever and the screen proved easy to read in any light. It didn't count her steps or alert her when someone texted, but she didn't worry about either of those things.

She'd managed to make it the first two hours without incident, only having to combat the caverns of her mind and the limitless bounds of her creativity. Gabe blissfully slept the entire time. He trusted in her, it seemed. And while of course she would protect him, Miriam still didn't understand his willingness to so readily put his life in her hands.

She nudged at his shoulder. He lazily batted away her hand. She tried again. "Gabe. It's your turn."

His eyes opened, and he raised his hand against the onslaught of light. He blinked a few times, then pulled himself up.

"It's been two hours already?" he asked.

"Yeah," she said. "Nothing happened."

He nodded groggily. "Good. That's good."

Standing, he shook out his whole body, as if forcing faster blood circulation. Miriam couldn't help but notice that he appeared to be psyching himself up. Though his fear had disappeared while they laughed the previous day away, it now crept back in.

Gabe asked, "Was it scary?"

"No," she quickly lied. Did she do it to calm his nerves, or to hide her insecurities? Even she didn't know.

"Okay," he said. "I got this. I got your back, Mimi."

Miriam smiled and shimmied into her sleeping bag. It felt good to lay down. She didn't have a pack to use as a pillow, since hers propped up her bad ankle, so she reached for Gabe's.

"Who said you could use my pack?" he asked.

"Oh," she said. "I just... I'm sorry."

Flustered, she pushed it back to its starting location and tried to find a comfortable spot for her head to lay against the rock.

"Geez, *chica*. I'm joking. Here..." He picked up the backpack and shoved it under her as she raised her head. "Sweet dreams. I got this."

He pulled the top of the sleeping bag closer to her neck and patted the front of her shoulder. The touch was unexpected, and jarred her.

Twice now he'd insisted that he *had this*. She hoped he really did, but the fatigue drew on her so strongly that she knew she wouldn't be able to stay awake all night to make sure. She'd have to trust him the way he'd trusted her.

For a few minutes Miriam watched him pace the cave, finding herself mesmerized by him. His nervous energy somehow made him more endearing.

He was scared—there could be no doubt about it—but he pressed on anyway, resolute on doing his part. On protecting her. On letting her sleep. Memories of thinking him a coward earlier rushed blood to her cheeks.

Though she worried that she might stay awake and watch him forever, her brain started getting fuzzy. Her thoughts meandered. Silly things popped into her head, only to be pushed aside by shadowed wings and grimacing, sharp-toothed versions of her father. Her mind tried to escape by forcing her back awake, but it only lasted a few moments before she started drifting again.

Against all odds, Miriam slept.

***

Something other than Gabe jarred her awake. Her eyes shot open and she jolted upright, surprised when his arm flew off her. He grumbled and turned in his bag. She ignored the mixed emotions of waking up to Gabe's arm around her, quickly dismissing it by telling herself that they'd ended up so closely cuddled together for warmth only. She instead focused on trying to ascertain the source of whatever she'd heard.

Nothing. Silence. Too much silence, maybe.

Sun clawed through the tent canvas. Morning had come. The waking haze evaporated. Frustrated and panicked, she turned and hit Gabe hard on the shoulder.

"You fell asleep!"

He slowly opened his eyes, looking as if he wouldn't respond to her at all before throwing off his sleeping bag and jumping to his feet. He seemed prepared for a fight. When it became clear that there was none, he sank back down beside her and rubbed his head.

"I... I didn't mean to," he muttered. "I'm sorry."

She tried to contain the frantic beating of her heart. She searched inside for forgiveness and levity. Instead, she exploded. "We could have been killed! This isn't a game. There's something out there. This isn't some TV show where you hang out in the desert and try to get the girl, Gabe. This is real life!"

"But we didn't. We're fine."

She wanted to get up. To pace and threaten and hover over him for intimidation, but she could still feel the dull pain in her leg. Without even looking, she knew she wouldn't be standing without extreme effort.

Miriam forcefully pushed his chest, but he leaned into it and hardly gave any ground. She yelled, "I trusted you!"

This time, he just offered a silent apology with his dark brown eyes and a solemn expression. She found it infuriating. Everything about him. He thought he could charm his way through life, but no monster ever went down from a breathtaking smile or a winning sense of humor. He just didn't get it. And he never would, would he? She'd gotten too close to him. Too fast.

"Get out of here," she said, more quietly. "Get some help."

He just sat there. Miriam turned away and looked at the cave wall, trying to sort out whether she was madder at Gabe or herself. Her eyes felt wetter than she wanted, and her breathing just wouldn't slow down. She might be sick. Her body, in an attempt to repair her ankle, must've left her unable to control her emotions.

Stupid bodies.

She heard him stand up behind her. Good. If he could just leave, then she'd compose herself and this whole mess would be over. It startled her when she felt his hand on her shoulder. Even as he turned her towards him, she refused to look him in the eye.

"I stayed awake through my shift," he said. "But you were sleeping so well, and your ankle... I didn't want to wake you up, so I just decided to stay awake through your shift, too."

She didn't want to honor anything he said with more words, causing her to take a while before answering, "But you didn't."

"I know. I messed up. I'm sorry."

He sounded sincere, but then again, she suspected he was very good at sounding sincere. If she couldn't trust him to watch her back when she needed it, then she also couldn't trust him to tell her the truth.

Eager to end the conversation, Miriam looked at him. At his ear, really, before saying, "It's fine. It's fine. Just go get someone."

She looked back down, feeling the heat of his stare for what seemed like an eternity before he stood from his crouch. Hopefully, she could at least trust him to send someone back for her. If not, though, she'd find a way to get back to civilization. She could always count on herself when it really mattered.

Quickly gathering his backpack, he pulled one side of the tent down and turned back to her. "You sure you'll be okay?"

"*Yes,*" she said. "I've got rations. I've got a weapon. I'll be fine."

He sighed and stepped out into the desert, leaving the makeshift door hanging open. He wouldn't be able to reattach it from the outside. Gingerly, she slid out of her sleeping bag and looked at her ankle. The swelling had gone down a bit. She pushed up to her good foot, tried to put weight on the bad one, and winced in pain. Pushing through it, she hobbled to the mouth of the cave.

Gabe stood speechless just outside. As if he sensed her behind him, he choked out, "What? How?"

Miriam supported her weight against the wall and tried to make sense of the pile of bones in front of her.

Not a small pile, either. A huge one, at least three feet high. A pole stuck out of the center with a chimera of skulls attached to it. The center skull of a longhorn stared forward from gaping eye sockets, flanked by a coyote. An owl. A rabbit, maybe? Above the crown of the longhorn, a carefully-posed rattlesnake skeleton arched forward, shaped into what looked like a scorpion tale protruding from the totem. Under the skulls lay what looked like a human ribcage.

She swallowed hard, her mind racing to understand when this could have happened. Was it fresh? Had the work on this monument woken her?

Dammit. If Gabe would have just stayed awake. The anger collided with the fear, and Miriam couldn't make sense of how she felt. They were just bones. Placed here to scare them. By skinwalkers? Maybe, but she refused to be intimidated. Whether people or monsters, she could kill them.

Gabe turned toward her with huge eyes. "I can't leave you here."

She certainly didn't want to be left alone. Not now, especially. But she couldn't walk the miles back to the road. It would take forever, likely stranding them in darkness without the shelter of a cave. Gabe could make it out and back before dark if he hurried.

"You have to," she pleaded. "There's no other choice. Just get back before dark. With help."

He motioned to the bones in front of him. "But whatever left his. It might come for you."

She ignored the tears welling in his eyes and the fear that coursed through him so strongly that she could feel it emanating into her. He wouldn't leave if she showed weakness.

"Just hurry," she said, as stoically as she could. "I'll be fine. I killed a kraken, remember?"

He didn't look convinced. Not surprising. She was trying to look strong standing on one foot, leaning against a cave, holding up an ankle the size of an orange.

She expected him to protest at least one more time, but instead he said, "Be careful."

"Always."

With that, he took off in a jog. He wouldn't be able to keep up that pace, but she appreciated the show of effort. Even at a brisk walk, he'd get back to her before nightfall. And then... she couldn't decide what she wanted to do next. Give up? Or take a few days and then get to the bottom of this? The pain begged her to choose the former, but something deep in her bones told her she wouldn't be giving up.

The hawk. The totems. The mimic.

It all felt personal now.

CHAPTER 12

Faster!

The speedometer pushed past ninety, but Gabe pressed for more. On reaching the highway, he'd received service long enough to listen to a frantic message from Brynn, insisting that her and Skylar had been attacked by someone. Or something. It was hard to make sense of it.

Now he raced to save not just one, but two women.

And Skylar.

Paying less attention to the road than he should have, he pushed some buttons on the steering wheel and waited for his phone to ring. He desperately wanted to hear the measured voice of 911 dispatch, but his phone couldn't connect. The brief window of signal had passed, and he was left to deal with his own problems.

A *honk* jolted his attention back to the road, where he swerved back into his own lane to miss the truck barreling towards him. The Jeep veered off the highway and Gabe fought for control. He almost lost to the speed, but the four-wheel drive caught traction and stabilized just before he struck the roadside barbed wire fence. He swallowed hard, took a few deep breaths, then pulled the Jeep back into his lane, keeping his speed at a reasonable seventy.

He couldn't help anyone if he was dead.

According to Brynn, something had slashed the tires of the other Jeep. Once Gabe got there, he could pick them both up, go back to get Miriam, then they could regroup. The four of them.

The roadside fence changed to pipe—evidence of Skylar's property. Just another half-mile. He pushed the gas, revving ahead.

Something flashed by on his right. He stiffened. His hands felt clammy. His heart throbbed in his throat. Briefly as he'd seen it, it'd looked like a shadowy humanoid. With horns?

A glance in the rear-view mirror, however, revealed nothing at all.

He came up on the entrance faster than he should have and practically stood on the brakes to slow down, barreling down the driveway and screeching to a halt next to the other Jeep. Sure enough, all four tires were flat and useless. He threw open the door and jumped down into the dirt, bounding towards the house.

From this vantage point, nothing looked out of the ordinary. Maybe Brynn had exaggerated. He hopped the steps two at a time, pulled back the screen door, and turned the handle.

It didn't budge. Locked.

It was then he noticed that the glass had been broken out of the door. He could easily reach through to unlock it, but he didn't want to startle Brynn and Skylar inside.

He knocked hard on the door and almost immediately heard someone coming. He didn't see the relieved face of Brynn or Skylar. He saw the muzzle of a gun, and, barely visible past a long arm, he could just make out Brynn's bloodshot eyes.

"Brynn!" he yelled through the door. "Let me in."

The gun didn't move. Neither did he.

She wouldn't shoot him, right?

"Gabe?" she asked, strangely hesitant for a person who could clearly see him.

"Yeah. Let me in. Where's Skylar?"

Instead of answering, she said, "Prove it."

She thought he was one of them. He guessed he couldn't blame her, but that level of paranoia hadn't yet hit him. He quickly sifted through memories and "Brynn factoids" to find something only he would know. He landed on something personal. He kept his voice low in the hopes that Skylar wouldn't hear what he said.

"Remember that night in Papua New Guinea?" he asked. "On the pterodactyl expedition? Skylar wanted us to go out and look some more while he tried to find information in the village. But there were no pterodactyls. We both knew it. So we rented that tree-house in the jungle and spent almost two days holed up together. Then lied to Skylar about finding nothing."

A sniffle, then: "It wasn't really a lie. We didn't find any pterodactyls."

"No," he said with a laugh. "I suppose we didn't."

The gun finally dropped, and she took a step, fumbled with the lock, and opened the door. Once inside, she slammed the door behind him and turned each deadbolt with a loud *thud*; not that they'd do much good with the window broken like that. Gabe looked around the room. Obviously, something bad had happened here. Skylar must have been lying down. She'd said in her message that he'd been attacked.

As he turned back to ask, his face ran right into Brynn's closed fist. He reeled back and clutched his cheek.

"What the *hell*, Brynn?" he yelled.

She lunged at him and hit him in the chest this time, then the shoulder. Tears poured from her eyes as she pummeled him. He grabbed at her wrists, unable to stop her punches at first but then finally exerting enough strength to hold her back. Still, she flailed and squirmed to get away, eventually giving up and melting against his chest, sobbing.

That didn't last long before she backed up and yelled into his face, "You *left* me!" He felt droplets of her spittle. "We needed you! I needed you!"

He tried to stay calm, but he felt the heat rushing up his neck. This wasn't his fault. He didn't do this. Whatever this even was. She'd become unhinged, unable to process reality.

She slapped him in the head. "You abandoned us just so you could get with some girl you barely knew, didn't you? You're a pig!"

He lost brief control of his temper and pushed her away from him. Not hard enough to knock her down, but enough to clear some distance.

"I abandoned you?" he asked. "*Skylar* abandoned me. You saw what he did. Accused me of planting that thing. What kind of shit is that?"

Instead of advancing on him, she crossed the room to his uncle's wing-backed chair and sunk down low, cradling her head in her hands and sobbing.

Muffled, she choked out, "They took him."

Took him? Skylar? Rather than question her about it, Gabe yelled Skylar's name and ran down the hallway, searching each bedroom for any sign of his boss. When he came up with nothing, he returned to the living room, careful to stay a few feet away from her.

"Who took him, Brynn? And where?" He spied the satellite phone on the floor next to her. "Why didn't you call the police?"

She raised her head from her hands, but didn't look at him. "I did. Twice."

"Have they come yet?"

"No."

"How long since you called?"

"The first time?" she replied. "Last night."

Gabe's heart sank as the realization of what Brynn had been through finally dawned on him. She'd been alone in this house for an entire night, without any help. Now he felt bad for not taking her beating with more grace.

"I'm sorry, Brynn," he said. "I didn't know."

It seemed impossible that the police wouldn't have arrived yet. Each officer out here would certainly be responsible for a lot of miles, but that didn't explain the lack of response. Something seemed off.

"We need to go," Brynn said quietly. "To the nearest town. To a police station. This is more than we can handle."

Gabe's heart broke from the desperation in her voice, but he wouldn't leave. He couldn't. Not with Miriam waiting for him in that cave. He didn't want to tell Brynn that, though.

She stood and walked past him towards the door. "Let's go."

He held his ground, clenching his jaw.

"What's wrong?" she asked. "Let's go. Now."

He closed his eyes to avoid looking at her. "I can't. I have to go back for Miriam."

When the silence stretched on for too long, Gabe opened his eyes to see Brynn fuming at the door. He had the keys. She couldn't take the Jeep from him. He could almost see that realization playing out across her face.

"She didn't leave?" Brynn asked.

"No. We went out in the desert together. To find one on our own." He could see the anger welling up inside of her. This time, though, he'd take the punches. "She got hurt. She can't walk. I came back to get help."

Instead of attacking, Brynn pushed a lock of hair behind one of her ears and tightly composed herself. "We'll send the police back for her, too."

"No," he said emphatically.

"Gabe. She's alone in the desert. I saw what these things are capable of. She's already gone."

"If you think that, then you don't know Miriam."

She threw up her hands, before storming outside and hollering back, "Neither do you!"

The statement stung, more painful than her physical attacks. It's true that he hadn't known Miriam long, but he knew enough.

Gabe followed Brynn outside, where she'd settled on the end of the porch, staring out towards Gray's Point. She leaned against the handrail, her normally regal posture giving in to the weight of her ordeal. He didn't love her anymore. Maybe he never had. But he still found it hard to disappoint her.

"Is that where you went?" she asked, motioning towards the mountain in the distance.

"Yes."

"Where is she?"

"In a cave. She's got weapons. And rations."

Brynn glanced over her shoulder and shot him a glance. He thought he caught the slightest hint of a smirk before she turned away from him again. "Can she fight otherworldly animal-men?"

Gabe tried to imagine what she meant. He pictured the odd footprint in the sand. The shadow creature he saw on the highway. The phantasmagoric bird that Miriam shot down. Brynn nursed a hole deep inside of her somewhere that he'd never been able to fix. But she wasn't a liar. And she didn't stage attacks for attention. Though these creatures had remained largely in his periphery so far, Brynn had seen them. Fought them. Lost to them.

He felt certain that Miriam could fight off anything, but, in a moment of clarity, he understood that saying so would wound Brynn in a way that he couldn't fully empathize with. Instead, he answered, "I don't know. I think she'll try."

Brynn turned toward him, leaning her backside against the railing and folding her arms across her chest. He followed her long, bare legs down to the ground where she planted her feet with purpose. The tears had dried up now. She almost looked like herself.

She raised one of her perfectly shaped eyebrows at him. "I can't talk you out of this, can I?"

"I promised her I'd come right back."

She walked towards him, her shoulder brushing against his as she made her way back inside. He followed, as she went straight to work gathering up supplies, in the process unplugging the satellite phone. "We all know that Gabe Castillo doesn't break his promises."

He detected the sharpness of her sarcasm, but he knew better than to challenge it. Instead, he scooped up the pistol on the kitchen table, pausing only briefly to stare into the eyes of the strange skull totem. It felt like a lifetime since he'd found it in the backyard. Now it seemed devoid of power. Something worse than this inanimate object waited for them.

Grabbing water from the fridge, Brynn asked, "Does the Jeep have gas?"

"I filled it up before Miriam and I left. Haven't used it much since."

"You walked?"

"Yeah. Didn't want you and Skylar to find us."

"We weren't looking," she said sharply, slinging her pack over her shoulder. "We should take that."

Gabe looked down at the totem. "This? Why?"

Brynn shrugged. "I don't know. Maybe it means something to them. Maybe they'll respond to it."

Gabe had a hard time seeing how it might help them, but he gingerly picked it up and rested the butt of it on the floor. If nothing else, it made a badass walking stick. Maybe he'd keep it as a souvenir.

He followed Brynn as she moved towards the door. On the way, he noticed a notebook on the end table. He'd never seen it before, but it looked old and personal.

"This yours?" he asked, picking it up.

She spun and froze, clearly unsettled. She crossed the space between them in record speed and snatched it out of his hand, quickly hiding it away in her backpack. "It's uh... my journal."

"Oooh. Like your secret diary?"

"Something like that."

"What's it say about me?"

"That you're an asshole. Come on."

CHAPTER 13

He listened, waiting for the rumble of the Jeep to fade into the distance. Only then did he climb up the ladder, pull down the hatch, and push on the rug above. It took extra effort to slide the heavy wing-backed chair above him out of the way, but it eventually buckled under his insistence. He moved up the ladder, letting the rug fall over him like a cloak. Once he got his knees up high enough, he scrambled along the floor and emerged into the light, out from under the rug and into the living area of the old cabin where they'd fought just hours earlier.

Behind him, the deer followed. Together, they stared out the window and watched the yellow Jeep hurtle through the desert towards Gray's Point, the back wheels kicking up a massive cloud of dust. Eventually, it began fading into the distance.

Now they were safe. Now they could search.

Each of them headed to a different area of the house, overturning furniture and ripping up floorboards. They emptied bags, tore mirrors from the wall, and upended beds. As they met again in the living room, the goat watched as the deer stared quizzically at the mounted buck above the fireplace. After a shared glance, the deer cocked his head, motioning for the goat to pull down the long-dead beast.

As commanded, the goat followed orders, scaling the mantle, ripping down the head and letting it fall to the floor. Using his non-skeletal hand, the deer rummaged through the hole in the back of the mount, waiting for the goat to get down and help. The goat only vaguely knew what they were meant to find, but he found nothing out of the ordinary. Frustrated, he tossed the buck-head aside.

He shuffled back to the hole in the floor and shrugged. The deer returned the gesture.

The deer veered off into the kitchen, opened the refrigerator and scanned the contents. The goat watched and waited for a nod. The confirmation came quickly and sharply. If the deer were capable of smiling, the goat felt certain he would have just then. It was time to go. He dropped down into the hole and descended the ladder, the footsteps of the deer echoing above.

After the deer met him in the cool caverns below, the goat climbed up the ladder again and used the rug to pull things back into place as best he could. It might not be perfect, but it would be good enough to remove any suspicion.

He spryly scuttled back down and met the deer. Together, they made their way through the darkness. Down the narrow passageway, and deeper beneath the desert brush. They didn't find what they wanted, but it didn't matter. They already had what they needed.

In silence, they rushed back to Gray's Point, eager to return to their quarry.

CHAPTER 14

Miriam waited for either a savior or a monster. Maybe both, if Gabe brought her father.

She didn't care for the waiting. It gave her far too much time for the fear and uncertainty to scratch its way into her belly. There'd been no time for fear in Cape Madre or Rose Valley. No time to sit and ponder the worst possible outcomes. She'd never thought of herself as a particularly pessimistic person, but she started to wonder if maybe that was only because she'd never stopped long enough to think about it.

The wind whipped the canvas of her makeshift door. Without Gabe's height, she couldn't manage to attach the top corner, so now it continually billowed and buffeted against the stone, occasionally sending a *pop* echoing off the walls. Miriam rubbed her eyes, trying to encourage more lubrication to stave off the dry, scratchy discomfort. She needed to blink more, but if she did that, she might miss a shadow cross in front of the cave. And missing that might mean the difference between life and death.

She tried to play games in her head, recalling fun facts about cryptids or reliving the few good memories she could conjure. Most of them were recent and involved Macy, but she mined a few from her childhood, from a time when all the hunts seemed like fun vacations. Somewhere, further back than she could clearly remember, she even managed to feel the safety and warmth of her mother's presence.

Damn her stupid ankle. She didn't want to think about her dead mother.

With the pain starting to flare up again, Miriam looked at her watch and did some quick math. Not quite four hours. Oh well.

She tilted a couple of ibuprofen into her hand, then swallowed them with half a bottle of water. She didn't often take medication, and wondered whether her stomach's uneasy rumbling came from the drugs, or the worry.

She'd tried her best to keep the water to a minimum. Too much water meant she'd have to venture outside to relieve herself. Thirst managed to win, though, and she'd downed two bottles in the last hour. As much as she didn't want to, she pushed herself up to her feet. Or foot, as the case happened to be. She couldn't be sure, but she thought maybe she managed it faster than last time.

Using the cave wall for balance, she scooped up everything she needed and hobbled her way to the mouth of the cave. Halfway there, she stopped, certain she'd heard something.

Holding her breath, she scanned for a hint of what she'd heard, but saw nothing.

A rattling noise outside. Miriam swallowed hard. Bone scraping against bone? Something must have been digging at the pile outside. Maybe just a scavenger. Nothing big enough to cast a shadow through the tent. Still, her heart pounded in her chest.

She inched forward, slowly. As she did, a form manifested itself on the other side of the tent, followed by a low growl. She heard more bones against bones as the shadow grew larger. At first, she thought it might be a person, but then it seemed to sink down on four legs. Maybe just a coyote, though it seemed larger than that.

Miriam dropped everything except the gun. The shadow moved closer. She didn't want to kill an innocent animal, but she also didn't want to wait to see what it might be. She leveled her shoulders and steadied herself as best she could. It was going to hurt when she pulled the trigger, but she couldn't concern herself with that.

With practiced grace, she squeezed the trigger evenly until the bullet tore from the gun, through the canvas, and into whatever creature stood outside. It yelped and fell to the ground, but didn't stay still. The growling stopped. She couldn't be sure of her angle on it now, but she fired again. The miss startled the dog-like shadow on the other side and caused it to spring back to its feet. Too quickly to be too injured.

Miriam tried to make sense of another shadow that came into view from the top of the canvas. She assumed a bird, but then it melted down from the sky into something distinctly humanoid. The craggy outline of feathers clung to the silhouette, like a person with wings.

She needed to see her stalker, so that she could put a bullet in its head. She lunged forward, ripped the canvas down from the mouth of the cave and whipped the gun out in front of her. Pain shot up her leg, as she used her bad foot to brace herself.

The bird-person was gone, but the growling started up again, giving her just a few seconds to zero in on the dog-thing rushing towards her. Sharp fangs protruded from its mouth, but its face looked more human than dog.

Not a coyote.

She forced herself to wait. If it closed some distance, she could be surer of her aim. She hovered her arms loosely to follow its head with every loping step. From three feet away, it jumped towards her. She tracked up. Fired. Blood exploded outward. A good hit, but its momentum didn't slow.

With only one good leg, she couldn't pivot in time. The full weight hit her in the chest, knocking her to the ground, forcing the wind out of her. Its chest heaved against hers. She could smell rank breath between them.

It wasn't dead.

Where it had once seemed almost human, the thing's face had now grown a long, canine snout. It snapped at her, but she managed to push up on its chin and force its jaw closed. She dropped the gun on the ground and wrapped her other hand around the snout, struggling to keep it at bay. It thrashed on top of her, but the shot had damaged it enough that it seemed incapable of finding its footing.

Bucking hard to the right, she forced the weight of the dog-thing to the ground next to her, then rolled over to straddle it. She half-expected that it would turn into something else. Keeping one hand as tightly against its chin as she could, she reached for the gun, pointed it straight up into its chin, and pulled the trigger. Warm blood sprayed her, sprayed everywhere. Without another sound, the thing went limp.

Trying to catch her breath, Miriam wiped the blood from her face and quickly rolled onto her back, ready to shoot the next thing that came through.

Nothing else in view.

She scrambled backwards with her one good foot and free hand, until her back hit the cave wall. It felt safer, having only one direction to protect.

The pain in her ankle throbbed, but she didn't have time to worry about that. She used the cave wall for support to pull herself back up. She tried to calculate the likelihood of Gabe's return. But this wasn't a movie. She wouldn't be lucky enough for him to show up and save the day. She drew strength from the pile of fur in the middle of the cave.

She'd killed that thing. She could kill the others, too. She wouldn't be stopped so easily.

Resolute, Miriam moved forward. She'd lost count of how many bullets she'd spent, but knew a few more remained in the clip. For double safety, she reached down and grabbed a leather case containing a Bowie knife. Despite having to constantly survive in the face of danger, Miriam really didn't relish this. Why couldn't cryptozoology go back to studying questionable evidence and shaky camera footage?

Whether the bird thing still lurked outside the cave seemed almost irrelevant. Her current abode was no longer safe, and that meant she needed to find a new home. If she went too far, though, Gabe wouldn't be able to find her. The decision tore at her. Certainly, making her stand here at any cost might ensure that Gabe could find her, but that hardly seemed worth anything if he only found her dead body.

She sat for a few more minutes, alert but slowly feeling her breathing return to normal. If there'd been another one, it seemed to have disappeared. When she felt confident enough, she crawled over to the dead one in the middle of the cave and poked at its belly with the muzzle of her gun. The fur gave way easily.

Next, she holstered the gun into the back of her jeans and pushed hard to roll the thing over on its side, its head lolling against the rock.

It didn't look like a coyote or a wolf. More like a dog of indeterminate breed. Was this the key to the skinwalkers? Did they die as the last animal they mimicked? It certainly would explain why no one had ever found a carcass. She didn't have the time or the inclination to perform a makeshift autopsy on this one, but she did pull herself around the carcass, taking pictures with her phone. The red flashing battery in the corner told her these pictures might be the last she'd take, at least until she found power.

With so much time having passed without another skinwalker, Miriam almost felt safe again, but she still needed to vacate the cave. She considered just starting back. Her ankle hurt, but she'd been able to maneuver well enough. She didn't know exactly where Gabe would be coming from, though, and that made the direction hard to choose.

Disgusted with her situation, she let out a frustrated growl that echoed out of the cave. Why did stuff like this always happen to her? She wasn't religious, but in that moment she considered joining a convent. Surely, the monsters wouldn't find her there.

If she wanted to move fast, she'd have to pick and choose her supplies. She decided to leave the tent and sleeping bag behind. They were too bulky, and, if it came down to it, sleeping in the desert air wouldn't kill her. She needed water, protein bars, and weapons. She jettisoned everything else from the backpack, including the samples from the bird autopsy. Maybe she'd come back for them once she had the safety of numbers.

With her pack much lighter, Miriam stood and looped it over her shoulders. The pain still pulsed up her leg, but the backpack didn't seem to add to it, at least. She needed help walking, and as she scanned the cave for a makeshift crutch, she came up with the perfect solution.

Eyeing the pile of bones in front of the cave, she estimated the totem in the middle to be just about the right height, assuming she could pry the skulls and ribcage off the stabilizing pole in the middle.

She hobbled over to the pile, careful to draw her gun and watch her flank as she exited the cave. Nothing. Not even a breeze.

Once she made it to the mound, she fell to her knees and scaled the mountain of bones. Some of them gave way underneath her, but she managed to get far enough up to get the totem in the middle. She reached through two of the ribs and pulled up on the shaft. It gave way easily.

Rolling over to her backside, she slid to the ground and went to work disassembling her prize. Unlike the totem Gabe found at the house, this one seemed more intricate. Some of the parts were fused together, others were tied. She put her face close to the totem to derive the material in the ties, immediately feeling the hackles raise along her spine. Metal wiring. Manufactured somewhere.

Surely, the skinwalkers weren't shopping at Home Depot.

None of it made sense, yet, but solving the mystery couldn't be her chief concern. She continued to work until she got the pole out of the middle. It seemed carefully made. Leaving the skulls and ribcage behind, Miriam stood and shifted some of her weight to her bad side, using her arm to take some of the weight off her ankle. It didn't have the padded comfort of a crutch, but as a walking stick it would work quite well.

Now—where to go? Gabe would have gone back the way they came, for sure, in order to get the Jeep. But she doubted he'd return from that direction. She wished that they'd talked more about where and how he meant to get the help, but somehow that never seemed important. Even if he'd dozed off during his watch, she still trusted him to ultimately do the right thing. Why exactly had he gotten so easily under her skin?

The sun beat down on her. She hadn't put on any sunblock before leaving it on the cave floor along with the other non-essentials. A sunburn seemed the least of her worries, though. Given the life she seemed destined to lead, she didn't need to worry about living long enough to develop skin cancer, anyway.

She decided to move toward the house. Though she didn't want Skylar's help, it made sense that Gabe might see that as the best course of action. Even going in the correct general direction, though, hardly guaranteed she'd run into him. The desert plain was vast, and their timing could be completely off. For all she knew, he'd taken a different route and would come up behind her without her ever knowing. She tried to imagine his reaction to finding a cave with one dead dog and no Miriam.

As she started forward, something caught the corner of her eye. Nothing scary. Just a scrub bush that looked disturbed. She stopped and studied it for a second before she realized that something lay beyond it, almost completely obscured.

It looked like a path. She scrambled over to get a better look. The narrow pathway gently sloped upward to the top of Gray's Point. She couldn't be sure that it went all the way up, but any height would be an advantage.

If she could gain elevation, she could see Gabe coming from much further away.

It took her only a few seconds to make her decision. She pushed past the bush and started the sloping ascent. Moving up proved more difficult than scrambling across the flatland, but she pushed away the pain and forced herself forward. She turned a corner and steeled herself to go even further, but then she saw an archway leading out to a small plateau.

Inching her way through the archway, she made it to the other side and looked at the desert beneath Gray's Point. She tried to orient herself, quickly finding the highway and the gas station far off in the distance. Further away, she could just barely make out the ranch house as a brown speck on the landscape. She cursed herself for leaving the binoculars behind.

From the house, she moved her eyes towards her location, and felt her heart leap in her chest when she saw a cloud of dust kicking up in the distance. At the front of the cloud: the unmistakable yellow of one of the Jeeps. Miriam's eyes filled with tears of relief. It would be a handful of minutes before they got to her, but she couldn't move quickly, so she needed to start back down.

She turned towards the archway, ecstatic to finally have a way out of this nightmare.

But something now blocked the archway. Crouched low to the ground, its antlers curled upward. The creature made a strange clicking noise as it tilted its head and scraped the antlers against the stone.

The deer-head's black eyes bore into her, as it swirled the sand with its long skeletal finger.

Miriam pulled the gun from her waistband and fired.

CHAPTER 15

Gabe leaned forward over the wheel, peering through the dust but unwilling to slow down. He didn't like the idea of leaving Skylar behind much more than he could stomach leaving Miriam, but he didn't know how long Brynn would be able to stay with him. He worried she'd gone into shock.

Brynn remained silent in the passenger seat, her expression disconnected and dispassionate. She jolted with every bump, not even bothering to hold onto the handle jutting from the A-pillar. As Gray's Point grew larger with every mile, she seemed to grow more and more agitated. This was it, he supposed. Everything they'd been training for.

Halfway to the Point, Brynn exploded, "You're not even going to be able to find her. Did you leave breadcrumbs?"

"There's a giant pile of bones in front of a cave," he responded less calmly than he would have liked. "I think we'll see it."

"What if she's dead?"

"She's not dead."

From the corner of his eye, he saw her turn towards him, could feel the heat of her gaze. When she spoke again, her tone was more sympathetic. "You don't know that."

"They didn't kill Skylar," he said.

"Not in front of me."

On that horrifying note, the conversation fell silent. Brynn returned her gaze to the sand and brush ahead. Brynn was just scared, spouting nonsense to try and convince Gabe to turn back for the police. He could understand that. Fear coursed through his veins. But he couldn't let that make his decisions for him. Once they got to Miriam, she'd calm them all down and come up with a sensible plan.

Gabe welcomed the silence as they drove the last couple of miles. They came in at an angle, and every rocky face of the crag looked the same. Right or left? He couldn't remember, so he trusted his instincts and pulled off to his right. It didn't matter. He would drive around the whole thing until he found her. He tried to make sense of the landscape as he pushed ahead. Tried to find any hint of a landmark he recognized.

He thought maybe he'd see the bloody carcass of the bird splayed out on a rock, but there was no sign of it. A little further on, he slammed the brakes. This had to be it. He could see the entrance to the cave. The view looked about the same. But no bones. No skulls. No tent hanging from the rock.

"What? Are we here?" Brynn asked.

He put the Jeep in park and got out without answering. Surely, multiple caves dotted the base of Gray's Point. Maybe this one just looked like the one where Miriam waited. He tried to convince himself by looking off into the distance and trying to place bigger landmarks, but such things were few and far between, and ultimately of little help.

His head spun. He barely noticed when Brynn also got out of the Jeep. When he slowed down enough to pay attention to her, he resented her fixed, patronizing gaze.

"Is this it?" she asked.

"I don't know," he mumbled. "It can't be."

There didn't seem to be any indication of where Miriam had gone, but Gabe hoped to gather more information. He moved towards the cave.

Scanning the ground, he could tell the brush and the sand had been disturbed. It could have been a clue that he'd found the right cave, or it could have just been the work of the wind.

Inside the cave, déjà vu washed over him. This had to be it. *Had* to be. Every inch of that cave looked exactly like he remembered. For over two hours, he'd stayed awake doing nothing but staring at it. Miriam could be stubborn. He could accept that she might have hobbled out of the cave for some reason, but why would she take everything with her?

And how in the hell could all those bones be gone already?

Had he lost his mind? His body was running on fumes, with little sleep and even less food. Maybe his mind just played tricks on him.

Gabe sprinted out of the cave and back to the Jeep. Brynn greeted him with a narrowed stare, lithely slipping into her seat once he opened his own door.

"So?" she asked, as the Jeep rumbled to life.

"Wrong cave."

She sighed, but Gabe ignored it, pressing the gas pedal and surveying ahead. The bones. He'd find the bones.

The minutes ticked by, with no new discoveries. He rounded the end and came back up on the other side. Everything felt wrong. Backwards. In fact, he found no caves at all. Could it be possible that their cave had been the only one?

The frustration boiled up from deep within. He banged on the steering wheel, cursing under his breath. Brynn still seemed too pissed to empathize, sitting silently as if waiting out a storm that she knew would pass. It wasn't the first time she'd seen him frustrated, but he missed the warm way she used to bring him back down to earth.

Before long, they came back around and Gabe stopped the Jeep in front of the same cave from earlier. Still no bones, or Miriam, but he had no doubts now. This *was* the place. He couldn't explain where she'd gone or what had happened to the macabre monument, but he would find out.

"We've already been here," Brynn said, as Gabe killed the Jeep.

"I know." He turned sideways in his seat, bringing one knee up over the console between them. Brynn avoided eye contact. "This is the cave. I don't know what happened, but she was here."

Brynn looked past him towards the gaping, shadowed maw of the cave. "Well she's not here now. She's gone. We need to go get the police."

"They didn't come when you called. They're not going to come now."

"Then we'll get the police from somewhere else."

Gabe knew the wisdom of her words, but also knew they were, ultimately, on their own. Was it smart to stay here and look for Miriam and Skylar? Probably not. But it was the right thing to do.

When he didn't respond to her, Brynn continued, "We're out of our depth. It's dangerous. We could die. It's not worth it to stay. We don't know what we're doing."

Anger grew in him, only sharpening his determination. She droned on in protest, but he ignored her. Eventually, he snapped at her, "¡No seas tan llorona!"

She fell quiet. Gabe continued before she could: "This is what you signed up for, right? This is what we trained for? You wanted this job."

Her usual, even complexion faded to red, her nose flared, and her hazel eyes shaded over. "¡Estás siendo un maldito idiota!"

He'd forgotten how good she was at Spanish, and immediately hated the intimacy it drew out of him. He spat back, "I'm not an idiot!"

"Well, I'm not a crybaby!" she huffed, crossing her arms over her chest. "This isn't some stupid expedition. This is real, Gabe. Skylar's in trouble. Miriam's in trouble."

"I know that! That's why we have to stay here. We have to find them. We have to find clues or tracks or something. We can't give up! If we leave now, we'll lose time."

She breathed out a long sigh and leaned back against her door, putting as much distance between herself and him as she could without leaving altogether. Gabe mirrored the action.

He forced himself to look at her, trying to conjure up some rousing speech, but she spoke first. Her eyes softened just a little, and her tone brought the conversation back down to reasonable volumes. "You can't save the world, Gabe. I know you want to. But you can't. The world can't be saved. It's a chaotic cesspool of disappointment."

Same argument, different day. He didn't want to have it again. Whatever convincing he'd hoped to muster died unsaid, as he chose to remove himself from the situation. He took the keys, though, to make sure she couldn't leave without him.

He slowly inched back towards the cave, studying the ground and hoping to make sense of the swirls of sand that might show him Miriam's fate. He couldn't interpret it, but that didn't stop him from hoping for some tiny sliver of a clue that might point him in the right direction. She couldn't have just vanished. Either they had taken her somewhere, or she'd left of her own accord.

Behind him, Brynn stepped out of the Jeep. He braced himself for the argument to continue, but she said nothing, just hurried toward him at a brisk enough pace that he could hear the friction of her shorts. When she got to him, she knelt and studied the ground. Gabe had never taken to tracking, but it was Brynn's specialty.

"We're going to regret this," she said with finality, making it clear that she expected no response. The argument seemed to be over for now.

She stood again and moved to the cave. Gabe followed. The ground inside didn't have nearly as much sand to be disturbed, but she still studied it as if she could see everything that he couldn't. She pointed to a part of the stone that looked darker. Almost wet.

"Blood, I think."

Shivers shot through Gabe's veins. "Miriam's?"

"No way to tell." Brynn shrugged and looked around. "Was there this much fur in here before?"

He couldn't remember any, but even now it just seemed like a few tufts here and there. She didn't wait for a response before squat-walking backwards. When she got to the entrance, she stood back up.

"Whatever bled here was dragged out, but then... no blood out here." She motioned towards the dirt. "That seems odd."

Gabe didn't want to face the obvious. Though the bloodstains were mostly absorbed into the stone, the amount still seemed staggering. Could she have survived that?

He stood, while Brynn kept creeping along the ground. Clearly, she didn't care if Miriam lived or died. If these things did kill Miriam, though, why did they take her body? And why did they take Skylar alive? No. She had to be alive. Somehow. Somewhere.

"Gabe!" Brynn hollered. "Come here."

She'd moved a considerable distance away. He jogged to catch up, then crouched down beside her. He expected to see another of the cloven hoofprints from before, but instead he saw the soft imprint of a size-seven Vasque hiking boot. Only one, though. It had no companion, though the sand beside it seemed to be disturbed in some other, indistinct way.

"You said her ankle was hurt, right?" Brynn asked. Gabe only nodded in response. "Whoever left this was clearly walking on one foot. With a crutch of some sort."

So she was alive. Was she bleeding out, though?

"Why did the blood stop?"

Brynn stood up and dusted off her hands. "I don't know. Either it isn't her blood, or she managed to get it under control by the time she left the cave."

"Let's follow."

She didn't move right away, squinting her eyes in the sun as she looked back to the Jeep. "We really should get some help, Gabe. We don't know what we're walking into. There's blood now."

Perhaps she saw the wetness of his eyes, or the determination in his features, but when he didn't answer, she immediately gave up and looked back at the ground and the footprints there. Gabe followed, ignoring the scenarios playing out in his head. He wanted to save Miriam—and Skylar—but he didn't think he'd recover if they ended up only finding dead bodies.

He pushed the thought away, refusing to allow for that grisly possibility.

After rounding the corner, Brynn took a sharp turn towards the walls of Gray's Point and stopped when she came up to a small scrub brush. At first, it seemed like they'd hit a dead end. The footprints ended there, with no signs of Miriam anywhere.

When Brynn barreled right over the spindly branches of the bush, it caught him off guard, but he followed dutifully as they meandered up a narrow pathway cut in the rock. Man-made? He couldn't be sure.

Almost no sand here, and no footprints. The only way was up, though, so that's how they went, soon finding themselves at a crossroads between an archway leading out to a rock plateau and a curve leading further up the path. Brynn veered off onto the plateau. He stopped in the archway.

She picked up a gnarly stick that reminded Gabe of the creepy totem in the back of the Jeep. As she stood and looked at him, her eyes went wide. He followed her gaze to the ground behind him, seeing nothing at first but then catching the reflective glimmer of something metal buried in the earth. He knelt to pick it up, noting the heft and density of the small object.

It was smashed now, but this thing had once been a bullet.

"¡*Maldito!*" he exclaimed. "She has to be close."

"Can we turn back now?" Brynn asked.

If her protests weren't enough, he could tell by her demeanor that going forward meant flirting with a panic attack. He'd never seen her have a full breakdown, but she'd described them. She always seemed so poised, but under that cool exterior brewed a fragile constitution that could betray him at any moment.

"I'll take you back to the house," he said. "But I gotta come back. There were no prints out, so she has to be up, right?"

"I'm not going back to that house," Brynn said flatly.

Gabe reached into his pocket and pulled out the keys. He tossed them towards her but they came up short, hitting the ground and careening across the rock. She stopped them with the toe of her boot.

"Just let me have some supplies," he said. "Then you can go get the police."

He didn't want to be alone, but he wouldn't go back. These skinwalkers clearly had some sort of plan, and if it required Skylar to be alive, then it meant Miriam, too. He now accepted the fact that she'd been captured, at the very least, but that didn't mean he could give up. In fact, it meant more than ever that he shouldn't.

They stood in silence, both staring at the other as a range of emotions played on Brynn's face. Eventually, she pursed her lips, bent over and picked up the keys. He thought he detected disappointment in her eyes, and it stung to think that she might assume he was abandoning her. He didn't want to abandon either of them. He wanted to do right by Miriam *and* Brynn. But he couldn't do both.

"Fine," she said.

In a huff, she pushed past him back down the path.

CHAPTER 16

Miriam awoke to oppressive, shadow-less darkness. Few places on earth got this dark. She had to be deep underground.

Flurries of memories played out in her head in full color and full violence. She'd missed her shot. Somehow. And then another skinwalker had come from behind her. It didn't make sense. The second one seemed to appear out of thin air. She never stood a chance, really, but at least she'd put up a fight—the throbbing in her knuckles testified to that.

She couldn't feel her pack anywhere nearby. A quick check of her pockets and she realized they'd taken her cell phone. She felt behind her head. Her ponytail was still intact. A hair tie, then. Her only weapon. As skilled as Miriam could be in all things, she certainly didn't have MacGyver talents. A hair tie seemed of little use other than to keep the hair out of her eyes, which seemed especially unimportant in total darkness.

She felt around and made a mental map of the surroundings. A cold and damp rock wall sat to her left and to her back. But to her right...

She tried to make sense of the sensations running through her fingers. She felt something cold and smooth, almost like metal bars. She pushed to her knees and scrabbled as far forward as she could, eventually hitting more steel. By touch alone, she presumed a roughly three-by-six-foot jail cell, built into the back of a cave.

Something rustled. She stiffened. What else shared this darkness with her? At least whatever it was currently was outside of her cage. She listened, knowing that it hardly mattered. She'd already made too much racket exploring her cell. There could be no doubt that she'd already given up her location.

The thing in the dark gasped for air, but not like it had been holding its breath. It sounded almost like crying. Likely not a skinwalker, then. With her ankle, she'd need help getting out of this mess, and maybe this crying person could be her legs.

"Hello?" she asked tentatively.

"M-M-Miriam?" a deep voice echoed back.

"Dad?"

She asked the question before she even processed the voice, too shocked to stop herself from calling him by the name that she wasn't sure he deserved. Her mind raced. How did he get here? And, maybe more importantly, could she believe that it was really him?

As if reading her mind, Skylar said, "Is it really you?"

Neither could trust the other. The fact that he questioned her identity seemed to be a point in favor of his. But then, maybe the skinwalkers were smart enough to act paranoid. She shut down that circular line of thought before it started. Paranoia would get her nowhere.

"Yes," she said. "How'd you get here?"

She could hear the fear in his voice when he spoke. "They... came to the house. Attacked us. We couldn't hold them off."

"Where's Brynn?"

"I don't know. I didn't see," he said.

Miriam wondered if Brynn also shared the cave with them, possibly unconscious — or worse.

Skylar asked again, "Is it really you?"

Frustrated, Miriam exhaled sharply and answered, "Yes. It's really me. Stop asking so we can find a way out of here."

He didn't respond right away, so Miriam filled the void by pulling herself up to her feet and trying to reach the top of the bars. Nothing but air and steel above her. Her father was taller, though. Maybe he'd be able to feel something she couldn't.

"I need you to stand up," she said into the darkness. "See if you can reach the top."

She didn't hear him move. After a few more seconds of silence, she heard soft sobs. Their situation was certainly dire, but it hardly called for uncontrollable crying. Sure, courage didn't often describe Skylar Brooks, but this still seemed out of character for him.

When he spoke again, it came out in a hoarse whisper. "I saw her. She's down here."

"Her who?" Miriam asked. "Brynn?"

"No," he replied. "Your mother."

Miriam's heart jumped into her throat, then fell into her stomach. Even though she knew it couldn't be true, she felt the tears stinging at her eyes. Less for her mother, she thought, and more for the trauma it must have caused Skylar. She tried to handle the unexpected pang of empathy, tried to decide on the proper response. She didn't remember much about her life with her mom, but she remembered the day they laid her into the ground.

"Dad," she said. "You couldn't have seen mom. Mom's dead. She's been dead a long time."

More crying and sniffling. "I-I know. I just... it had to have been one of them, right? But how do they know?"

Miriam considered the question as rationally as she could. Her mother had been long dead when they'd come to look for the skinwalkers the first time. Even if these things could shape themselves into anything they wanted, it didn't explain how they could morph into someone they'd never even seen.

"I don't know," she answered. "That's why we're here, right? To get to the bottom of it."

"We're going to die down here," he said grimly.

Miriam shook her head in the dark, as if Skylar could see the gesture. "No, we're not. We survived that beast in Rose Valley. We can survive this."

He let out a sharp, mirthless laugh. "You survived the beast in Rose Valley. It was gonna kill every last one of us."

The admission shocked Miriam more than the mention of her mother. In all the interviews, all the official reports, all the speaking engagements, he'd always taken credit for the kill. Always. Miriam's annoyance at his spreading lies had faded long ago, and been totally buried when she finally got her due for the Cape Madre kraken. It hardly mattered anymore.

"Stand up," she said, hoping to change the subject. "See if you can feel the top."

He moved this time. She could hear him pushing to his feet. His search moved slowly as she waited for him to report back, leaving her time to wonder about Gabe. He'd be back with help of some sort, but how would he possibly find her? She didn't even know where she was.

Skylar finally answered. "If I stretch, I can feel rock above. The bars go all the way to the top. Seven feet or so, I'd guess."

Miriam sighed. "Well, they didn't kill us. They must be keeping us alive for something."

"Dinner, maybe?" he asked. He meant it as a joke, she knew, but the possibility was strong enough that it came across as morbid. Still, though, a joke meant he'd started to pull himself back together.

It seemed unfair that she had to be the adult, but then that'd always been the case. Certainly since mom had died. Before that, in the very corners of her memory, Miriam remembered her father as strong and invincible. If only she could have that man with her now, then maybe they'd have a better shot at escape.

Skylar didn't seem to be interested in talking, which Miriam felt totally fine with. She curled up in the corner of her cave cell and tried to make sense of everything. Maybe they couldn't escape directly, but surely the skinwalkers didn't capture them for the sole purpose of letting them starve in the dark. They'd be around eventually.

And that's when she needed to be ready.

***

"How's Tanner?" Skylar asked, breaking what seemed like hours of silence.

Seriously? This is what he wanted to talk about right now?

"Fine."

"He still dating the Mayor's daughter?"

"Macy. Yes."

"Good for him. She's pretty."

As if that's all that mattered. "She's also really smart, fiercely loyal, and the most empathetic person I've ever met."

Miriam's father didn't seem to have an answer for that. She realized he came from a different generation, but she didn't understand how having a daughter of his own hadn't made him at least a little less chauvinistic. Maybe quiet starvation would be preferable to conversations like this.

"And..." he started, pausing for a curiously long time. "How is Miriam?"

Her stomach roiled at the question. Hot blood flooded into her cheeks. Under normal circumstances—from anyone else—it would have seemed a perfectly pleasant question, but somehow it made her angry coming from him. Granting Skylar any insight into her life felt like it would somehow give him power over her again. She'd fought too hard to take back that power to give it up now.

"Fine," was all that she could muster.

"School going well?"

"Fine," she said again.

School wasn't fine, of course. She faced the very real possibility that she'd fail her classes if she didn't get out of this mess and back to her finals again. And even if she did manage that, the trip hadn't exactly afforded her much study time.

Before he attacked her with another veiled question, something creaked far away, echoing off the cave walls.

Then, a light. Faint, but enough for Miriam to barely see the outline of her hands. She took control of her breathing, listening for more sounds. And then: the patter of feet across the rocky floor.

Skylar stood, his shadow vaguely visible as he moved towards the light. Miriam fought the urge to do the same, instead choosing to keep off her ankle. She might need her strength for an escape later.

When she could make out the expression on her father's face, she realized the light source had moved closer. Soon, a flickering candle flame illuminated the cavern. It sat on a makeshift wooden holder, carried by a figure wearing a pelt that had been fashioned into a cloak. Or, given its size, the pelts of many animals sewn together. On the figure's head hung the dead face of a coyote, drooping downward and obscuring the face beneath. It stopped in front of the cells, and stood in silence.

Desperate to get a closer look, Miriam crawled to the bars, lifted herself up and moved to the front of her cell. Only one inch of steel cylinders separated her shoulder and Skylar's. Through the pounding of her own chest, she could hear his panicked breathing beside her. Miriam didn't often process fear, but it prickled up her back now.

Her new vantage point didn't provide much new information. The figure before them wasn't large for a human. About Miriam's height. Maybe a slimmer build, though the pelt made it hard to tell. Slender fingers wrapped around the base of the candleholder. A female, almost certainly. Further proof revealed itself in the faint outline of breasts beneath the cloak.

"What are you?" Skylar asked.

A distinctly feminine voice answered under the hood, "Ancient."

Miriam's eyes widened at the answer. She didn't expect them to be able to talk. The cloak provided the figure with an otherworldly presence, but the voice seemed ordinary. The hands, typical. The bare feet, distinctly human.

"Let us go," Miriam demanded, realizing that such a request would likely go unmet.

The voice answered, "One of you will go free, but the time has not yet come."

One of them? Miriam shared a quick look with Skylar, only to see his eyes even wider than hers. She wasn't about to play some messed-up torture game where they had to decide which one of them lived or died.

Nope. They'd both live, and, in the process, kill the bitch in front of them. To spite her, if nothing else.

From the shadows, two other figures emerged. Miriam swallowed hard when she realized they hadn't come in with this one. Had they been there the whole time? They both stood taller than the cloaked woman, each decidedly less human. These two were the ones who'd attacked and dragged her here. One with a deer head. The other, a goat.

"They will bring you bedding," the cloaked woman said. "Food and drink. It won't be much longer until the ritual."

"What ritual?" Miriam asked.

"The one that must be done."

Great. They'd gone from cryptids to cryptic.

The woman spun with grace and glided back up the tunnel. The animal-men followed her, no doubt to retrieve the promised bedding and food. Miriam's mind stretched in a million different directions, unable to land on one satisfactory theory as to what they faced.

"What are they talking about?" Skylar asked.

The light went out entirely, plunging them back into darkness.

Miriam answered, "I don't know."

As much as she wanted to hash out a plan with her father, she worried that the two skinwalkers hiding in the shadows weren't the only ones. There might be more. Waiting for them to say the wrong thing, or make the wrong move.

The way she saw it, only two options presented themselves. Either they found a way to overpower their captors during the ritual, or Gabe miraculously found them and brought an entire cavalry. The latter seemed unlikely. Miriam's ankle hadn't healed, but it had already gotten stronger. If this mysterious ritual took place far enough in the future, she might be at full strength. If he had to, Skylar could hold his own—if he had to.

Yes. They had a shot.

As she settled back into her corner, Skylar spoke. "I don't think these things are skinwalkers."

Miriam agreed, though she couldn't rule out some interpretation of the myth. Whatever they were dealing with certainly seemed otherworldly.

Unbelievable.

Impossible to explain.

CHAPTER 17

The local police department looked suspiciously empty. The double doors were locked, and glancing through the small windows revealed nothing but darkness. What kind of police department didn't staff employees during the day?

She pounded a fist against one of the doors, more in frustration than in the hope that someone would come to her aid. The guilt of leaving Gabe behind threatened to overwhelm her. She had to get *some* help. She slid her phone out of the back pocket of her cargo shorts and checked the time. A little early for lunch, but maybe the staff ate early. Brynn decided to wait in the Jeep in the hopes that someone would return to the rinky-dink station.

Sinking into the driver's seat, she gripped the wheel so hard her knuckles turned white. When that didn't help, she slammed her palms repeatedly against the wheel. She felt lost and defeated. If they managed to find Skylar, she'd resign and go find a quiet office job where she couldn't get anyone killed. It's the least she could do after what she'd done to him...

And Gabe.

Brynn glanced at her pack in the backseat. She hadn't even worked up the courage to tell Gabe about his mom's journal. Now she worried that he'd never get a chance to see it. Keeping it from him was tantamount to lying, she now realized. After all he'd done for her, she owed him more than hiding this.

A lock of hair fell across her eye and stuck to her sweat-beaded forehead. She cranked the Jeep's engine, then the AC. Her brain nagged her not to waste gas, but she didn't care. It didn't matter now. She couldn't be trusted with the responsibility of saving them, so all she needed to do was to wait to pass on that responsibility to someone more capable.

She sank in her seat and tried to relax, in vain. Needing a distraction, she reached her long arm around to the backseat, unzipped the side pouch of her backpack and removed the weathered journal. At one time, she'd wanted to read this account so she could find information to help hunt the skinwalkers. Now, she just needed it as an escape.

Opening to where she'd last left off, she skimmed through the Spanish for something interesting. Most of it detailed the day-to-day life of Ana and Gabe, much of the happiness overshadowed by the ambiguous menace of Hector. Each day seemed to bring with it another weird request, or an ominous visit from the men in suits. Very little of it read as overtly dangerous, though, and Brynn couldn't help but wonder if Ana had become paranoid—until she remembered her own circumstances. The feeling of safety seemed to evaporate as Ana fully understood her isolation.

Flipping page after page, Brynn finally settled in on another account of a visit from the men, but this time, they brought someone new.

***

Hector seems increasingly frustrated by my resistance to join his church. My name for it, not his. He calls it a brotherhood sometimes, but mostly leaves it nameless. His friends came again today, looking as sharp as ever in their suits.

This time, however, they brought a woman with them.

She wasn't terribly tall, but her presence filled the room and commanded my attention. When she spoke, her words dripped over me like honey. She is their priestess. The leader of their brotherhood. Hector expected me to be very impressed that she chose to visit me. It's apparently an honor that few outside the brotherhood ever receive. When she spoke to me, she took my hand in hers, as if we'd been friends for the entirety of our lives.

Her dark eyes swallowed the light of the room, and her face exuded an ageless quality. I would guess her to be no more than thirty years old, but she spoke as one who had experienced a lifetime. She told me of the beauty of nature, and of the flexibility of time. She insisted that if I joined their brotherhood, I, too, could share in her wisdom. She promised that Gabriel and I would always be cared for.

An enticing offer, to be sure.

Hector and his two friends sat on the edge of their seats as she spoke, equally mesmerized by her stories, though surely they had heard all of this before. Our conversation meandered for hours, but I didn't want it to end. Every word she spoke felt more important than any I had ever heard. She made promises, and imparted prophecies. She peered into my soul and revealed its inner workings in ways that I had never considered. I have never felt so completely understood.

She asked if she could meet my little Gabriel. At the time, I harbored no reservations, quickly fetching him and placing him in her graceful arms. She cuddled him against her bosom as only a mother could and stared into his eyes for a long time.

"Does Hector help you with him?" she asked me.

I nodded. Hector has always cared for Gabriel as he would his own son, even though his countenance sometimes unsettles me. She seemed pleased with my answer, running her hand gently across Gabriel's face before handing him back to me.

Then, she looked at Hector and said, "Take care of him. He's important to our cause."

Hector assented with a nod. I could see tears welling in the corners of his eyes. I had never seen him so moved before. For the first time, I saw what this brotherhood meant to him. What it did for him. Why he needed it.

When the priestess rose to leave, she embraced me in a warm hug, then left a soft kiss on my lips. It caught me off guard, but when she did the same for the men, I realized that it must be their custom. When they left, a great peace descended upon the house, the likes of which I've never experienced. Gabriel slept for hours afterward, and Hector retired to his chair and spent the rest of the day in quiet meditation.

Though I could never fully believe as they do, perhaps such a loving environment would be good for Gabriel. I don't know what exactly she meant, but I do believe the priestess that he is somehow important to their cause. He deserves more love than I can provide. Perhaps these people have children of their own that he can be friends with.

They seem to want harmony and balance. Even if I can only worship the Lord, I can appreciate their beliefs. Even now, with some distance from the whole experience, I yearn to talk with the priestess.

Perhaps she will visit again.

***

Brynn sat the journal down on her lap and stared out the windshield, trying to make sense of Ana's words. None of it seemed actionable, but some element of it begged to be further analyzed. It felt like a puzzle that desperately needed the edge pieces in order to take shape.

She sighed. The police department remained empty. Brynn thought back to her frantic phone calls, wondering if maybe the few officers in the area were currently canvasing the house. Surely, the disarray left behind would have worked them into a panic, and that might mean hours of investigation and evidence-gathering. As much as she didn't want to return, it seemed worth a shot.

She backed out of her spot and maneuvered the Jeep onto the highway. If there were no police cars, then she'd just turn around. She wouldn't go in, or stay in that cursed place without others. At least looking for the police gave her something to do. A way to stave off the guilt and adrenaline a little longer. She tried to ignore the grisly images of Skylar's and Gabe's dead bodies that rose to her mind's eye.

She pressed hard on the gas pedal and surged forward down the asphalt. Desert miles blurred by. She didn't see another soul on the road, and only Miriam's Sentra occupied the gas station parking lot. Gray's Point had never seemed more desolate than it did right now.

She slowed to turn down the driveway, and almost sped up instead. Something in her gut urged her away. But she couldn't just run. She'd done enough of that already, and this course provided the safest of those presented to her. The most sensible. She told herself that her chosen path wasn't cowardice. She sought the most necessary path. The rational one.

The Jeep rumbled down the driveway. She took it slowly, carefully scanning for any sign of the skinwalkers. As she approached the house, she didn't see any police cars, but she did see a car. An old, green Toyota Camry sat parked next to the porch. The front door of the house sat wide open. Brynn hit the brakes. A plain-clothes officer, maybe? She would have expected them to run in nicer cars. Maybe a neighbor, then.

Unwilling to take any chances, she turned the Jeep to face back down the driveway. She pulled her pistol from her pack, unbuckled, and exited the vehicle cautiously, arms raised and ready to take a shot. She ignored the wobble in her hands, trying to remain stoic even as a replay of the goat-man attacking her scrolled through her memory. She didn't want revenge, really. She just wanted it to be over.

She sprinted silently towards the house, walked up the steps gingerly without a creak, and flattened her back against the wooden beams next to the door.

She waited and listened.

A cute Texas drawl, female and anxious, echoed out: "This is really bad. Where are they?"

"I don't know," said a masculine voice. "But we'll find them."

Two people then. The girl sounded weak enough for Brynn to take, but she couldn't be sure of the man's size. They didn't sound like cops. Or dangerous, for that matter. Brynn shifted her weight, freezing when the boards groaned underneath. She held her breath, but it didn't sound like the people inside had heard.

After a few seconds of silence, the girl started singing loudly. Some current love anthem that Brynn vaguely knew but didn't care for. The girl's voice wasn't half-bad, but it seemed an odd time to sing. The crooning masked other sounds, but Brynn thought she might have heard a door open somewhere in the house.

It suddenly dawned on her that maybe the singing was meant as a distraction. While she focused on the song, the man might be —

Brynn heard the click of a gun beside her, and spun as fast as she could. He had the drop on her, though. She stared down the muzzle of a pistol held up by thick, muscular arms. Blue eyes studied her under close-cropped blonde hair.

Brynn could tell instantly this guy wouldn't miss his shot.

"Drop the gun," he said.

She lowered her arms and squatted down, dropping the gun on the porch. He took a step forward and kicked her gun to the other end.

Motioning behind him towards the porch swing, he commanded, "Go over there. Sit down."

His gaze drifted away for the briefest moment, and Brynn took the opportunity. She slapped at his wrist as hard as she could. The gun wobbled away from her momentarily as she lunged forward, past his arms so that the muzzle ended up behind her. She grabbed at his throat, wrapping her long slender fingers around his neck and hoping her weight would bring him to the ground. He stumbled backwards, using his free hand to grab at her hands.

Drop the gun, dammit, she thought, waiting to hear the thud on the ground.

Instead, she heard the sweet—but angry—voice of the southern girl, "Get off'im!"

Both the guy's arms now worked at her wrists. He hadn't dropped the gun, though, and that could only mean that the girl had it now. With no other options, Brynn released her grip and slowly turned around.

The girl pointing the gun at her stood at least six inches shorter, her arms shaking from either the weight of the gun or the fear of wielding it. Her bright red hair popped above her head into a high ponytail. These two made a perfect pair. Though they were sensibly dressed now, Brynn could imagine the two of them showing off their beach bodies on Instagram.

"I will shoot you, bitch," the girl said, her pretty face contorted into a forced snarl.

Brynn gave in to the guy pulling on her wrists from behind. He wrapped her arms around and held them tightly along her back, forming makeshift cuffs with his vice-like grip.

"Hey, bae," the guy said as he held an empty hand over Brynn's shoulder. "Give me the gun."

The girl's eyes locked onto Brynn's, and she feigned a lunge. Brynn flinched, and a smile spread across the girl's face. Then she passed the gun over to the guy and backed away.

The guy jerked Brynn towards the old porch swing, shoved her down into it, and stood across from her, relaxing the gun enough that it didn't present an imminent threat, but his grip insisted that he'd use it in an instant if Brynn made any sudden movements.

The red-head joined him, the menace that she'd mustered seconds before having completely melted away. In that moment, Brynn realized that the entire tough-girl facade had been an act. This shapely it-girl appeared now to be exactly as she looked. Small and weak.

"Look," he said, motioning with his head out to the yard.

The girl's face scrunched up. "Isn't that one of Skylar's Jeeps?"

"Uh-huh," he said.

The red-head shrugged. "That's handy. Mom would have thrown a fit if we drove her car through the desert."

Muscle-boy turned back to Brynn. "Are you with Skylar?"

Brynn nodded.

He slipped the gun into the waistband at the back of his jeans, cracked a huge smile and offered a calloused hand. She hesitated before offering hers in return. He pulled her back to her feet with ease, then pumped his arm up and down.

An effortless giggle erupted from the red-headed bimbo. "Damn, girl, you scared us," she said.

Brynn mumbled out an apology, still not entirely sure whether she could trust this duo. Somehow, though, she felt guilty for trying to kill them. Neither of them seemed threatening now, though, and the smiles implied that they didn't hold a grudge.

The guy let go of her hand and made the introductions.

"This is Macy. I'm Tanner Brooks. Where's Miriam?"

CHAPTER 18

Gabe's chest heaved up and down, trying to recover as much oxygen as it could after his sprint up the trail to the top of Gray's Point. From here, it felt like he could see to the ends of the earth. Flat land stretched out in every direction, pockets of shimmering mirages dotting the landscape. Given the recent encounters with skinwalkers, these false watery veneers seemed a potent reminder that he couldn't always trust his eyes. Knowing *when* to trust them might prove the bigger challenge.

Somewhere out there, Brynn scrambled for help if he was lucky—for safety if he wasn't. He still couldn't believe she'd left him.

Laying his skinwalker-made walking stick on the ground, he cracked the top on a bottle of water and chugged half of it, before turning around and studying the plateau. If he ignored the view, it looked almost as flat and uninviting as the rest of the area. A few scrub brushes managed to pull sustenance from the rock below, and some boulders sat scattered about. He didn't see much that would give him a clue as to where they'd taken Miriam.

And they *had* taken her—alive. He refused to believe anything else.

He finished his water and crushed down the bottle, soon regretting the loud *crunch* of the twisting plastic.

Until he met Miriam Brooks, Gabe would have said that he knew everything he needed to make a living as a cryptozoologist, but now his every decision seemed short-sighted and reckless. How could he hope to find her when she was the one person he needed to actually solve any of this?

He wondered if Miriam might find that funny, the irony.

He slowly walked around the plateau, studying the ground and hoping for something to jump out at him. As he wandered, his mind started concocting a chart comparing both Miriam and Brynn. They did have some things in common, to varying degrees. Before Brynn, Gabe had never met a woman so confident and capable. He didn't even know the trait would appeal to him, having spent a life around girls who seemed to go out of their way to at least act like they needed a man, even if they didn't. Girls who wore too much makeup and skimpy clothes that demanded attention. Girls who hung on his every word, then split when the next guy showed up. But now, he found the idea of a girl who didn't need him—or maybe even want him—intoxicating. Brynn showed him the template, but Miriam...

Miriam may have perfected it.

Having made it once around the top of the plateau, Gabe felt the frustration creeping up his neck. His shoulder muscles tightened. Why couldn't he figure this out? She had to be here. The sun made him tired, and his mind felt fuzzier than he wanted.

"*¡Maldito sea!*" he yelled into the dry air.

Behind him, something grabbed his wrist. His heart jumped and he looked down to see bony fingers pulling on his arm, giving him no choice but to spin towards it. The fingers gave way to a skeletal wrist and forearm, the white bone leading all the way up to a shoulder. The dark eye sockets of a deer skull stared at him, sitting atop a barrel-chested human frame. Chittering echoed out of the skull, straight into Gabe's mind.

His gun sat out of reach, tucked into a zipped pocket of his backpack—one more amateur mistake—so he drew back the walking stick he held in his other hand and swatted the thing right in the cheek. The wood rattled against the bone skull of the creature, whipping its head sideways. Gabe pressed the attack, pulling back to take another swing at its legs, just as the thing evaporated into a cloud of black dust.

Before he could process the disappearance, something grabbed his wrist again, causing him to spin back in his original direction and see the same creature before him. How the hell did it do that? Gabe swung again at the cheek, again hearing the bones rattle together, again watching as it disappeared into dust.

The air around him turned into fevered whispers, assaulting his senses. The black dust of the vanquished skinwalkers swirled around him, then dispersed in every direction. In a panic, he retreated to the center of the rocky precipice, giving him more area to protect, but also more safety from the threat of falling to his death.

The dusted remains didn't follow, instead seeming to multiply and disperse. Soon, a thick line of dusty particles encircled him. He shook his head, unwilling to believe his eyes. This surpassed anything his imagination had ever dreamed up.

A part of the dusty circle dipped down to the ground, forming into legs, a torso, and then one seemingly normal arm. Next, the same vacant deer skull grew out of the neck, followed by the same skeletal arm that had already grabbed him twice. Gabe pulled the totem up like a baseball bat, ready to take it on. It didn't advance, though. It just stood and chittered the same bony, raspy sound from before.

It's okay. He could defeat another one.

Next to it, the ring dipped down to the ground again, forming an exact duplicate of the one before. Then another. And another until the circle of dust became a circle of vicious skinwalkers, each one emitting that same penetrating sound, amplifying together into a deafening roar of clicking.

Gabe tried to count, but his mind seized up with adrenaline and fear. The number didn't matter. There were enough of them that his chances of surviving had dwindled to near zero.

They simultaneously took a step forward, tightening the circle around him. Maybe if he charged, he could break through the line, but he'd lost track of how to reach the downward path. If he chose poorly, he might end up with his back against open air, and a long drop. Deterred from that course of action, he slung his backpack to the ground and dug for the gun.

They took another step inward.

He couldn't think. The sound confused his senses. By the time he managed to get back to his feet, he couldn't focus long enough to aim. He fired wildly towards the ring of skinwalkers, confident he'd hit at least one of them. The shot rang out into the sky, and within moments one of them disappeared into dust, then almost immediately reformed.

Another step inward.

In a brief moment of clarity, he realized the physics didn't work out. The circle couldn't be closing on him without losing some of the skinwalkers. On the next step, he paid attention and saw that they were disappearing as they moved in. The numbers slowly started shifting in his favor with each step. He forced himself to breathe, understanding now that the gun didn't provide him the best protection. The totem did. A few more steps and he could get them all in one swinging arc.

The circle closed by another step.

He knelt on the ground, leaving the gun behind and rising with the skull-headed totem. He'd give these skeletal fiends a taste of their own medicine.

Another step.

They'd nearly drawn close enough. Their bodies stood so close together now that Gabe couldn't make out anything on the other side of them. Their height matched his own, and as the ring closed, his vision became more and more obscured. It would be over soon, though. One way or another.

They strangled him in with yet another step.

¡Ahora!

He swung hard, putting all the hard gym-training into one smooth, arcing motion that struck the first one squarely in the head. He pushed through, following his swing until the skinwalker disappeared in a cloud of dust, leaving nothing but air so that another took the brunt of his blow. One by one, they fell like dominoes, each one exploding into a black cloud of dust that sparked and shimmered before fading away entirely and leaving only the dry desert air.

Once they were all gone and he'd completed his spin, he let the head of the totem fall to the ground, still clutching it in case of another attack. Sweat poured from his hairline. His chest heaved. His heart pounded. His muscles tensed and spasmed, eager to continue the fight.

But the skeletal apparitions didn't return this time. Just when he thought it had all ended, his periphery caught another shape off to his right. He turned to see the huge shape of a bird landing on a rock outcropping. Its talons touched down, and its lithe body stretched upward as its wings shrunk down until they resembled human arms. The claws of the talons flattened out, and the spindly avian legs morphed. Left in front of him, he saw the silhouette of a tall, lanky man with poor posture.

On his hunched shoulders, the man wore a feathered cloak. The hood stretched down over his head, obscuring most of his facial features, its tip ending in a beaked point. Only when he saw the beak did Gabe register the beady eyes sewn into the hood of the cloak.

Gabe lifted the totem again, ready to charge but aware that his momentum could send him to his death if he wasn't careful.

" *¡Aléjate!*" he yelled at the new skinwalker.

The bird-man didn't press forward. Instead, a stick fell from the sleeve of his robe, hitting the ground as he collapsed his weight onto it. A cane. Unlike the deer-man from before, this one seemed old. Elderly, even. He used his free hand to brush back the bird-shaped hood and then greeted Gabe with sharp eyes and a tired grin.

Gabe's breath caught in his chest as he tried to make sense of what he saw, as he tried to process those familiar eyes. That smile. That quiet, prideful confidence.

When his breath escaped his chest, Gabe fought through the confusion to tentatively ask: "*Tío?*"

***

The last time that Gabe had seen Hector Castillo, the old man could barely get out of bed. He'd hobbled to the bathroom on occasion, and managed to make his own meals, but most of his day-to-day tasks relied on the dutiful attention of the caretaker that would check in on him a few times a day. Gabe had never harbored any resentment for his uncle spending all the money on that retirement community, only guilt for not visiting him more often.

The man in the bird cloak, though, seemed at least ten years younger than that Hector. Hardly spry, but the cane only provided a steadying force for him as he cleared the distance between them. Clearly aware of the unbelievability of the situation, the man stopped five feet away and regarded Gabe warmly.

Gabe swallowed hard, narrowing his eyes and trying to make sense of it all. Surely, the skinwalkers couldn't replicate those eyes. He could see his *tío's* soul in there, and the force of it couldn't be mistaken. Or maybe the fear goaded him into making poor decisions.

"Is it... really you?" he asked.

The man nodded slowly. "It is."

"*No entiendo,*" Gabe said, rubbing his temples. "*¿Cómo estás aquí?*"

"*Es difícil de explicar,*" the man answered before switching back to English. "But maybe it's time that you knew the truth."

Tears stung at Gabe's eyes. His *tío* knew Spanish, but always seemed to prefer English. As a kid, Gabe had begged for his uncle to speak Spanish more; he always felt like the language tied him to the mother he never knew. Surely the skinwalkers couldn't know about such a mundane quirk.

Gabe fought the urge to hug the old man in front of him. Even though every muscle in his body told him that, despite all logic, this man was the very same that raised him. But Miriam wouldn't let her guard down so quickly, and if he hoped to survive this, he needed to think more like her.

Hector nodded, as if he read Gabe's mind, then moved towards a boulder nearby. He sat on it, leaned on his cane and motioned to the ground in front of him. The strange, feathered cloak reflected the light, giving the black feathers an almost greenish hue.

"We haven't got much time, Gabriel," the old man said gently. "Come here. Let me explain it. Or try, at least."

Memories of story time flooded through Gabe's mind. He would sit cross-legged on the rug, enamored with the tales of folklore. Later in life, he learned that most children learned about nursery rhymes and fairy tales, but not so with his *tío's* stories. Gabe remembered more the mystery and intrigue, the wonder and awe. After what he'd just witnessed, he started to think that maybe not all his uncle's stories came from fiction.

Realizing that he'd been standing dumbfounded for the entire interaction, Gabe let the totem fall to the ground, then bent to pick up the gun. Hector seemed unconcerned with the action, and why wouldn't he? Apparently, he could turn into a bird and fly away.

The world didn't feel real anymore.

Hesitant and exhausted, Gabe moved towards this man so much like his uncle. Once there, he collapsed to the ground and curled his legs underneath him. Though he kept the gun loosely in his hand, he didn't feel any urge to use it. Whether the old man was a skinwalker or not, Gabe vaguely understood that the gun provided only comfort—not protection.

Hector leaned forward on his cane, almost looking like a wizard from some fantasy movie, with the billowing feathers of the cloak capturing a gust of wind and ruffling around him. Gabe half-expected him to conjure a magic potion, or open a portal to summon a vicious hellhound.

But Hector did none of that. He just fixed his gaze, took a breath, and started the craziest and most important story that Gabe would ever hear.

CHAPTER 19

The odd animal apparitions did return, as promised, with bedding and food. At first Miriam tried to resist the food, but her grumbling stomach insisted. Skylar dug in right away. She could hear the slurping and chewing in the dark. Eating seemed much more disgusting when reduced only to sound. She only nibbled at first, but eventually gave in and took larger bites. She'd need her strength for the eventual escape, and the peanut butter sandwich provided pretty good calories.

She ate only half of the sandwich before stopping, ignoring the side of what she guessed to be potato chips. Deep in thought, she stretched out on the sleeping bag they'd provided, her head propped up on a soft feather pillow. Not exactly a fancy hotel room, but she could see herself getting some sleep this way. She tried to work out the situation. Whatever this "ritual" was, she didn't figure it would mean their death. No reason to provide sustenance to people you just meant to kill.

After Skylar finished munching on his own feast, she heard him also settle down, rustling around a bit before finally leaving them both in silence again.

Miriam had decided that there were no more skinwalkers hiding in the dark. Too much time had passed. No living creature could remain quiet that long. She was fairly certain they were alone, and that meant they could talk freely to devise a plan. It still presented a risk, of course. Perhaps they had night vision cameras, or audio recording devices.

While she schemed, Skylar fell into a soft snore. How the hell could he sleep at a time like this? She supposed she never would understand him.

She rotated her wrist and felt for the button on the side that made her watch glow a bright green. They'd been here a while. Long enough that Gabe should have gotten back. Maybe he stood above her, unable to find a way down. She'd been unconscious on the trek downward, so she couldn't even picture him finding the entrance. She found it difficult to remain hopeful when she had to put so much of her faith and trust into someone she barely knew. Someone without any of the skills necessary, really. Still, she yearned for him to find her, some part of her desperate for his easy companionship.

Did she have a crush?

She didn't really know how to process that. For as long as she could remember, boys generally annoyed her, especially when thought of in a romantic or sexual way. It's not that she didn't sometimes find them physically attractive; it's just that their mouths tended to destroy that attraction with the first word. Her life worked better when she only had to rely on herself, but getting close to Macy had started to soften up that conviction... a little. Though still novel, having someone to rely on that wasn't obligated through family carried with it certain intangible benefits in which Miriam still had a hard time putting stock.

She pushed Gabe out of her mind. Thinking about him wouldn't get her out of this mess, no matter how much comfort she derived from it. No, the only way out was to be ready for an opportunity, though that course of action didn't provide much for her to think about. At the very least, she knew she couldn't afford to sleep. As Skylar's snores grew louder, she longed for the cloying silence again.

Before long, as Miriam tried to will herself to safety, a creaking sound echoed into the cavern. The flicker of the candle slowly built again, reminding her that her eyes still worked. A glance over at Skylar revealed him still softly sleeping, seemingly undisturbed by the approaching skinwalker. She didn't really know if that's what they were anymore, but she had no other way to describe them yet.

The woman wearing the coyote cloak rounded the corner, this time alone. No sign of the deer or goat. Miriam wondered if maybe they'd been dispatched to capture Gabe.

"Dad!" Miriam hissed. He didn't stir, so she tried again. "Skylar Brooks. Wake up!"

The woman answered Miriam's pleas instead. "He won't wake up. Not for a while."

Miriam growled towards the shadow of the lady. "What did you do to him?"

"He's fine, child," the woman said. "He's your biological father, yes?"

What an odd question. Though her first instincts drove her to avoid answering, she tentatively responded without thinking. "Y-Yes. Why?"

The lady didn't answer that question either. Miriam pushed slowly to her feet. If she couldn't get verbal answers, then she wanted to get close enough to read something from the woman's body language, or maybe get a glance at the face obscured by the hood.

"Hoping to get a better look?" the lady asked, as Miriam hobbled to the bars.

Holding the candle with her right hand, the woman used her left to lift the snout of the coyote and push it up over her head, letting it fall against her back. The flickering light danced across the woman's face, illuminating her striking features and dark, vacuous eyes. Her raven hair covered her ears before sweeping back into a low ponytail. She wore make-up, too—a lot of it—darkening her eyes and lips and giving her an ageless glow that Miriam suspected to be a ruse.

"There," the woman said. "See. I'm not a monster."

Miriam's defenses wouldn't let her believe that yet. Not all monsters wore fur or tentacles.

The woman stood as straight as an arrow, never wavering. The mere presence of her chilled the air. If she didn't know otherwise, Miriam would have sworn the temperature in the cave had dropped by at least ten degrees.

"I loved that dog," the woman said.

Miriam pictured the gnarly, dark blur of fur that she'd shot down in the cave. The one that somehow morphed into a dog upon its death.

The woman continued, "I've had it for twelve years. Gabe loved it."

Miriam's heart almost stopped. Gabe knew this woman? No. Impossible.

"Yeah, well..." Miriam answered. "Maybe don't order it to attack people."

The woman clicked her tongue, her lips turning up in a faint smile. "He wouldn't have killed you, but you clearly don't have the same restrictions."

Miriam wasn't about to apologize or even feel bad for killing that thing. Dog or not, it presented a threat, and she did the only thing she could have in the situation.

"I know a lot of things," the woman said, seemingly unfazed by Miriam's rising anger. "But I didn't expect you to be so strong."

Skylar sawed out a particularly loud snore, halting the conversation for a minute before the woman spoke again. "I never doubted that he'd come through, though. That he'd deliver you to us. And here you are. Right on time. Gabe's very reliable."

The witch's faint smile grew into a taunting one.

Miriam reacted by gripping the bars on her cell tightly, the blood draining from her knuckles. She wanted to scream, but held it in. Mentally, she rifled through everything she knew about Gabe. About the house. The weird way he ended up working for Skylar. How he'd found that strange totem. He'd followed her when she tried to run. Why hadn't she seen the signs? She hadn't had all the facts, and somehow she'd accepted that instead of probing deeper with questions and research.

A pain welled up from Miriam's chest. She felt as though her heart might explode and that she'd never breathe normally again. Tears stung her eyes. Her knees felt weak. The pain in her ankle throbbed harder than it had for hours. It had been a long time since she'd felt this way. So utterly betrayed. Since... Rose Valley, when her father didn't even stop to mourn Cornelius' death.

The lady reached out and patted Miriam's knuckles. Her hands were frigid, sending iciness through Miriam's veins. "I'll be back, my child. For the preparations."

Then she blew out the candle, plunging them into total darkness. For a second, Miriam wondered how the woman would navigate without being able to see, but her mind wouldn't let her focus on that. Not now.

With no one to watch, she slid down the bars to the ground and leaned her head against the cold steel. She let the tears flow out, streaking down her cheeks. It all felt so hopeless. Gabe wouldn't come. No one would come.

She searched for resolve. It had always been there when she needed it the most. But in that moment, Miriam couldn't find it.

***

Somehow, the tears lulled her into sleep. She woke with a start, immediately alert and listening for anything that might have startled her. When she heard nothing, her chest relaxed and she tried to regain her wits. She never liked being reduced to tears, and now the burning embarrassment stoked that resolve that she'd desperately lost when she'd found out about Gabe.

Part of her didn't believe it, but she couldn't afford sentimentality. She only hoped that her escape didn't result in a direct confrontation with him. She didn't know if she could handle that.

"Are you awake?" Skylar asked into the darkness.

"Yes," she answered quietly.

"I think they drugged our food," he said. "I couldn't stay awake."

"They drugged your food, not mine. I got a visit from that coyote witch."

Skylar chuckled. "You're funny. Like your mom."

Miriam's shoulders tensed up. What was up with him bringing up her mom every chance he got? They'd barely talked about her back when Miriam lived with him. Her mom had always been this taboo subject that never got mentioned or acknowledged, as if ignoring her memory could somehow erase her from existence. Miriam couldn't remember much, but the shadow that loomed over the family would have been evident even if she remembered nothing at all of her mother.

"Did you learn anything new?" he asked.

Miriam didn't want to share anything about the encounter. If she talked of Gabe out loud it would make his betrayal real, and she didn't want to accept that yet.

Afraid that he might ask for more information, Miriam tried to head it off with meaningless information, saying, "She was mad I killed her dog."

"You killed her dog?"

"Yeah. Back before they caught me."

"Good for you," he said.

The conversation fell silent, but it didn't feel over.

"We might not make it out of here, Miriam," he said, his voice projecting with a sense of resigned finality.

"Yes we will."

Another beat of silence before he replied, "Maybe. Maybe we will. I shouldn't underestimate you. But if we don't..."

Miriam felt her defenses go up. She wanted it to stop there. For him to trail off and never finish his thought. She sensed that she wouldn't be able to handle whatever he meant to say.

He continued, "I want you to know—"

"Dad," she interrupted. "We're going to get out of here. You can go back to Rose Valley. I'll go back to Dobie. We can just pretend like none of this ever happened."

He didn't immediately respond, and she thought for a second that she'd made herself clear, but then he said, "It was really hard after I—after we—lost your mom."

Adrenaline coursed through her veins, every bit as strong and urgent as the kind she got from fighting cryptids. She needed to run. Or fight. She felt like maybe if she used it all in one push of strength, she'd be able to bend steel. Blood rushed up to her cheeks and the cool air of the cave seemed to evaporate away. Her eyes burned.

She wanted to scream. But she stifled it, choosing instead to remain silent. She had no answer, anyway.

Thankfully he couldn't see her flushed cheeks or her good leg bouncing up and down, but he did keep talking. "She was always the better parent. I never quite took to it."

No. No. No. Skylar Brooks wasn't human anymore to her, and she refused to listen to this. She would not let him worm his way back like that. Caring about people hurt too much, especially when they had a high likelihood of hurting her. She pulled her knees up and hugged them.

"I didn't know what to do. And you..."

Shut up. Shut up. Shut up.

"You're just like her. And that hurt, Miriam. It hurt. A lot. I don't believe in ghosts, but seeing you every day after her death was like looking at one."

"Dad," she said, not nearly as forcefully as she hoped. "Please. You don't need to do this. Let's just come up with a plan to—"

It was he who interrupted her this time. "Miriam. Dammit. Listen to me. You think this is easy? Me telling you this stuff. We might die down here! And I have so much to atone for."

She couldn't offer him atonement, though. She didn't have it in her. She didn't remember a broken man who saw ghosts. She remembered a harsh critic who pushed her to study, learn and train. A man who required a hefty toll for his pride, and an impossible sum for his love.

She remembered a monster.

Still, his outburst took her enough by surprise that she halted her protests.

"Your mom died because I took her out into the field without enough training. She made a rookie mistake."

"It was an accident," Miriam whispered.

"One that could have been avoided. If I had paid more attention, maybe. If I'd made sure she was ready. Given her the skills she needed. And then... it happened again... with Cornelius."

Miriam had never blamed her dad for her mother's death. Never even considered it. She didn't blame him for Cornelius' death, either, really. Just for the way he'd handled it.

He continued, "I didn't set out to do it. I didn't mean to push so hard. But it seemed important. Necessary. Especially if you were going to take up the trade. And I knew you would. I could always tell. You took to it so quickly. Tanner and Cornelius, they had a passing interest. But it consumed you. And I knew I wouldn't be able to stop you from following in my footsteps."

She hardly noticed when she started rocking back and forth. The tears that pushed their way down her cheeks didn't register. She'd stopped analyzing, and started feeling.

And she hated it.

"Sometimes," he said. "Sometimes I just lose sight of it all. In the moment, I just react. I give in to the... fear, I guess... and I just... I just wanted you to be safe. I wanted to protect you. And making sure you could protect yourself was the only thing I knew to do.

"I don't expect you to understand, really. But we might die. We might, no matter how stubborn you are. And I wanted you to know. I just couldn't tell you before. I... I didn't even know, I don't think. But... it's been so long since we talked, and it gave me a lot of time to think, and..."

Her crying became audible. Embarrassed, she tried to contain it, but she couldn't. She'd lost all control. She couldn't think about the future or the past. She felt like she'd lost the ability to think at all.

"If we don't make it out of here alive, I just want you to know that no matter how poorly I showed it, I —"

She heard him shuffle in the dark, interrupting himself. Maybe he'd stop there. Maybe he'd leave her to the silence so she could collect herself.

His voice sounded shaky when he finally said, "I'm so proud of you... and I... love you."

CHAPTER 20

As Tanner and Macy hatched a plan to head back to Gray's Point, Brynn held her head in her hands. Why did everyone want to return to that evil place? Even the little prissy girl seemed to want to get in on the action, but Brynn convinced herself that Macy just didn't understand the threat. She hadn't seen the weird animal-people. She hadn't heard the weird noises. Or watched them drag away her mentor.

Brynn had told them all of that, of course, but somehow it didn't scare them, leaving her to question her own fortitude. They seemed to think they were taking the Jeep, but she hadn't relinquished the keys yet and she didn't intend to. They could walk. Or take that crappy old Toyota. Brynn still had every intention of finding the police, though she'd started to question whether this god-forsaken place even had any.

"We don't have a lot to go on," Tanner said to Macy. They'd stopped directing any of their conversation to Brynn. She couldn't really blame them. She'd checked out, and couldn't find the will to get back on board.

"No, we don't," Macy said, always seeming a little cheerier than warranted. "But you can track them. You're awesome."

Tanner leaned over and gave Macy a peck on the lips.

The whole interaction sickened Brynn on some visceral level, though she didn't really know why. By all accounts, they seemed to be in a healthy relationship.

Still, she couldn't stop herself from rolling her eyes and letting out an audible sigh. She leaned into her hands again and rubbed her eyes. Before she knew it, the couch cushion next to her sank under the weight of someone else, and a small hand rubbed her back. She tried to shrug it off, but the girl persisted anyway.

Tanner crossed the room and fiddled with something in the kitchen.

"You okay?" Macy asked. The authenticity of her voice infuriated Brynn.

"I'm fine. We just need to find the—"

As if she'd summoned them from her imagination, a knock echoed through the door, along with a forceful announcement: "Police! Anyone here?"

Finally! Brynn practically sprinted from the couch and threw open the door. Two officers took up her view, both dressed in khaki uniforms and black Stetsons. One older, with a mustache, and the other shorter and younger, clean-shaved and exuding a nervous energy.

The older one stopped chewing on his toothpick long enough to flash a fake smile. The name on his chest said Davies. "You the one called us in?"

"Yes, officer," Brynn said. "There's been an assault. And a kidnapping."

She stood aside as both men shuffled inside. Neither took off their oversized aviator sunglasses as they surveyed the room. Davies rested his gaze on the other two people there before hooking his thumbs into his belt and nodding at Tanner. He offered no such greeting to Macy.

The younger cop's name tag said Grimes. He spoke with a surprisingly high-pitched voice, and a bit of a stutter. "S-sorry we didn't get here s-s-sooner."

Brynn wanted to chide them for their tardiness, but she held in the anger. She didn't want to explode in front of Tanner and Macy, or cause any trouble with the cops she'd been seeking for the better part of a day. Instead, she nodded as if she understood. "It's okay. You're here now."

Davies said, "An assault, you say?"

"Yessir."

"Do you have a description of the assailants?"

Cautious to how she'd be received, Brynn started slow, describing two men. She eased into the fact that they had the heads of a deer and a goat, couching her description by suggesting that maybe they wore masks. She didn't think so, though. She distinctly remembered the otherworldly presence of the goat staring at her through that broken window—an image surely to haunt her for years. She finished her story by recapping what she'd learned from Gabe and how Miriam might be missing as well.

Neither Davies nor Grimes wrote down a single thing. Grimes nodded occasionally, and seemed to be paying more attention. Davies kept his head faced towards Tanner, as if preparing for a sudden attack.

Eventually, she found it annoying. "Are you going to write this all down or something?"

Davies turned towards her and cleared his throat, motioning to his right hand without moving it from his side. For the first time, she noticed the plastic sheen of his strangely curved fingers.

"I-I'm sorry," she stammered out. "I didn't..."

She trailed off as she realized that Grimes had two functional arms, and could just as easily take notes.

"Who are your friends here?" Davies asked, changing the subject.

Tanner crossed the space before Brynn could react, deftly offering a left hand for shaking instead of a right. Davies glanced at Tanner's outstretched hand but didn't take it.

"I'm Tanner Brooks. My uncle is the one that got kidnapped."

"So the missing girl's your cousin, then?" Davies asked.

"Yessir."

"D-d-didn't know Mr. B-b-brooks brought such a b-b-big group," Grimes said, glancing up at Davies. Brynn thought she caught the slightest hint of annoyance on his face. How would they know how many people came on the expedition?

Tanner piped in, "Yeah, my girlfriend and I just came down from Dobie. Skylar wouldn't have mentioned us—or my cousin—on his paperwork."

Paperwork? Brynn had never considered that Skylar might have coordinated efforts with the local law enforcement. She supposed it made some amount of sense, especially in such a close-knit community, but they weren't doing anything illegal. Didn't seem like they'd need permission.

"Uh-huh," Davies said. "Well, Officer Grimes and I will certainly keep an eye out. See what we can find out."

"They might be in danger!" Brynn protested. "We need to act fast."

Davies made a show of staring her down, chewing his toothpick decidedly slower. Grimes looked on with worried bewilderment. She felt Tanner's warmth against her as he closed ranks beside her. It made her feel safer, at least. Macy's quiet footsteps indicated that she, too, moved closer.

This whole encounter seemed especially bizarre. Why were they being so difficult? Did they not believe her?

"Listen, Miss," Davies finally said. "We know how to do our jobs. We'll be in touch if we find out anything."

Calmly, Tanner said, "She didn't meant to snap at you, officer. It's just been a while now, and we're really worried about them."

"Yeah, well, I'm sure they're fine," Davies said with a chuckle. "What'd he say when he came in, Grimes? That he was a world-renowned monster hunter or some such? Surely he can take care of his own self."

Grimes returned the laugh nervously. "Y-y-yeah. A cryp-c-c-cryptozoologist. Said he was really famous."

Davies nodded. "Yessir. That's what he said."

Brynn expected Tanner to press the issue further, but he didn't. She followed his lead and chose not to goad the officers on any further, either, but she didn't quite understand why. She'd worked so hard to get in contact with these guys that it seemed strange to let them go so easily.

Davies touched his left hand to the brim of his hat and dipped his head just slightly. "Sir. Ladies. We'll be in touch."

Grimes jolted out the door without a word and Davies followed close behind. They didn't talk to each other before climbing into their squad car and leaving the property.

Flummoxed, Brynn turned to Tanner. "What just happened?"

Macy answered instead, "Those guys are creepy. Something isn't right."

"They know something," Tanner said with a nod. "And they aren't interested in helping us."

***

Here she was again, begrudgingly gearing up for an expedition to Gray's Point. This time with strangers, though Tanner did seem more capable than Gabe. Brynn caught herself studying his sinewy frame more than once. He was the kind of hot that didn't quite seem real. She wondered what he saw in the redhead. Sure, she had some nice curves and a cute face, but Brynn considered herself a better specimen.

She got so lost in thought that she didn't notice when Macy entered the room. Brynn looked up to meet those piercing green eyes staring her down. She worried it meant confrontation. Surely Macy had caught on to some of the admiration for Tanner that Brynn seemed incapable of hiding. Instead, Macy flashed a big, gorgeous—and somehow infuriating—smile.

"You doin' okay?" she said. "You can stay here if you want. Tanner and I can totally handle it."

Brynn hadn't relinquished control of the Jeep yet, and she considered just leaving though she knew she wouldn't. As much as she wanted to run from this nightmare, she couldn't handle the weight of any guilt she'd feel for not helping where she could. That didn't mean she had to go with them, of course, but she also didn't relish the idea of staying behind in the cabin.

"They'll try to stop you," is all that Brynn could think to say.

"Then we'll stop them right back," Macy said matter-of-factly.

She admired the courage. A little. But Brynn didn't think Macy understood the gravity of the situation.

Tanner sidled up behind Macy and flashed a smile of his own. Brynn liked his better.

"Brynn's gonna be great," he said. "Skylar trained her. She knows what she's doing."

The vote of confidence rattled something deep inside of her. She couldn't be sure if it touched on a loyalty to Skylar or a need to please Tanner. She knew in that moment that she'd definitely be going on this adventure whether she wanted to or not. And she'd be fine, she told herself, if she could just pull it together.

The visions of the skinwalkers lurked in her mind. The feelings of shame for abandoning Gabe. The shadow of helplessness when she couldn't save Skylar. It was all spiraling out of control. She'd tried to run from it, but events had conspired to keep her tethered to this place, and now to these people. Running had become exhausting. But fighting sounded overwhelmingly difficult.

"What's the plan?" she asked, trying to sound upbeat.

"Go to Gray's Point," Tanner said. "Look around. You know where your friend Gabe was headed. So, we'll go that way. Between you and me, we can surely find some kind of lead."

"And what if we don't find them?" Brynn asked.

Tanner shrugged. "We'll figure that out if it happens. All we can do now is the now."

How very zen of him. She glanced at Macy and asked, "Does anything rattle him?"

"Not much." Macy giggled. "But he's kind of a bear when he's hungry, so we gotta keep him fed."

Brynn carried her backpack into the kitchen and dutifully started filling it with protein bars and bottled water. "It's not the best, but it should get him through."

"I'm right here," Tanner said. "And yeah, protein bars are fine. But when this all over, we're going out for burgers."

"Good luck with that," Brynn said. "They don't have restaurants out here."

"We'll make it work," he said, lifting one of the heavier backpacks and heading out the door.

Brynn watched him go, only realizing it when she caught Macy looking at her out of the corner of her eye. No smile this time, but neither did she look threatening. Brynn thought maybe she saw amusement, instead, which only caused her cheeks to flush. She supposed that with a guy like Tanner, Macy might be accustomed to the ogling.

Flustered, Brynn kept her head down and moved towards the door. She could hear Macy following behind. Monsters or not, this was clearly going to be a long trip.

CHAPTER 21

Grimes stared ahead as the cruiser slid over the pavement. It didn't take much to make him car sick, so watching the road provided his best chance at keeping his stomach from revolting. The acid down in his belly rumbled, but he didn't think the ride could be blamed.

"W-w-what are we g-g-gonna do, now?" he asked.

Davies held his left hand at ten o'clock, far more rigidly and formal than usual. His prosthetic rested on his thigh, bumping and rolling with every imperfection on the road. Grimes had worked with Davies for years now, and he didn't think he'd ever get used to that weird fake arm. It gave him the creeps.

"It'll be fine," Davies said, not sounding quite sure enough for Grimes' liking.

"S-s-she's not gonna be happy."

"No," Davies relented. "I don't s'pose she will."

Grimes respected her. Loved her, he guessed. But that didn't mean he wasn't scared of her. Truth was, even being around her made his blood run cold. Sometimes he wondered if that meant he should separate himself from the whole thing, but he knew that wasn't really how it worked. She'd let Hector go, but he'd always had a special place in her inner circle, and that'd always meant he got some of those special privileges. Privileges that Grimes could never hope to receive.

"W-w-we should t-t-tell her," Grimes suggested. "S-s-sooner rather than later."

Davies rolled the toothpick over to the other side of his mouth, clenching and unclenching his jaw. He flipped on the turn signal, and took the cruiser off the road and parked it behind the police station.

Grimes popped open his door and moved towards the back of the vehicle, where Davies soon joined him. Davies took off his aviators, regarded him with those dark brown eyes of his and sighed. He clapped Grimes on the shoulder.

"Let's just play it by ear. See what happens. If we do it tonight, then it'll all be over before those kids can catch up, anyway."

Grimes nodded, still scared to be anywhere near her when they gave her news that could derail her plans. But it wasn't his place to question things. He just followed. Did his job. Kept his head down. It might not have been the life he wanted, but it was the one he got dealt and the only thing he could do was play it. He still believed, mostly. It's just that he couldn't control those impulses that made it all feel wrong sometimes.

He hadn't been there for the last ritual, but his dad had been. Davies, too, and he said the experience changed his life. So Grimes hoped that maybe soon all of his misgivings would evaporate away.

Davies pulled open the doors leading down to the cellar underneath the station, not even bothering to let them down lightly. The metal banged against the concrete of the parking lot and echoed into the distance. Not many buildings out in this rocky part of Texas had basements or cellars. This one was commissioned special. Davies descended and left Grimes to the business of retrieving the doors and closing them behind as he descended. By the time he'd done so, the lights beckoned him downward.

Once he moved through the heavy steel door that Davies had left open, Grimes turned and secured it closed, turning all three deadbolts and the handle lock for good measure. He took the bench across from Davies and started unbuttoning his shirt.

"Just follow my lead, okay?" Davies asked. "We'll tell her when we need to, but not before."

Grimes nodded, leaning over to slip off his boots. He sat up with a jolt when he heard the racket across from him, looking up just in time to see Davies' prosthetic crash to the ground. A few choice expletives flew out of Davies' mouth. Grimes scrambled forward and picked it up, placing it on the bench without saying a word. This sort of thing happened frequently, but it still frustrated the hell out of Davies every time.

In silence, Grimes undressed down to his boxers, carefully hanging his uniform on the hooks along the wall. He placed his Stetson on a top shelf, then slipped on worn jeans and a denim shirt. Both smelled to high heaven. He made a mental note to wash both his and Davies' soon. They didn't usually do so much work in them as they had lately.

Once Grimes was dressed, he stood up just as Davies presented his back so he could get help attaching the other prosthetic. The one that gave Grimes even bigger creeps. When he finished up, Davies didn't offer up a thank you, but they were way past that. Grimes didn't take offense.

He hung back and let Davies try to dress himself, gently offering help when another hand was needed. Before long, they were both ready to go. They shared a look, as they always did. The last, unspoken acknowledgment of their humanity. Sometimes,

Grimes wondered if it might be the very last time he ever looked into Davies' human eyes.

Davies offered a comforting nod, indicating that it was time to go. Grimes turned, grabbed the goat head off the hook on the wall, and pulled it over his scalp. Through his obscured vision, he now looked into the haunting eyes of what he'd almost started to think of as the true form of Davies.

Together, the deer and the goat descended into darkness, down a winding underground path to the lair of their master.

CHAPTER 22

Miriam steered herself away from the emotion the same way she always did. She focused on action. After Skylar had barraged her with decades of painful feelings, he'd fallen into silence again. She preferred it. Welcomed it. The tears dried up when she turned her thoughts back to Gabe.

She considered herself an excellent judge of character. Naturally suspicious, few people managed to fool her. But he had. And look where it had gotten her. She tried to understand why she'd let her defenses down. How she could trust a stranger so completely. The reason scratched in the back of her mind, but the truth was uncomfortable. She'd never really been attracted to anyone before. She'd come to terms with it. She didn't fear a life devoid of romance.

But somehow, he'd gotten through at least one layer of her defenses. Though she tried to ignore it, her mind had wandered down that path while she waited for him to return. In that cave, she entertained the idea that maybe she could have a normal, healthy relationship. What Tanner and Macy had. What her mom and dad might have had at one point. But she knew that Gabe had betrayed her. This was exactly why she never had any interest in relationships.

"Why did you hire Gabe?" she asked suddenly into the darkness. Probably not what Skylar wanted to talk about, but it's all that Miriam could handle. Anger was so much easier than love.

"He needed work," Skylar said.

"Yeah, but, how did you come to hire him?" she asked. "Did you seek him out?"

"Hmmm," he said. She could imagine him stroking the edges of his handlebar mustache as he sometimes did. "After Rose Valley, I was looking for assistants. I got a call about him."

"A call? From who?"

"Hector."

"His uncle?"

"Yeah. He called me and said that Gabe had a dead-end job at a mechanic shop. Asked if I'd mind hiring him. Promised that he'd be a good, hard worker."

"Has he been?" she asked.

"Yeah. He's been good. Integrated quickly. Gets along well with Kent and Brynn."

Of course, he got along well with the latter. Maybe too well. Miriam wondered if Skylar knew about Brynn and Gabe's failed relationship. Wondered if Brynn knew how dangerous Gabe really was.

"You went to Papua New Guinea after you hired him, right?" Miriam asked.

"That's right, though..."

Skylar trailed off in thought, and Miriam let him. She'd learned deduction from him, and knew the interruption meant that he'd also started to follow her line of thinking.

"From the beginning, he advocated for this mission. To come back out for the skinwalkers. I assumed it was because he grew up here. That he wanted to visit his childhood. Work on something familiar. He said he saw one as a kid."

"Yeah. He told me."

Skylar sighed and moved positions, his bedding rustling in the dark. "You think Gabe set this up, don't you?"

"I don't know," Miriam said, telling the objective truth, but still feeling as though she lied. She didn't have all the pieces. She didn't have the confirmation. But, somehow, her capture, Skylar's capture—it had all been part of some plan.

"How, though?" Skylar asked. "How could he know you'd be here? No one could have predicted that."

"Because... I've been coming out here to study for months."

Miriam closed her eyes and waited for the assault. She felt certain Skylar would yell and lecture. Tell her that she had no right, especially given the nature of their relationship after Rose Valley. He said nothing, though, and the silence felt just as chiding as his ire. Every time she took a study break out to that cabin, she felt justified in sharing his property, but now she couldn't help but feel a little guilty about the deception.

When he spoke again, she detected no judgment in his voice. "So you think someone's been watching you?"

"I don't know. Maybe. Whatever they've got planned, it seems like they need the two of us. So maybe Gabe got you here, knowing that I'd show up. Why did you come out here now? You said Gabe had pushed for it since you hired him."

"We'd been back from Papua New Guinea for a few weeks. No new leads had come in."

"Why not just come out here right when you got back, then?" she asked. "I've never known you to sit idle."

"Let me think," he said. "I wanted to get back out in the field, but Gabe argued that we should wait. Until Brynn and Kent finished their semesters."

"But Kent's not finished. That's why he didn't come, right?"

"That's right," Skylar said slowly.

"Then why the sudden change? Why didn't you wait for Kent?"

"I-I don't remember, exactly. Brynn finished. And we all seemed ready to do something."

Miriam fought back the frustration of not knowing the full story. Skylar might not remember, but evidence pointed to Gabe insisting they'd come here. Now. Not before. Not after. But then, they'd all gotten here days before she had. It would have all been on a hunch that she'd come to Gray's Point for a study break at this exact time. But the finals schedule for Dobie Tech would be easy enough to dig up. Was there someone there watching her? Following her to class?

It felt surreal, being targeted. She hardly felt important enough for someone to put that much effort into capturing her. What could she possibly offer?

"Okay," she said. "So, at the very least we know that you got here at least partially because of Gabe."

"I guess so."

"And when I tried to leave, he followed me. Did you tell him to do that?"

"No," Skylar said quietly. "But I should have."

She didn't want to get into talking about their relationship again. She didn't care if he meant to let her go or not.

"Okay. So that was his idea?"

"Yeah. He was mad at me, I think. And insisted that you needed your gear."

Miriam chuckled lightly at the thought of calling textbooks and notes by that name. "Just school things. Not gear."

He laughed. "Right. Sorry. Been in this business too long."

"When he caught up to me, he convinced me to stay. Even offered to abandon you to stick with me."

"And you stayed. And then you got captured in that cave. Did he pick that cave?"

Miriam's ankle suddenly throbbed, reminding her of the need to find that cave. Gabe hadn't done that to her. She just took a bad step on uneven ground. And it had been she who insisted they find a cave for shelter. Gabe seemed happy enough to just sleep in the tents.

Then again, she hadn't been able to walk on her own. He had more control over their destination than she. And once they chose the cave, Gabe had been the one to put the tent up over the cave entrance. Could that have been some sort of signal to the skinwalkers?

"I don't know," Miriam answered. "We kind of picked it together."

"Was he eager to leave you there alone?" Skylar asked.

He hadn't been. At all. She'd processed Gabe's reluctance as fear then, but now her mind framed it differently. Maybe it had been nerves. Maybe staying with her until the right time was part of his job.

Every memory started to heat up Miriam's blood.

"No. Not exactly. He seemed scared to head out on his own."

"That's a strike against your theory, then."

"Unless he needed to stay with me until they were ready."

Skylar shifted again, this time moving closer to her. She could hear his breathing now, but still couldn't see him in the pitch black. He must have moved towards the bars between them.

"Maybe this is all just paranoia. Gabe's a good kid. He had a rough life, but he's never done anything that made me doubt his loyalty."

"Not even when he left you for me?" Miriam asked pointedly.

"I can be a bit much to take sometimes. And Brynn thought maybe... she thought maybe he might have took a liking to you."

Took a liking to her? No. What a silly idea. Sure, she'd found herself a little bit attracted to him, but Gabe could have his pick of women. He wouldn't choose her. If he took an interest in her at all, it had to be for whatever plan these creeps had in store for her. Besides, what did Brynn know?

Brynn dated him. She knew a lot about him.

Miriam shushed that inner voice. Somehow, she found the prospect of someone *like*-liking her more terrifying than the idea that they meant to sell her off to monsters.

When she didn't respond to Skylar's last bombshell, he started talking again. "At any rate, it doesn't really matter."

"It matters a lot," she said. "He promised to come back for me."

"How would he find you? We don't even know where we are."

Her dad was, of course, right. Whether Gabe wanted to find her or not, he probably wouldn't be able to. If they were going to get out of this mess, they'd have to do it together. They only had each other.

The idea of working with her father to secure their escape had once seemed unfathomable, but she almost imagined a scenario where they could work together in harmony. Or at least, effectively.

"This is nice," Skylar said, as if he could read her mind. "Being able to carry a conversation. Solve a problem."

Oh no. She wasn't going to let him go down that path again.

"How long until they come back, you think?" she asked.

"I don't know, but until they open the cell door, there's not much we can do."

"True," Miriam said. "But eventually they will. And when they do, we should be ready."

"Don't worry," Skylar said. "I am."

CHAPTER 23

It took her no time to find the path. Brynn managed to park the Jeep within just a few feet of it. She'd always been blessed with a good memory and a knack for remembering terrain. She pointed at it from the driver's seat. Tanner leaned in towards the windshield, studying the brush that hid the entrance. From the back, Macy watched, as well.

"It's hot out," Tanner said. "We should all make sure to keep hydrated."

"There's water in the packs," Brynn said.

Without being instructed, Macy unzipped a few pouches before she found the sweating bottles of water, then handed two up front. Brynn cracked the top on hers as Tanner followed suit. They both took long drinks.

Tanner threw a glance to Macy. "Drink some water, babe."

"Nah," she said. "I'm good. I've got this."

She held up a bottle of flavored tea she'd brought with her all the way from Dobie, Brynn assumed. Certainly nowhere to get such a fancy drink out at Gray's Point. Macy's choice wasn't nearly as hydrating as water, but what did Brynn care? If the stupid girl wanted to flirt with heat exhaustion, so be it.

"All right," Tanner said. "Let's go."

Making sure that she had her gun before shuffling out of the car, she met Macy and Tanner on the driver's side. If they were having second thoughts, they showed no sign of it. Their confidence emboldened Brynn a little, but she still fought to keep her heart from beating straight out of her chest. She didn't know what they'd find, or whether they'd be equipped to combat it. All she knew was that she desperately didn't want to die.

She waited until Tanner made them move by striking out towards the path. Macy followed quickly, leaving Brynn to take up the rear. They pushed past the brush and started upward until they came to the plateau where Brynn had fought with Gabe.

A fresh wave of guilt washed over her as she saw her own boot prints, and the thin line the keys had etched in the sand when sliding toward her boot. Gabe would never forgive her, she'd already decided, but she at least hoped they might find him alive. That maybe he could go on with his life, rightfully pushing her out of it, sure, but at least she wouldn't have to blame herself for his death.

Brynn hung back and waited while Tanner and Macy studied the plateau. Gabe wouldn't have stayed here. He would have gone up. She found a bit of irony in the fact that Skylar had hired her to replace Miriam, and now Gabe sought out Miriam just to replace her. A cruel circle of life that Brynn didn't like. She tried to imagine Skylar's research team working without Gabe, but the very thought seemed joyless. Gabe brought the muscle, sure, but he also brought the humor. The heart. Without him, life would be bleak. Whatever the reasons for the breakup, she wished she'd seen how much he'd enriched her life before now. Before it was too late to do anything about it.

She zoned out and didn't pay attention to the conversation between Tanner and Macy. Before she knew it, they both moved past her and up towards the plateau at the Gray's Point summit. By the time she started after them, a sizable gap had formed between them. She could hear them ahead of her, but the path wound in such a way that she lost sight.

By the time she turned the corner, Tanner and Macy were around the next, leaving Brynn feeling like she'd never catch up. Blood started pumping in her ears. Her vision narrowed. She felt suddenly claustrophobic, despite the open air off to her right. Picking up her pace, she turned the next corner, still unable to see them. Except now, she couldn't hear them, either. Her mouth ran dry. Her head pounded. Something felt wrong.

She turned to look behind her, and the path seemed to wind down forever. She couldn't judge her altitude anymore. Was she near the top? The ground below all looked the same. In her confusion, she started descending, before realizing that was the wrong direction and turning back. She rubbed her temples. She couldn't afford a panic attack now. She coaxed herself to pull it back together, closing her eyes and trying to think calm thoughts. Occasionally that worked.

Something rattled her inside, and it took her a few seconds to identify it as a growl. Not from her. From something else. Close. Too close.

Brynn slowly opened her eyes and saw nothing in the path upward, which left only one possibility. She reached for the gun she'd been smart enough to hide in the waistband of her shorts. She pulled up the gun, spun, and fired off a shot before she could even properly aim. Unsurprisingly, she hit nothing. The shadowy thing before her didn't budge.

It stood on all fours, with huge broad shoulder blades and shimmering fur. It had the general appearance of a canine, but the front legs were longer than the back, giving it an almost hyena-like appearance. Its standing fur looked as pointed as blades. Its yellow-hued eyes stared out over a long snout, its white teeth revealed in a rippling snarl. She tried to steady her gun, but couldn't push the fear down long enough to keep from shaking. Her second shot missed again, causing the beast to step forward. It looked to its left, stepped to its right.

Another one appeared beside the first. Brynn blinked away tears she couldn't control to try to make sense of it. Fighting became secondary.

Brynn turned and ran.

She could hear the two creatures gaining ground behind her, snarling and snapping their jaws. She felt slow and ineffective, so she shimmied off her backpack and let it fall to the path behind her, hoping it would buy her some time and increase her speed. She kept the gun. It made her feel safe, despite her inadequacies with it.

Another few steps and she saw the plateau, but took the last corner too wide. One boot slipped in the sand and careened her out towards the edge. She tried to keep a grip with her left foot, but her momentum proved too much to fight. She pumped her right foot to find traction, but only found air instead. She screamed, knowing it might be her last.

She wouldn't survive the fall.

As her other leg left the ground, she flailed, digging her fingernails into the dirt and ignoring the pain in her ribs when she struck the earth. She could find nothing to hold onto, and though she managed to slow herself down, her weight still pulled her ever-closer to death. She left the gun in the dirt, using both of her hands to save herself. She couldn't see the dogs now, but she knew they'd be there. Waiting for her if she managed to pull herself up.

She slid further and finally found purchase, her arms almost pulling themselves out of their sockets as she dangled from the precipice. Brynn spent a lot of time in the gym, but her upper body strength would only be able to hold her so long.

She pulled hard, managing to lift herself a little, but then the sand shifted under her fingers and she had to let herself back down to keep from losing her grip. She knew she shouldn't, but she looked down to see what faced her. The fall alone would kill her, but the number of crags and rocks she'd hit on the way down would be far more painful.

As she contemplated her last moments of life, she found her thoughts turning away from herself. To those she'd never quite treated right. To her mom. Gabe. Miriam.

Maybe they'd all forgive her in death.

Her left hand slipped and fell. The agony of holding herself up with just her right hand showed itself by the sweat on her brow. The jabbing pain in her side. She considered letting go.

On giving up.

"No you don't," Macy said, the melodic sound of her accent tumbling over the cliff.

Then two hands on Brynn's wrist, pulling hard. Brynn wondered if her shoulder might dislocate before Macy could haul her over the edge. Slowly, though, Brynn inched upward until she could get her left hand back up. She used it to grab Macy's wrist, giving them that much more power to get the job done.

When Brynn's eyes crested the side, she saw Macy face down in the dirt, straining with everything she had. Some of her wild red hair had escaped its ponytail and snaked down the side of her face, matted down with sweat. She grimaced and pulled again, this time giving Brynn enough of a boost to get her elbows over the side, to change the balance of her weight. She pulled up quickly to her feet, as Macy scrambled to do the same.

The dogs. Where were the...

The growls echoed from down the path. Brynn searched the ground, found the gun she'd left behind and bent to scoop it up. She didn't want to tear her eyes away from the dogs staring at her from the downward path, but with only Macy at her side, she desperately needed to know where Tanner was. She found him quickly, squaring off against one of the strange creatures from the house. The deer dodged and weaved as Tanner repeatedly tried to get a hit in, occasionally landing a blow that the deer countered before retaliating with even harder blows that seemed impossibly quick. Convinced that the goat would be nearby, Brynn scanned the plateau but came up with no one else.

Why hadn't these dogs attacked? They'd certainly had ample opportunity.

"We need to help Tanner," Brynn said, surprising herself with the panic in her voice.

"Tanner can take care of a one-armed dude in a mask," Macy said.

Brynn thought she must have misheard. These things weren't merely men in masks. They were some other spawn of Satan. Demons infused with the bodies of men and the heads of otherworldly animals. With unnatural strength, and the ability to transform and appear anywhere. Macy, once again, seemed to be severely underestimating the situation.

"You gonna shoot these things, or what?" Macy asked, snapping Brynn out of her confusion.

She'd tried before, and only managed to create two where there had been only one. Another shot might make even more, and then what would they do?

"I can't. They multiply when you do that," she told Macy.

Macy looked at her like she'd lost her damn mind. Given the pounding pain behind her eyes and the overwhelming feeling of hopelessness, maybe she had. But that didn't make the demon dogs in front of them any less real.

"They're just dogs," Macy said.

Brynn looked again at the creatures in front of them, just to confirm that her eyes hadn't played tricks. No, these weren't dogs. Their eyes still glowed. Their proportions were still wrong. The fur still emanated a deathly black glow. She could shoot and kill animals, but not these monstrosities.

The dog on the right lunged forward, clearing an insane amount of ground before snapping its jaw shut mere inches from Brynn's face. She should have pulled up the gun and fired, but she couldn't find the courage. She just froze.

Macy sighed, then snatched the gun out of Brynn's hand. Before Brynn could react, Macy fired a round into the chest of the approaching dog just as it lunged again towards Brynn's throat. With a heart-breaking yelp, it fell to the ground. A yelp that sounded curiously normal.

Like a... dog.

The other held its ground, barking and snapping. Brynn held her breath, waiting for another of the apparitions to spawn. It didn't happen, though. Only one of the creatures remained, and it seemed keen to keep its distance. She kept her eye trained on it, waiting for Macy to pull the trigger again, but no shot came. The dog continued barking.

Behind them, Tanner groaned in pain. Brynn turned to react just in time to see Tanner hit the ground hard, landing on his back with a thud. The deer-headed monster straddled Tanner, pinning him down by placing a forearm across Tanner's neck.

Macy jerked the gun towards the deer and yelled, "Get up, or I'll shoot you!"

The deer stopped, loosening his grip enough for Tanner to gasp for air.

"I'm serious," Macy warned again.

The deer regarded her quizzically. Though it was hard to discern an emotion from such an inhuman creature, Brynn thought maybe it looked confused. Brynn jumped when Macy fired the gun. It quickly became clear that Macy intended the shot to miss.

"Up!" she commanded.

The deer stood, putting both its skeletal hand and normal hand above its head. Tanner scrabbled backwards, crab-walking to safety before getting to his feet. He made his way over to his girlfriend and stood beside her, not demanding the gun from her this time. Brynn kept one eye on the barking dog, sure that either it would attack, or the deer would vanish.

The deer chittered and clacked, its ungodly "voice" searing into Brynn's brain. Perhaps on command, the dog-like monster raced forward towards Macy's back, moving at a speed that Brynn could hardly process. Without thinking, and perhaps more bravely than she ever had, Brynn lunged forward and pushed on the dog's midsection just as it leapt from the ground.

Together, she and the dog tumbled down, wrapped together into a ball of fur and limbs. Pain seared up her arm as it clamped its jaw on her forearm. She punched at it with her free hand, to no avail.

As she fought, she started to lose the advantage, rolling to her back as it stood over her. It let go of her arm, and surged its many-toothed snout towards her neck, but she managed to deflect the bite just in time.

Then, a shot rang out and the dog went limp on top of her. Only then did Brynn realize that she'd been screaming. She heaved the dog off to the side and rolled away, too scared and tired to stand up, but desperate to clear as much distance between them as she could.

"Babe!" Tanner yelled.

Macy spun again towards the deer, but he loped away, disappearing behind a boulder just as Macy fired again. The bullet ricocheted off the stone and echoed into the empty air.

Brynn sat in shock, her chest heaving up and down as she nursed her arm. The wound looked bad, her arm covered in blood and throbbing. She only vaguely registered Macy handing the gun to Tanner and kneeling beside her.

"I think you're ok," Macy said, rubbing Brynn's back. "We've got a first aid kit, right?"

Brynn winced and breathed out, "Yeah. In my pack. Down the path."

Macy nodded and disappeared as Tanner closed ranks and stood nearby.

"What were those things?" Tanner asked, to no one in particular.

"The skinwalkers," Brynn answered. "It's what you wanted, right?"

While she struggled to catch her breath and process the pain, Tanner stood resolute and seemed completely unfazed by the beatdown he'd received at the hands of the deer-man. His skin glistened with sweat, and his shirt was covered in dirt. He looked like a Greek hero, there to save her.

"What do you mean?" Macy asked, returning with the first aid kit. "It was a guy in a mask and two dogs."

Tanner arched an eyebrow, "No way. That deer guy moved weird, and the dogs were... glowing?"

Brynn nodded, "With yellow eyes."

"You mean red eyes," Tanner said.

Macy looked at each of them in turn, concern etched all over her face. "They both had brown eyes. Like a lot of dogs. They're just mutts."

Tanner looked as confused as Brynn felt. Macy motioned to the dog carcass closest to them.

Brynn looked at it—really studied it—and realized for the first time that Macy happened to be right. It just looked like a dog. A large, dead dog. It must have changed when it died. Morphed into something real. There could be no other explanation. Surely, she and Tanner couldn't have shared a mass hallucination.

"I don't understand," Tanner said. "They didn't look like that before. And that deer-thing. It jumped and teleported and moved around like nothing I've ever seen."

"And one if its arms was a living skeleton," Brynn added.

Macy knelt and started tending to the wound on Brynn's arm. If it came from a dog, then there really wouldn't be anything to worry about... unless they had rabies. But if it came from a skinwalker, she had no idea what it might do to her in the long run. She needed a hospital, right? Surely they'd have to see reason now. Surely, they'd agree to leave.

Macy looked up at Tanner and commanded, "I think you should sit down. Something's wrong with the both of you."

Tanner followed her orders, his brow furrowed in thought as he did. "Ok, babe. So you're saying you didn't see any of that?"

"Well, I mean, I saw the two dogs and the man attacking us with a weird costume on," Macy said, intently focused on her bandaging job. "No glowing, or teleporting. Dogs trained to kill people are no joke, though. I was a little worried, there."

"What about the weird skittering sound it made?" Brynn asked.

"Huh?" Macy asked. "You mean the whistle to sic the dog on me? Thanks for that, by the way."

Brynn felt too confused to acknowledge the sentiment. Finished wrapping Brynn's arm, Macy stood up, dusted off her hands, and pulled the bottle of tea from her backpack. She twisted the top off and finished what was left, then retrieved a couple of fresh bottles of water and offered them to Tanner and Brynn.

Just as Brynn raised it to her lips, Macy retracted the offer, leaned over and batted it out of Brynn's hands, sending the bottle to the ground. The water chugged out onto the sand. She followed suit by quickly doing the same to Tanner.

"What the hell?" Brynn exclaimed.

"This water," Macy said. "Y'all drank it. I didn't."

"So?"

"This stuff is bottled here. In Gray's Point."

"Yeah," Brynn said. "We bought it at the gas station. Most bottled water is just from municipal water supplies, anyway."

"Hmmm," Tanner said, following Macy's lead. "What if this stuff is spiked?"

"That might explain things," Macy insisted. "I don't know what's in it, but it had you guys seeing things... differently."

Brynn tried to make sense of the supposition. Tried to remember how much of the water she'd drank. *When* she'd drank it. Could she explain every skinwalker encounter that way? It hadn't seemed an important enough detail to remember, so she couldn't be sure. The tap water tasted horrible, though, so they'd made most everything from the bottled water. Could they really just be facing people? Dogs?

The impossible started to feel possible.

Before the conversation could continue, they heard growling from the boulder where the deer had disappeared. Brynn looked up to see another of the dogs rounding the corner.

This dog, however, looked much like the dead ones. Huge, fearsome, and dangerous, but not supernatural. She couldn't be sure whether she saw them clearly because she knew the truth, or because the effects of the water had worn off.

Nonetheless, this new turn of events was manageable. They could surely defeat a single dog.

But when another appeared, the odds went down.

And when four more crept out, snarling and gnashing their teeth, Brynn wondered if they had any chance at all.

CHAPTER 24

Grimes watched the last of their hounds race up the path, while Davies whispered a string of choice expletives fit for the very worst sailors. The priestess didn't like it when they talked with their masks on, and they weren't allowed to take off their masks within the Sanctuary, but Grimes wouldn't tell anyone. He was just grateful that he didn't have to go up and fend off those kids.

"Are y-y-you ok?" Grimes asked in his own whisper.

"That little red-head was gonna shoot me," Davies whispered back. "I had to retreat."

"S-s-she must not have d-d-rank none of the w-w-water. I-I-I told you I didn't think she drank none."

Grimes had been on lookout when the trio had arrived, and he watched very carefully for them to drink. Of course, in this case, they could hardly wait for that anyway. The walls were closing in around them, and they didn't have the luxury of waiting until the hallucinations kicked in.

"I was hopin' to just scare'em off," Davies said. "But I guess it's dog food for them."

Grimes shuddered to think of the hounds ripping those poor kids limb from limb. There weren't many choices left, though, so he didn't question Davies' decision to release them.

"S-s-should we t-t-tell her now?" Grimes asked.

Somehow, even through the mask, Grimes could tell that the questioned irked Davies. He stood with an uncharacteristically rigid posture, and his shoulders seemed uncomfortably tight. Telling her would surely bring down her wrath, but it would be worse if the kids somehow got down into the Sanctuary. But six hounds, trained to kill. Each outweighing the girls, and almost the guy. Surely, they wouldn't stand a chance.

"No," Davies answered. "Not yet. We need to get down for the initiation. If we're late, she'll know something's up."

Fair enough. Davies called the shots, and Grimes followed orders. He couldn't complain really. He didn't yearn for responsibility. Especially in this organization. He worried that leaving those kids unattended would come back to bite them in the ass, but he didn't have the courage to protest any more than he already had.

Davies led the way and Grimes followed, down deeper into the cave, their way lit only by torches mounted along the cave wall. He'd grown quite accustomed to finding his way in dim light, so it didn't bother him that he couldn't see the detail of the ground or the length of the path in front of him. Before long, they stood outside of her office. He strained his ears to try to hear whether the initiate had already arrived.

The door parted, seemingly on its own. But standing on the other side was their priestess, dressed head to toe in her ceremonial coyote robe. It looked heavy, but also comfortable and luxurious. Far more appealing than the heavy mask and denim that she made them wear. Still, Grimes had a hard time feeling the jealousy that tried to push through. Her inviting smile and mysterious eyes drew him in and made him forget a lot of things. Most of all, himself.

She motioned inside and they both nodded in the way that she'd instructed, halfway to a bow, but not dipping so low as to lose sight of what stood in front of them.

As they entered, Grimes landed his eyes on the hawk. He hadn't seen that old bugger in years. Surely, he should have been dead. Grimes couldn't remember a time when Hector had been young. The old man's watery eyes regarded the two of them with the reverence Grimes had come to expect from other members of the Brotherhood.

In the chair next to the hawk sat that Mexican kid that came in with Skylar Brooks. Gabriel. The one they'd been expecting for all these years. Probably about the same age as those fighting the hounds up top. Nicely trimmed beard. Shrewd, alert eyes. A fair bit of muscle on him, too. It'd be good to have another worker-bee. The duties he shared with Davies already worked him to the bone. He wondered what animal spirit this kid would be blessed with. Probably something more badass than a stupid goat.

Grimes and Davies stood next to the door after she closed it, guarding it from intrusion that almost certainly wouldn't come. The hawk and the kid sat across from them along the opposite wall, comfortably sitting in the hand-carved chairs that Grimes' daddy had made. He'd always admired the intricate woodwork, and sometimes lamented that he'd become a cop instead of going into the trade. He would have loved to spend the time learning it from his daddy. She'd insisted a cop would be more valuable to the Brotherhood, though.

"Gabriel Castillo," the priestess said suddenly. She paced back and forth in front of the kid, briefly cutting off Grimes' view with every lap. "Do you come here of sound mind and body?"

The kid shared a glance with Hector before answering, "Yes, ma'am — I mean, your grace."

Grimes held in a snicker, but luckily didn't have to fight to hide the smile behind his mask. This kid didn't have any idea what he was getting into, did he? Hector probably gave him the rundown minutes before, and now the poor thing had to walk on pins and needles, hoping he didn't screw up and say the wrong thing. She could get unfairly angry when someone said the wrong thing.

The priestess continued, "And you understand the responsibilities you will be taking on? To serve the Brotherhood. To protect the lands of Gray's Point. To forgive your brothers for all of their trespasses against you?"

"Yes, your grace."

"All of your brothers?"

"Yes." The kid nodded his head, seemingly confused by the double question.

"No matter what they may have done to you?"

Again he nodded. "Yes."

"We shall see," she said, stopping her pacing to sit at her stone desk along the cave wall. She sat in the huge, wooden, throne-like chair. She motioned towards the hawk.

"Brother Hector. Have you told him?"

"No, your grace," the old man said. "I don't think this would be the best time."

A smile curved up on her red lips, and her piercing eyes twinkled with mischief. The woman was supernaturally beautiful, Grimes supposed. Perhaps it was how she managed to keep this thing going when, by all rights, it should have ended decades ago. He thought back to all the time spent in the squad car trying to guess her age. Davies placed her at almost sixty, but she looked closer to thirty-five, even though Grimes knew that couldn't possibly be true.

Either way, neither of them could remember a time when her presence didn't lord over Gray's Point, mostly from the shadows. Davies said she looked older before the last ritual, but Grimes didn't buy into that crap. He appreciated the ceremony, and understood that it kept them all strong to abide the Brotherhood. He didn't believe in magic, however, dark or otherwise.

"We don't have secrets in the Brotherhood," old hawk, she said. "Not from each other." She seductively drew out her words, as if what she meant to force out of Hector brought her some sort of perverse sexual pleasure.

The old man looked at his nephew and Grimes could see decades of regret and fear reflected in those aging eyes. He didn't envy Hector. There were better than average odds that it would end in them having to kill the poor kid and bury his body out in the desert. Grimes didn't wish for that. Digging a six-foot hole in sandy desert rock proved difficult work.

"Tell me, *tío*," the kid said. "I can handle it."

For the briefest of moments, Grimes got the distinct impression that maybe the kid already knew. But surely not. Hector could be a crazy old man, but he wouldn't give away his darkest secret. Not when it might cost him so much. That secret provided the key to the Brotherhood. They all knew what Hector had done, and that meant loyalty. They all had something damning on each other. That's how the whole thing worked. Except for the priestess, of course. No one knew much about her at all.

Hector sucked in a deep breath, released it, then turned in his chair to face his nephew. The kid mirrored the action, and didn't protest when Hector placed a hand on the kid's knee.

Grimes had been charged with watching Skylar Brooks' whole crew for days, and he still couldn't quite believe that this kid meant to turn on his friends. But the prophecy was very clear. Clearer than most. And everything so far had happened exactly on schedule. The arrival of Gabriel. The return of Hector. The delivery of Skylar and Miriam. It fulfilled a promise the priestess had made decades ago, before this kid could even walk. It was hard to argue with that kind of accuracy.

"Many years ago," Hector started, "when you were just a baby, your mother ran into some trouble in Mexico. And so I arranged for her to be brought here to America. To me. She didn't know that at the time, though. I just made sure certain people listened to her. Agreed to her requests."

The kid nodded. Didn't look like any of this news surprised him.

"But back in Mexico, she would have been killed," Hector said. "Her life was as good as over... and yours as well. But she found a home here. And she eventually came to love this place. I introduced her to my family."

Hector gestured around the room, motioning to the coyote priestess, the deer, and the goat. Grimes hadn't really been there when Ana joined. He'd never met her, but he supposed the gesture was largely symbolic.

Hector continued, "You mother came to love this family. And she chose..."

He trailed off and looked again to the priestess. Grimes didn't suppose Hector wanted to say the next part, and who could blame him? Living with that sort of thing was hard. Grimes certainly didn't like to talk about his own experiences in this family. The priestess gave a subtle nod, but the sharpness of her gaze conveyed more than subtlety. She really did enjoy this.

"She chose to make the ultimate sacrifice for her family," Hector finished.

The room sat silent for a while. The kid didn't talk or say anything, and that seemed suspicious. Maybe the priestess thought so, too. She could be so hard to read. Surely she meant to make Hector unveil the entirety of the story. The really juicy bit. The part that would prove the mettle of this kid and, most likely, result in his death. The kid had come too far, and though he might not know it, he could only move forward. Not back.

When Grimes thought that they might just leave it at that, the priestess finally spoke up, her words dripping out of her mouth like honey. "That's not the end of the story, old hawk."

The look Hector gave her screamed volumes, but he reacted in his usual, measured way. He turned towards his nephew next to him. "She went into it with full consent. That's important for you to know."

Gabriel's face twisted up. If Grimes didn't know any better, he thought maybe the kid was gonna cry, and he hadn't even heard the really good part yet.

"We have a ritual here," Hector said. "It keeps the brotherhood strong. It keeps our priestess strong. It requires blood, Gabriel. Blood spilled by blood."

The priestess whispered an *amen* as he spoke the last line. The sacred line. Grimes watched Gabriel's face, trying to see whether he'd connected the dots yet.

"In this ritual, a person must be sacrificed to the earth. And their death must..."

Hector stopped and turned to the priestess. "Surely, your grace, this is enough. He understands the meaning."

"Does he?" she asked, addressing Gabriel next. "Do you understand what the old hawk tells you, boy?"

Gabriel swallowed. He closed his eyes and exhaled. "That my mother died. Here. For the brotherhood."

"Yes," the priestess said. "Sacrificed, though. Not died. Sacrificed by your uncle's hand. Blood spilled by blood."

Gabriel's jaw tightened. Either this kid was a damn good actor, or he really didn't know that last bit. Even in the dim light, Grimes could see the flush on Gabriel's cheeks. He pushed Hector's hand off his leg and stood up. Beneath his mask, Grimes smiled. This might be fun.

Standing over his uncle, the kid clenched and unclenched his fists. If he threw a punch, Grimes and Davies would be obligated to step in. But he didn't. He just stood and fumed, clearly considering either an attack or a tirade. Grimes felt his own body tense up in anticipation of the fight. The moment stretched on forever, with nothing but heated, angry silence.

Then, in a move that Grimes would never have expected, the kid looked up at the priestess and said, "I forgive him."

Even she looked surprised by that, and she didn't often look anything but calculating. Grimes didn't believe him. No one could so easily forgive the outright murder of their mom, even if she'd chosen it. And she hadn't. That was just a stupid lie the brotherhood told itself so that it could continue to feel enlightened. Davies had told him the real story.

The priestess stood from behind her desk and glided towards Gabriel, embracing him in a tight hug. At first, the kid didn't seem to know what to do, but eventually he played into it and wrapped his arms around her. She gave good hugs. Grimes could attest to that. It always felt like she was somehow transferring part of her soul when she pressed her body against his.

She backed away from Gabriel and held his biceps in her small hands, staring into his face with that weird, crippling gaze of hers. "I'm impressed, Gabriel."

Grimes couldn't help but notice that Hector only stared at the floor, slumped in his chair as if he'd been defeated.

"Your spirit is strongly connected with the land," she went on. "We welcome you into the brotherhood, young snake."

Snake? How the hell would that work? That kid's noggin was a mite larger than a snake's skull. The priestess answered Grimes' question by moving to a trunk behind her desk, opening it, and removing a snakeskin cloak. Not the worker clothes that he and Davies wore. But one of the nice cloaks that she and the hawk donned. Not fair.

She helped Gabriel into it. Clearly, the cloak was meant for him. It wrapped nearly perfectly around his broad shoulders. For the first time, Grimes wondered where she even got all these things.

This cloak impressed even him, though. Shimmering rattlesnake scales lined the entire silhouette, and as Gabriel pulled the hood above his head, Grimes saw that the front of it sported a number of rattlesnake heads, the fangs of each dipping down over the kid's forehead. It certainly won for intimidation points, and with the hallucinations added to it, it would surely contribute to a lot of nightmares.

Likely, there would soon be stories of multi-headed rattlesnakes in the area. Those would be fun to add to the collection. They hadn't had a cloaked brother since Hector, and somehow it didn't seem fair that this kid would enter the Brotherhood at such a respected position. Grimes wanted to be mad, but he supposed the priestess had her reasons. Or maybe, Grimes supposed, she was paying back a debt to the old hawk.

"Thank you, your grace," Gabriel said. "I will uphold the strength of the brotherhood."

Damn. Hector really had coached him well.

"I know that you will," the priestess said with a smile. "Your family has always been a trusted protector of this family."

Next, she turned towards Grimes and Davies. "Deer. Goat. The time has come. Fetch our guests and prepare for the ritual."

CHAPTER 25

"Walk with me," the priestess said. Her eyes locked onto Gabe's, and almost hypnotized him. When she hooked her elbow under his, warmth shot up his arm. Somehow, she exuded both a comforting matronly presence and a predatory sexual hunger.

He swallowed hard and complied, slowly accompanying her down the darkened hallway carved through the stone of Gray's Point. Torches flanked the path. The goat and the deer had shuffled down ahead of them to prepare for the "ritual." Gabe didn't quite know what that entailed, but his hunch offered only one, grisly possibility, though he had a hard time imagining a world where Miriam would become a willing sacrifice.

Occasional misshapen wooden doors lined the walls, leaving him to wonder where they might all lead. Were Miriam and Skylar behind one of them? Or something worse. More dangerous. Perhaps something that the priestess meant to reveal to him.

His heavy, snake-lined hood tugged at his scalp and hair. He desperately wanted to pull it down to his shoulders, but he worried that the priestess wouldn't approve of it, so he bore the pain in silence. After passing a few of the doors, she stopped them at one that appeared more worn than the others, splintered and split. The dim light provided no opportunity to see through. She gripped the handle, turned it, and slowly pushed open the door.

Her torch revealed a large cavern with a long table in the middle as well as intricate, hand-carved wooden benches on either side. A tapestry unfurled on the wall opposite the door, from the top of the cave almost to the floor. In total, the room conveyed the qualities of a medieval mead hall, where heroes might have met to share some grog after a hard-fought war—or perhaps, conquerors after a vicious pillaging.

The priestess ushered him inside and shut the door behind them. Being alone with her in a closed room felt dangerous. As if she might devour him and leave no trace that he ever existed. But no. That didn't make sense. She'd chosen to usher him into this brotherhood. She wanted him here. To carry on the legacy of his *tío*.

She said nothing, but held the torch towards the tapestry, bathing it in a threatening orange glow. It seemed old. The edges frayed, and the colors faded. The angled figures looked Native American in origin, quickly reminding Gabe of cave paintings he'd seen on a trip to some old caves on the Texas-Mexico border. Three distinct figures stretched from left to right across the fabric.

The left-most figure stood with arms outstretched, offering what looked like a dog to the figure in the middle. The second seemed to have the same dog draped over its head, not unlike the coyote priestess standing next to him.

And the third... the third could only be described as a werewolf. Or a were-coyote, Gabe decided. With a canine snout and a human body. It didn't take a PhD in ancient cave drawings to understand the meaning of it, and as he fully processed the art, his cloak suddenly felt heavier.

Magic wasn't real, he told himself. He didn't need to worry about literally turning into a snake... did he?

"This has been in the brotherhood for generations," she said. Her seductive voice reminded him more of a snake than a coyote. Perhaps she wore the wrong cloak. "It depicts the first of our kind. The first to commune with nature."

Though her ethnicity was ambiguous, Gabe didn't think she seemed Native American. The goat and the deer may have been, for all he knew. But his uncle was Mexican, through and through. He had no doubt about that.

"With this power, we can do many great things, young snake," she crooned. "Tell me. What do you see?"

Gabe didn't want to answer. He feared saying the wrong thing. But she stood with infinite patience, never taking her gaze from him. Eventually, he cleared his throat and said, "I see someone handing the power over to another. The power to turn into a coyote?"

Her lips turned up in amusement. "More or less. But that power comes at a cost."

"The ritual," Gabe said.

She nodded and lowered the torch. "Yes. It keeps the power strong. I've been leading the brotherhood for a long time, young snake. A very long time."

She didn't look that old. Maybe fifty at the most, but a young, attractive fifty. He supposed "long time" could be taken relatively, but he sensed that she hinted at more than that.

Her presence kept him alert, but he couldn't stop his mind from going to the place he was trying to avoid. His uncle had killed his mother to protect this power. A confession that Gabe still couldn't quite grasp. A willing sacrifice, though, Hector had said.

Gabe would have thought the idea impossible a day ago, but now, with this silver-tongued seductress across from him, he could see how someone might be convinced of the cause.

He couldn't resist the urge to ask, "So you can change your shape?"

She reached under his cloak and placed a hand on his bicep, squeezing as she spoke, "I can do those things that are necessary to keep the family strong."

He tried to imagine this woman shimmering and shifting into some other form. How did that even work? Did her clothes change shape, too, or did she have to be naked when she shifted? He stopped trying to wrap his mind around the particulars, and again reminded himself that magic wasn't real.

"Do you want to see our menagerie?" she asked. "Where we keep all of the animals that we draw our powers from?"

Gabe nodded as she took him again by the arm and led him into the hallway. A few stops down, they stood in front of another door.

When she opened it, his senses were overwhelmed by a sharp, acrid smell. The torches in this room were already lit, casting shadows along the walls. Various cages lined the stone, in different shapes and sizes, each containing a live animal or two. Rattlesnakes, scorpions, and jackrabbits filled most of the cages, sleeping or eating, some of their beady eyes following him carefully. He thought back to the rattlesnake Brynn had told him about. The one that appeared when she and Skylar had been attacked. She'd assumed it was another skinwalker, but looking at this collection, he wondered if maybe they'd just used a snake to scare her.

"When you become one with these animals, you gain their essence," she whispered in his ear. "You can feel their power in you."

Her hot breath tickled his earlobe, like a forked tongue slithering out to touch his skin. He fought the urge to brush it away. He'd joined the brotherhood, yes, but he didn't feel this spirit of nature that she went on about. In front of him, he saw only sad, captive animals. With short lives sacrificed to make elaborate cloaks.

"Today you will witness something magnificent, young snake. You will understand the meaning of everything I say."

She took his arm once again, and her strangely comforting hand briefly washed away his doubts. What had he even gotten himself into? It seemed like the right course before. He'd felt certain it would give him an advantage. But now everything seemed to be slipping out of his control, and he worried what that might mean.

Retreating back the way they came, she eventually opened a door up to a huge cavern with torches lining the wall in rows, circling upward, higher than Gabe could imagine anyone climbing. Perhaps they could change shape. Maybe one of them had turned into a bird to get that high.

In the center of the room sat an altar. Simple, gray stone, easily large enough for a human to lay atop. On the ground, a strange symbol was drawn in chalk, encircling the table. The swirling circle consisted of leaves and snakes, winding back in on themselves, seamlessly entwined. There were no chairs. Hector stood across the room, his back hunched, his feathery cloak obscuring his face as he leaned on his cane.

"*Tío. ¿Estás bien?*" Gabe asked.

"He's fine," the priestess answered. "He's just tired. It's been a while since he's exercised the power of the brotherhood."

Hector raised his head and nodded, unveiling his bloodshot eyes.

"Take your place, young snake," she said. "Next to your uncle. The ritual will begin soon."

CHAPTER 26

Miriam filled the time by working through all the possibilities. Each minute that ticked by brought them closer to another visit. Thinking of Gabe's betrayal or Skylar's sudden need for a relationship annoyed her, so she studied out every eventuality in her mind, preparing for everything and still expecting to be surprised. She couldn't predict when their opportunity would arise, but it was coming. She felt it in her bones.

They'd only seen three people. Or skinwalkers. Whatever they were. The deer, the goat, and the coyote. That left her and Skylar outnumbered, but not hopelessly so, assuming Skylar could still carry himself in a fight. She hadn't seen her father do any fighting for years.

Then there was Gabe. He might prove another obstacle, tilting the odds in favor of her captors.

Skylar wanted to talk instead of think. "If they open the doors, we have to strike hard."

Miriam would not consider *if*. Only *when*.

"I'm fine," Miriam insisted, even as her ankle tired from pacing around her cell.

Her muscles tightened, and she could almost believe her knuckles got harder. Without any guns, she expected to do a lot of punching. Kicking would be out of the question.

"When we get out of here," Skylar said. "Maybe you and I can get together some time. You haven't seen the museum yet."

She'd been back to Rose Valley a handful of times with Macy, but Miriam had always made a special effort to steer clear of the *Skylar Brooks Center for Cryptozoological Research*. Visiting it—and him—always seemed like a painful, threatening prospect. Now, though, it didn't seem so scary. That museum surely contained a lot of memories of good times. Good hunts. Memories of a father that Miriam had long forgotten, but now caught glimpses of while trapped in the dark here with him.

"Yeah, maybe," she said. She stopped short of a promise, or letting him know that the invitation finally felt like it might be in the realm of acceptable.

The creak of the door echoed down the corridor. The amber glow of fire started filling the room. Antlered shadows danced off the hallway, before both the deer and the goat rounded the corner and attached a burning torch to the wall. As usual, they said nothing, stopping at the entrance to the cave and staring with those hollow eyes. The deer cocked its head, sending shivers up Miriam's spine.

Sometimes they seemed to shimmer and shift, but now they looked solid. Almost human. The skeletal hand of the deer didn't look like bone as it sometimes did.

After pausing for what seemed like only dramatic effect, they both moved towards Skylar's cage. The deer fetched a keyring from its pocket, unlocked the padlock, and let it drop to the cave floor with a threatening *thud*. Miriam followed the key that she so desperately wanted as the deer shoved it back into his pocket.

The two animal-people stood shoulder to shoulder as they pulled the door back, their feet firmly planted in case of an attack. But Skylar wouldn't attack. He didn't have the resolve for that level of heroics.

But then, much to Miriam's surprise, he did.

Skylar lunged forward, burying his shoulder into the stomach of the goat and driving him back. The goat lost its balance and fell to the floor, Skylar maintaining his own, spinning with a wild punch that missed the deer. Before Skylar could reset, the deer pulled back his non-skeletal hand and struck Skylar in the stomach and he doubled over. A follow-up blow on the cheek sent Skylar down to the cold stone.

The goat scrambled back to its feet, holding onto its stomach, while the deer leered over Skylar, daring him to get up.

This fight didn't make sense. Not now. The odds were against them. They needed to wait until they were both free and could mount a better attack.

"Dad," Miriam said. "Don't."

She hoped he took her meaning, but he clearly didn't, jumping to his feet much faster than she would have thought him capable and pushing hard on the deer's shoulders. Miriam jumped back from her cage door to avoid her fingers being smashed by the skinwalker slamming against the bars. Skylar rushed forward, barring his forearm across the creature's throat.

For the briefest moment, Skylar's eyes locked onto hers, then fell. Miriam followed the gaze.

The key. She could get the key.

In a flurry, she reached her small hand through the bars and felt around the hip of the deer until she found the opening of his pocket. His struggling and kicking made it hard for her to keep steady, but before long she felt the cool metal. She pinched her fingers around the ring just as the deer surged back against Skylar and stumbled out of her reach.

Unsure of her success, Miriam looked down and saw the shimmer of her prize. She palmed the key quickly and retreated to the back of her cell just as the goat pummeled Skylar in the back. The deer almost immediately sent him reeling the other direction with a clean uppercut that made even Miriam's teeth hurt. The goat caught him, and the deer went to work punching Skylar in the stomach over and over again, clearly intent on beating him into submission.

In between his groans, Skylar lifted his head and gave her a nod, subtle enough that the skinwalkers didn't notice. Miriam tried to fight back the tears. She never imagined him capable of such a sacrifice. She wanted to use the key now. She could even the odds by letting herself out, but she fought that urge, knowing that she'd fare better with an element of surprise.

She inched towards the door. Before she got there, the deer stopped his assault. Each of the creatures took one of Skylar's arms and dragged him towards the corridor. Skylar's head lolled. His toes scraped across the floor, his full weight relying on the deer and the goat.

"Where are you taking him!?" Miriam screamed after them.

They didn't answer. The deer grabbed the torch as they passed it. Within seconds, the light extinguished, the door closed, and Miriam was alone.

Alone, but with more hope now than she'd had for days.

She felt the key in her hand, and smiled into the dark.

***

Getting the lock open hadn't been terribly challenging without being able to see, but finding her way across the stone and up the corridor proved more of a feat than she expected. Every divot threatened to turn her ankle and upset her balance. Though the pain had now become bearable, she didn't think twisting it again would do her any favors.

In her mind, she meant to hurry, but the trek to the door felt like it took an eternity. She wasn't prepared to bump into it when she did, and that alone almost sent her backward to the floor. A sane person might have realized that fighting off mythical monsters would be impossible with only one good leg, but Miriam felt surer of her success now than she ever had.

She opened the door slowly, as quietly as she could, and blinked into the light of the torches lining the walls of another corridor. She considered her course. Left or right? She studied the ground, but the lack of any debris or dirt made any sort of tracking hopelessly impossible. Her success came down to a fifty-fifty guess. She chose right, despite the ground sloping upward in that direction, proving more of a challenge. At least this way, if it led in the wrong direction, she'd be able to get back easier.

As she shuffled upward, she heard rustling behind her. Miriam found the first door she could see, and quickly slipped inside a dark room. The room smelled horrible, like a barnyard or a poorly kept dog park. As she took a few steps inside, her good foot slipped on something wet and sent her down to her knees. From the ground, the smell overwhelmed her senses, triggering a gag reflex that even a seasoned monster hunter couldn't suppress. There could be no doubt as to what she'd stepped in.

Gross.

She pushed back to her feet and listened for the rustling she'd heard before. Nothing. Yes this was a kennel, but it seemed empty. She heard no breathing in the dark. No panting. No movement. Is this where the dog she'd killed in the cave came from? Either that was the only one, or the others had been sent out on an equally vicious mission.

Surely, the dogs needed tending to, though. And that meant that maybe she could find an extinguished torch somewhere. She needed light for the dark corners of this labyrinth.

Gingerly, she worked her way to the cave wall, until she felt cool stone beneath her palm. She turned on her watch's glow for any kind of illumination. She placed her wrist close to the stone and could still just barely make out the uneven surface. With every step she lost a little hope, but then the stone gave way to a bolt and bracket. Held within: an unlit torch. She took it.

As she turned back towards the corridor, a bang echoed towards her, followed by expletives. They knew she'd escaped. She crouched next to the door and listened, hoping for any hint as to which direction her assailants had crept.

"T-t-this ain't g-g-good," someone said in a hushed whisper.

Another, deeper voice answered, "Hell nah it ain't."

"T-t-hose kids musta g-g-got in. We n-n-need to tell her."

The gruffer man growled in disgust. He didn't seem to like the suggestion. But Miriam's bigger takeaway was the mention of kids. Miriam didn't have much hope that Brynn would mount a rescue. She almost refused to hope for what she thought it might mean. After the phone call at the gas station, Miriam and Tanner would have expected her home. And if she never made it home, then maybe...

Her chest lightened again. The odds tipped further in her favor if her suspicions were right. She just had to stay out of sight.

She could only surmise that the men outside the door were the deer and the goat. She'd never heard them talk, and they appeared more often as otherworldly apparitions than not, but Miriam had started to unravel the truth of it all. Though she couldn't rule out their ability to talk or shapeshift into humans, every experience pointed towards only one explanation. These were just people. Plain and simple. Though, she still couldn't explain everything she'd seen.

The two men sounded as if they'd shuffled away from her, so she stood back up and slowly opened the door. With it cracked, and the torchlight from the hallway filtering in, she waited and listened some more.

Only silence.

She crept out into the hallway with her unlit torch and once again found herself faced with a decision. Based on intuition and the keenness of her hearing, she decided that the men must have gone down further into the cave, opposite of where she'd been heading, so she doubled down and continued up the path away from where they'd gone. She lit her torch, using one of the burning ones along the wall.

Miriam had no idea where Skylar might be. Probably not this way. But if she could find the "kids" that they talked about, then she'd have help. And with a busted ankle, she could use some.

She found no more doors, and the path started to corkscrew upward. To the surface? Her heart jumped at the thought of escape, but she knew she couldn't take that path. She couldn't abandon Skylar. And the possibility now existed that Tanner and Macy were somewhere nearby as well. No, this was the end of the line. She had to turn around and head down into danger.

As she turned, something scraped above. Stone on stone. Small bits of gravel and sand rained down, particles floating in the air and glowing in the light coming from the top of the corkscrew. Miriam prepared to rush back to the foul-smelling kennel, but then she heard a familiar voice.

Macy's sweet, eternal optimism filtered through the darkness. Even as a whisper, it immediately warmed Miriam's soul. Failure now seemed impossible.

Macy's voice struck a balance between chiding and teasing. "I can't believe you used up all our ammo."

"Are you questioning my methods?" Tanner voice asked back.

Macy said, "Well, you *did* get yourself squidnapped last time."

Someone shushed Macy. Not Tanner. Even with such minimal sound, Miriam could tell that it was another girl. Brynn, then?

Miriam didn't have to wait long before she saw three sets of ankles. She swallowed hard, wanting so much to believe that they'd come for her, but she couldn't push down the possibility that these three might just be another set of skinwalkers, expertly shifted into forms Miriam couldn't ignore. Instinct told her to hide again, but she'd never seen a skinwalker take someone else's form *and* talk like them.

Miriam chose hope over suspicion and stood her ground.

Tanner led the pack, jumping when he got to the bottom, his fists going up as he dropped into a defensive stance. From behind him, Macy asked, "Mir?"

Miriam couldn't stop the tears trailing down her cheeks, or the hoarseness in her voice when she replied, "Yes. It's me."

"You look like ass, girl," Macy said, jumping past Tanner to wrap her arms around Miriam's neck. "You don't smell so good, either."

As Macy backed away and Brynn reached the landing, Miriam studied the three of them. Tanner's clothes were ripped in countless places. All three sported scratches on their arms. Brynn had a particularly nasty one on her face. Whatever they'd been through, it hadn't been easy.

Miriam sniffled. "You don't look so good yourself."

"Fair," Macy replied with a giggle. "Let's get you out of here."

Macy took Miriam's hand and tugged back towards the corkscrew up, but Miriam stood her ground. She couldn't leave now.

"No," she said, with less hesitation than she could have ever imagined. "We have to save dad."

CHAPTER 27

Davies was dragging his feet, and Grimes didn't really blame him. He didn't want to deal with the priestess either. Not now. Not after they'd lost the girl somehow. He'd said from the beginning that they should have told her about the addition of the other two kids, but Davies insisted and now look where they were. They'd be lucky if they got off with just some yellin'. She'd never tortured them before, but he knew the brotherhood had a history.

"All right," Davies said. "Turn it on."

Grimes reached down to the knob on the tank at his feet and twisted it all the way, until it wouldn't go any further. He always thought knobs like this resembled flowers, which seemed weird in this case since this knob would hopefully tilt the fight in their favor and take those kids down a notch. Assuming they came. If he'd been in the same situation, he would have packed up and left. Sure, they'd lose the cryptozoologist by leaving Gray's Point, but it seemed a small price to pay for the lives of four.

"S-s-should we set up the other one?" Grimes asked.

"Yeah." Davies stood up and stretched his back, peering down the corridor in the direction of the ritual room where the rest of the brotherhood waited for them to deliver Miriam Brooks.

"She's gonna w-w-wonder where we w-w-went."

Davies didn't answer, so Grimes gingerly stepped over the tripwire and followed down the hallway until they came to the next trap juncture. In all his time in the brotherhood, these things had never been set, but she still made him and Davies attend to them every week to make sure they remained in working order. All great in theory, but that didn't mean they'd work properly now when everything depended on it.

On his side, Grimes shimmied the rock out of the way and thumped the glass on the other side. When the contents didn't move, he thumped again, this time jarring a handful of them awake enough for them to writhe and shift. Good. They didn't have time to replenish the stock.

"Move," Davies said in a hushed whisper.

Grimes stepped out of the way and Davies duck-walked the rest of the way to the wall with the almost-invisible wire. He attached it to the grommet set into the stone, stood up, and dusted off his good hand against his jeans. They didn't have time for a proper test. That would require clearing the glass tank so they could test the mechanism without injury. It would probably work. He just couldn't be sure that it would slow anyone down enough.

Back when they still had the girl, these traps would have provided plenty of time for them to finish the ritual, but they'd lost one of the more important components, and he didn't even know what they were gonna do now. Nor did he understand the ramifications of not going through with it. Obviously, it was important to the priestess, but no matter what she said he didn't believe she'd actually die without it.

That was it. No more traps they could set. No more preparations they could make. Grimes wondered what delay tactic Davies would use next.

"I'm hungry," he said suddenly. "We should get something to eat."

Grimes almost laughed. At least they could justify being cautious, but eating? No way. If she caught'em eating right now, she'd have their heads for sure.

"I-I-I don't think—"

He cut off his thought as he heard someone coming towards them. The priestess? God, he hoped not.

Grimes let out his breath when the young snake came around the corner. The kid pushed his hood off his head when he reached them, letting it fall back to his shoulders. She didn't like it when they took their hoods off, but Grimes supposed Gabe didn't know that yet.

"What do you want, rookie?" Davies said quietly.

Rookie or not, Gabe wore a cloak and they wore a mask. Talking to the snake like that wouldn't be tolerated. The kid didn't flinch though, so he must've been too stupid to realize his place yet.

"Where's Miriam?" Gabe asked.

"None of your business," Davies curtly responded.

Grimes didn't wanna hide no more. It'd only make things worse. "S-s-she escaped."

Gabe's stoic expression broke for a second, but Grimes couldn't decide what it meant. Davies punched Grimes in the arm—hard. He fought the urge to lunge back and instead just rubbed his bicep, waiting to see what the snake had to say.

"Escaped?" Gabe said, almost as if he didn't believe it. "She's not gonna like that."

No shit, sherlock. Of course she wouldn't like that. That's why they'd lollygagged in the corridor, making any excuse to avoid telling her.

"We can go get her," Davies said. "She can't have gone far. Not with that ankle."

True. Unless she met up with the three perfectly healthy and athletic kids they'd left up top. Then they'd all get their asses kicked. Grimes considered telling Gabe that part, but held back. Miriam escaping would be bad enough.

"No," Gabe said quickly. "Go tell her what happened first. Let her decide."

Maybe the kid did understand his place, after all. What did it matter to him whether they went after Miriam now or later? And what made him think that he could tell them what to do?

Davies grumbled. "Yes, sir. We'll do that. Right away. The goat would be happy to explain it."

What the hell? Davies was just gonna throw him under the bus like that? Fine. If Davies wanted him to tell the story, then he would tell the whole thing; see who was laughing at the end of that tale.

"Come on," Gabe said, turning back towards the ritual room.

The deer and the goat followed.

***

Grimes stood with his head down, talking only as loudly as he had to. He'd already been through the bit about the other kids, and the hounds that may or may not have managed to stop them. She probably already expected the last part, given they didn't have Miriam in tow.

"I-I-I told the d-d-deer that we should tell you right away, but he said w-w-we could handle it ourselves."

Her usually placid eyes seethed with anger. Her lips curled up in what Grimes could only describe as a snarl. But that horrifying gaze pointed straight at Davies. Just like Grimes wanted. She might kill the poor deer. Maybe she'd summon some of those magic powers everyone said she had and vaporize him on the spot.

She didn't move her eyes from Davies when she asked, "And where's the girl? You were supposed to bring the girl."

"Y-y-yes, ma'am. Somehow, s-s-she got out. W-w-we don't know w-w-where she is."

From the middle of the room, a bloodied Skylar Brooks let out a gurgled laugh. When he talked, it seemed to take all the strength he could muster. "You're so screwed."

Davies started towards the altar, no doubt to punish the outburst, but the priestess stopped him with an outstretched hand. Though Grimes expected her to get even angrier, the heat seemed to dissipate from her eyes. When she smiled, it raised his hackles.

"Well, the ritual has to happen today," she said. "It can wait no longer."

"Yes, ma'am," Davies said. "We'll go find the girl right now. We can kill those other kids if we have to. We won't fail you."

"Oh, but you already have," she said calmly, as if her plans weren't crumbling before her very eyes.

"I know, your grace. But, I can fix it. Me and the goat can fix it. We'll have her back before sundown."

"It's too late," she said. "Too dangerous. We'll have to proceed without her."

Proceed without her? How the hell would that work? The ritual clearly called for a sacrifice made at the hand of a blood relative. Either Skylar or Miriam had to die, and one of them had to kill the other. That's all they'd been working for. All the meticulous preparation. The research. The manipulation. They couldn't just move on with this intricate plan unless they got all the pieces.

The priestess floated across the room until she stood in front of Hector, who looked like he'd aged ten years just since he'd been back. "It's our only real choice. Wouldn't you agree, old hawk?"

The old man's chest heaved with a big breath before he raised his eyes to meet hers. His response came slowly and measured. "It's not what I would prefer."

"No. I don't suppose it is," she cooed. "But I'll let you choose. You can kill him, or..." She turned towards the young snake. "He can kill you."

Gabe's face tightened, and his jaw set. For all the poise this kid seemed to bring to the table, he clearly wasn't expecting this. Now they'd see what this young snake was really made of. Could he do it?

"I've lived a long time," Hector answered. He turned towards Gabe and reached out to take one of his hands. "Don't feel bad for this, Gabriel. *Es la única manera.*"

Gabe started shaking his head as tears squeezed out the corners of his eyes and down his cheeks. No one could really fault him for having a hard time. Grimes always wondered whether he, himself, would have been able to do this, but his old man had died of a heart attack before the ritual came around. He remembered staying up at night, wondering if that ultimate sacrifice would be asked of his family the way it had Hector's. Having to sacrifice one family member sounded bad enough, but now Hector's family would have to endure two.

"*No*," Gabe said. "*No lo haré. No.*"

Grimes became so invested in the exchange that he jumped when Davies tapped him on the shoulder. Davies gestured to the altar and Grimes took the meaning, moving over to it and helping to move Skylar to the ground. They propped him up against the wall so he could watch the whole thing. It would probably be the last thing the cryptozoologist saw. The priestess surely couldn't let him live, even if his death would be for nothing.

"So," the priestess asked. "What will it be, old hawk?"

"I will make the sacrifice," he said. "Gabriel will perform the ritual."

"The hell I will." Gabe dropped his uncle's hand and turned to the priestess. "I won't do this. You can't make me."

The priestess reached up and brushed her spindly fingers against Gabe's face. "Oh, young snake. It must be done. What difference is it whether it's your ailing uncle, or your employer over there?"

"I won't do it," Gabe said, standing his ground.

"Your loyalty to the brotherhood means everything," she said. "If you won't do this, then I can't trust you, and if I can't trust you, then..."

She trailed off. The possibility of what she might have said seemed more terrifying than any words that could have slithered out of her mouth. But Grimes knew what she meant, and surely the boy did, too.

"No," Gabe said again. "I won't do it."

The priestess turned away. "Very well. Deer. Goat. Would you please?"

Grimes grinned behind his mask and moved in unison with Davies over to the kid. It's what Gabe deserved, really. Coming into the brotherhood at such a high rank wasn't fair. This outcome seemed much better. After this, Hector would go back to his old folks' home and things in the desert would go back to normal. Well, once they hunted down Skylar Brooks' contingent of explorers, anyway.

Grimes took Gabe's right arm, Davies the left. Gabe squirmed and bucked, and Grimes dug his grip in. With only one hand, though, Davies' grip slipped and Gabe managed to wrench his left hand free, swinging it round to connect with the chin of Grimes' mask. The hard bone blunted some of the force, but it didn't stop from snapping his neck back. Before he could recover, he felt Gabe twist, then a knee right in the groin. Grimes tried to hold on, but the need to cup his crotch won out.

Free now, the kid turned back towards the deer. Davies had way more time to react and managed to dodge the punch and counter with one of his own. Gabe's head spun around and blood spewed out onto the stone floor. Davies didn't let up after that, alternating between the hard hits of his fist and the softer blows of his prosthetic. Gabe brought up his hands to defend himself, managing to redirect some of it, but enough got through that Gabe eventually fell backwards onto the ground.

Grimes hopped up and down, trying to clear the pain from his system. When he could maintain his balance well enough, he kicked Gabe in the side of the head. Hard. Sending the kid all the way down. Gabe didn't show signs of getting back up. Had they knocked him unconscious? Seemed unlikely.

Davies walked towards Gabe's face and reached down to pick him up by his shoulder, but Gabe suddenly came to life, grabbing Davies' ankle and jerking it out from under him. Davies went down, his head striking the stone wall as he did, fracturing the deer skull so that it revealed his human eye underneath. Somehow, that looked creepier. Grimes reacted by kicking Gabe in the side over and over. The kid inched himself up to all fours, scrambling towards the wall and spinning to sit. Grimes let him go.

Gabe spit blood on the floor, as Davies got himself upright. This kid wasn't a slouch at fighting, but he wasn't good enough to take on the two of'em.

"Gabriel. Don't do this," Hector said. "Don't give up your life. You have too much to live for."

Grimes tightened up when Gabe started pushing to his feet, ready for round two. Davies stood on the other side. The young snake didn't stand a chance.

It didn't stop him, though. He swung hard at Grimes, then followed it up with another swing towards Davies. Gabe wobbled on his feet, failing to connect either blow. When he tried again, Grimes grabbed his wrist and jerked him forward. Gabe almost lost his balance, but still tried to wrench his arms free. Grimes didn't let go.

Davies joined in and they worked on dragging the kid towards the altar. The resistance became less and less pronounced with every foot forward, and by the time they got him there, Gabe hung loosely between them. Awkwardly, they managed to get him up on the altar, even as he took a few more half-hearted swings and kicked his feet blindly in the hopes of connecting with something.

Skylar had been too beaten up to resist this much, and they'd left him on the altar unrestrained. Grimes didn't trust Gabe, though, so once he got the kid's back against the stone, he used the old, rusty manacles attached to the side of the altar. Davies did the same and before long, the threat of Gabe's arms were finally contained.

Grimes glanced towards Hector, wondered if the old man had killed his own niece in cold blood while she protested and writhed on this very altar, begging him to spare her life. He shuddered to think of it. Somehow it seemed worse than the other things they'd done. To kill someone so vulnerable.

With Gabe subdued, the deer and the goat backed away. From out of nowhere, the priestess summoned a knife into her hand. The blade reflected the torchlight, almost mesmerizing him. The hilt, pommel, and guard were all made of intricately carved wood. Grimes had never seen this dagger before, but he recognized his father's work when he saw it. But where had this knife come from?

It must have been up her sleeve. Surely she didn't just manifest it.

Expertly, she flipped the dagger into the air and caught the blade with her hand. If it cut her, she showed no signs of the pain. Handle out, she offered it to Hector.

"Do what must be done, old hawk."

Hector regarded her, and Grimes thought for a second that maybe the old man would refuse too, but then he took the handle, and looked up to meet the eyes of the priestess.

Resolutely, he said, "Your will be done, your grace."

CHAPTER 28

Tanner and Macy had already taken over, but once Miriam joined up with them, Brynn felt like she'd disappeared entirely. They marched through the darkly lit corridor on a quest to save Skylar. Brynn owed him a lot, and certainly didn't want anything bad to happen to him, but after surviving the dogs above, she felt more strongly than ever that they had tread way too far out of their depth. She feared they'd all end up dead before the end of the day.

As they walked, her mind turned towards the journal in her bag, prompting her to say, "Gabe might be down here, too. We should look for him."

Miriam stopped. Inches shorter, she had to crane her neck to look up at Brynn. "If he's here, then he's just another bad guy in our way. He's been helping them."

What? Brynn couldn't accept that. It didn't make any sense. Gabe didn't have a hateful bone in his body. His overwhelming zest for life and willingness to open his heart to virtually anyone were his most defining qualities. Plus, she couldn't reconcile having slept with someone who might join these things.

Tanner and Macy seemed to quickly take Miriam at her word, but why wouldn't they? They'd never met Gabe.

As the group continued onward, Tanner said, "So I think they're poisoning the water somehow."

He recounted the story of their first encounter on the plateau. Of the skeletal deer and the creepy, demon hounds. And how Macy had only seen a couple of dogs and a man in a mask. Brynn wanted to trust the theory, but she had a hard time believing that a hallucinogen could be so powerful. And if he was right, then...

"That squares with what I've decided," Miriam said. "I don't think we're dealing with monsters. I think this is just some sort of... cult, I guess."

A cult? Like Charles Manson? Or Heaven's Gate? Did those even exist anymore? Monsters or cultists, it only further solidified Brynn's belief that all of this was a horrible mistake.

They crept further into the darkness, stopping occasionally because Miriam insisted she heard something. Brynn wondered if Miriam had gone somewhat crazy in her captivity. Brynn heard nothing, and started to wonder whether anyone remained in these caverns. Perhaps they'd taken Skylar somewhere else.

They were moving too slowly. Miriam's bum ankle dragged them all down, and she refused to let Tanner carry her or even prop her up. When she lost her balance and fell, Brynn didn't even feign surprise.

Macy offered Miriam a hand first, and said, "You ok, Mir?"

"Yeah. I tripped over something," Miriam said.

Sure, she did. Her own two feet.

Tanner started coughing, just as Brynn registered a faint hiss. A foul-tasting stench unfurled through the air, and she breathed it in before she realized what was happening. Miriam didn't get up; instead, she buried her face into her shirt. Of course there would be traps. What kind of cultist lair didn't have traps?

Brynn worried that maybe she'd inhaled a poison, but as the air cleared and the coughing stopped, she didn't feel any different. She felt fine, strangely.

Tanner drew Macy in close to his chest and looked at Brynn, "Are you ok?"

"I... think so," Brynn replied. "What was that?"

Still on the floor, Miriam said, "If they've really been putting hallucinogens in the water, then I'm assuming it was an airborne version of that."

"But I don't see anything weird," Brynn said. "You all look normal."

"We don't really know how it works," Tanner said. "Maybe it takes a minute to kick in."

Miriam added, "Or maybe it only triggers when you see unexpected things. Weird things."

"Like guys in funky animal masks?" Macy asked.

Tanner pushed forward, "We'll deal with it when we have to. Let's go."

With Tanner in the lead, they group moved a little bit faster, Miriam now having given in to her stubbornness and leaning on Macy for support. They checked behind doors as they went. Most of them were empty, but a few had chairs or tables. One seemed to be a dining hall, complete with a creepy, worn tapestry. They found bathroom facilities, which amounted to a hole in the floor that Brynn could only assume led down to a deeper, now desiccated cavern.

No signs of Skylar. Or anyone else, for that matter.

The cave grew colder as they moved forward. Here, only every other torch burned, leaving them in more darkness than before. Brynn wanted to turn back. She even considered doing so, leaving her foolhardy compatriots to contend with whatever lay ahead. But something kept her glued to the others. Maybe fear. Maybe obligation or curiosity. Certainly, not desire.

"Crap!" Tanner exclaimed suddenly. He hopped on one foot, almost losing his balance, but righting himself just as a loud *pop* reverberated from both sides of the corridor.

And then, chaos.

The air filled with blackness, and buzzing, the ground squirming beneath them. Brynn lost sight of the others as something swooped at her face. A scorpion? With wings? She managed to swat it out of the way, but more came. She covered her face with her hands and screamed. Something flicked at her ankle. She kicked, but didn't connect with anything. When she planted her foot back on the stone, she felt a satisfying crunch under her heel.

None of this is real, she told herself. She backed up, moving the way they'd come. Vaguely, she made out the noises of the others fighting off the assault, strangely comforted by Macy's screams. Now, Brynn felt less embarrassed by reacting to the apparitions.

She lost track of her trajectory and backed into something squishy. Not the wall. She spun to see the stone undulating, covered in millions of creepy, crawly bugs of all sorts. Huge ones. Larger than any she'd ever known to exist. She could hear the skittering.

Something buzzed her ear and she swatted at it, twirling and spinning, hoping desperately for a way out of the haze of confusion. Another step, and she lost her balance, slipping on a cylindrical object that writhed beneath her feet. She landed hard on her chest as something wrapped around her ankle.

She felt a million pin pricks in her skin, all landing at once. Her arms. Her legs. Her face. Her skin stung and her heart raced, and she felt sure that whatever had grabbed her ankle would pull her down into the depths of hell.

She couldn't shake the feeling that, somehow, she deserved this. She'd ignored all good sense and come back to this god-forsaken place over and over, letting herself be swayed by zealots. Life proved hard enough when dealing with the known. Adding the unknown to it was a foolish idea that she now deeply regretted. In the fear and uncertainty, Brynn forgot that all of this could be attributed to some sort of gaseous drug she'd inhaled.

It all became completely real.

In front of her, a giant scorpion unfurled its stinger, ready to inject deadly venom straight into her face. Her stomach turned as she pushed up with her hands, crunching what felt like a bed of bugs. Pinches and burns and stings shot into her palms. More than she could count. More than she could separate as distinct attacks.

She managed to get back to her feet, but something still held to her ankle, tightening its grip with every passing second. A snake. It had to be a snake.

She looked down to confirm her suspicions. She kicked her feet and watched the abomination lose some ground, sliding back down to her ankle. She kicked the wall, crunching even more bugs under her toe and jostling the snake further down until she slung it off. It landed with a *thud* into a bed of cockroaches and quickly coiled up, hissing at her.

Brynn couldn't see the others. Only bees and wasps. Flying scorpions and snakes. Some of it made sense. Some of it didn't. Every inch of her skin burned like fire. Surely, she'd die from all these bites. Or stings. She couldn't even be sure which it was. Even if she made it to a hospital, she wouldn't be able to tell them what venom or poison to account for.

"Tanner?" she yelled. "Macy? Miriam?"

She received no answer. Had they all died already? Or maybe she'd just retreated around the corner. Too far away to see the torture they endured. She swatted something away from her face, but it came back for another pass. She couldn't see forward, so she turned back towards the way they came. That way seemed brighter. Clearer. Less creepy crawlies.

For a moment, shame pressed her to turn back for the others, but she ignored it—openly rebelled against it, really. She would suffer no more of this. The time had come for her to save herself. She'd send someone back for the bodies.

She didn't notice the tears until they tickled her cheeks, mingling with the feeling of bugs crawling all over her skin. She swatted them away as she would a wasp, rushing back up the corridor towards the exit. When her steps became too labored, and her pace too slow, she screamed and grunted through the pain. She would not die here. Not for these people. Not for this silly cause.

Onward, she passed doors that she recognized, but a glance into the dining hall revealed that the tapestry had come to life, the ancient figures dancing and morphing. Turning into hideous creatures that threatened to jump from the fabric into the real world.

This isn't real!

Her mind couldn't convince her body. The adrenaline pumped through her, pushing her forward, hopefully keeping the toxins at bay. Just a little further. Just a few more steps.

She finally found the spiraling ramp that led up to the plateau of Gray's Point. Her escape. Freedom. By the time she reached the top, she had fallen into a crawl. One of her eyes had swollen shut.

Then, with her one good eye, she finally saw it. Sunlight. She pulled herself out on the sand-covered stone and fell over to her back, staring up at the sweltering sun. The carcasses of all the demon-dogs they'd slain surrounded her, the Jeep waiting for her at the bottom. She felt for the keys in her pocket, relieved that she'd managed to retain control of them. She'd drive for help. Make sure she'd live. Then—and only then—would she ensure someone came back to make sense of what had happened.

First, though, she just needed a little break. She needed to catch her breath. The sun beat down on her face, and the heat ignited every bite, scratch, and sting covering her bare skin.

She needed to move.

She knew that.

She tried to roll over to get back to her feet, but her body felt so incredibly heavy that she gave up and fell back to the ground. She tried to yell, but only managed a groan. Her mind started to wander and she fought with it to focus. To save her. To give her just enough resolve to make it to the Jeep.

For a minute, she thought she'd done it. She felt the sand underneath her feet as she shuffled along. She saw the bright yellow paint job, welcoming her into the air conditioning.

But then her mind snapped back to reality and she realized she still hadn't moved. She was still alone, sprawled out atop a mountain that hardly ever received visitors. The only people who knew where she was had likely succumbed to their own horrors, and would die beneath the surface, deep underground.

But the fear started to dissipate, leaving only room for resignation.

Reluctantly, Brynn stopped fighting and gave in to a painful, fitful sleep.

CHAPTER 29

Bugs. They were just bugs. And snakes? Yes. Snakes on the ground. Tanner and Macy held tightly to each other just a few feet away, but the fear in Tanner's eyes told Miriam all she needed to know. The gas from before had certainly been a hallucinogen. But her fall and quick thinking had kept her from inhaling the bulk of it, and she could still see the truth in everything around them.

Behind her, Brynn retreated in a fit of frantic screams, but Miriam couldn't help everyone. Perhaps it was selfish, but she moved towards the people she knew and loved. The people she couldn't live without. She waded through a sea of insects, shaking each foot with every step to make sure none of them got past the tops of her boots. The bugs didn't bother her, much, but the snakes worried her, some of them coiled so tightly that they all but disappeared under the sea of chittering insects.

All the bugs that she could see seemed manageable. Even the scorpions were only the small, golden kind that barely threatened more pain than a bee sting. The snakes, on the other hand, could be deadly.

Tanner swatted at wasps and bees, while Macy tried to ignore the whole scene by burying into his chest. A rattlesnake slithered up the toe of Tanner's shoe, barely visible in the dim light, but Miriam saw it and got there in time, kicking it away before it could strike. Miriam grabbed Tanner's hand to pull him forward, out of the bulk of the trap, but he resisted and pulled away.

"No!" he yelled at her. "Stay away!"

Miriam wondered what he saw instead of her. Quickly, he shuffled Macy off him and turned his back to her. "I've got you, babe. Just stay right behind me."

He put his fists up, ready for a fight, but Miriam didn't have the time or inclination to get into a scuffle with him. He didn't seem to notice all the flying bugs that landed all over him, staying on his skin for a brief second before moving on. How many of those had stung him?

Miriam had her hands full keeping them off herself. "Tanner. It's me."

"No! You're dead!" he exclaimed. "I saw the beast kill you."

A lump formed in her throat: Tanner must have thought she'd become the zombie version of Cornelius.

"Miriam's brother?" Macy asked from behind.

Tanner took a step forward, throwing a slow right hook that Miriam easily evaded. Tanner had strength and height on her, but not wits. Not now, anyway. When he followed with an arcing blow to her side, she swatted at his wrist and rushed forward, ramming her shoulder into his chest.

He stumbled backwards, almost tripping over Macy before regaining his balance and trying to grab Miriam by the neck. She ducked under that, reaching up and grabbing his wrists as she did so. It all happened in slow motion, as if she could predict his every move, but he was moving more slowly than normal. Confused and scared.

"Tanner!" she yelled in his face. "Listen to me! This is Miriam. What you're seeing isn't real!"

Macy's head poked out from behind Tanner's bicep. "That's not Cornelius."

"You never met him," Tanner said, absently shaking his head to try to dislodge the bugs buzzing around his face.

"But it's a girl," Macy said. "A little girl."

Miriam should have known better than to think she could have held onto Tanner if he didn't want her to. He pulled so hard that she lost her balance, letting go of his wrists and stumbling down to the ground. She caught herself on her balled-up knuckles, ignoring the sickly ooze against her skin. She quickly got back to her feet and backed up.

Tanner could do some serious damage if she wasn't careful.

"Are you lost?" Macy asked. "Where's your mother?"

She wouldn't be able to force them forward, but Miriam quickly devised another plan. She turned and ran away from them.

"Wait!" Macy called after her.

Miriam rounded the corner, hoping that her gambit worked. She couldn't see them anymore, but she heard the footsteps of their approach. She felt a little bad for using Macy's good nature against her, but if Macy wanted to think that she needed to move forward to save a little girl, so be it.

They rounded the corner and beat off the last of the bugs. Some might follow, but they seemed mostly contained to the area where the trap had released them. None of them had been bitten by snakes, and that seemed to be a win.

"It's dangerous in here," Macy said, now pushing ahead of Tanner. "Give me your hand. We'll find your mother."

"Wait!" Tanner said. "Miriam?"

Finally. She doubted it had worked its way out of his system, but perhaps removing the threat of death by poison and venom had shaken some sense into him. She couldn't be sure, but it seemed that the hallucinogen caused more trouble when fear was added to the equation. Surely, that's why the deer and the goat wore those masks.

Eager to capitalize on the moment of clarity, Miriam responded, "Yes. It's me. We have to go get Brynn."

Tanner nodded, but Miriam worried that taking him back up there would only lead to more hallucinations. "Stay here. I'll get her."

He seemed hesitant, but when Macy grabbed him by the hand, he listened. Miriam rushed back towards the sea of insects and peered through the wasps and bees flitting around. She couldn't see Brynn at all, and wondered how far away she'd ran. Miriam didn't want to leave Tanner and Macy behind, but they could take care of themselves, right? She hesitated before crossing, unsure of which direction to go. She listened for any sign of Brynn nearby.

A scream rang out down the corridor. Not from in front of her, but from behind. A man. Her dad, maybe? She couldn't tell, but it made the most sense.

Brynn would have to wait.

***

Miriam rushed forward, blood thumping in her ears. Tanner and Macy trailed behind her, but she worried that they weren't in any shape to help. In fact, she worried that they'd make things more difficult. With no weapons, she didn't like what might lay ahead.

She braced herself for what she might see. The scream had been frantic, but she held out hope that it hadn't been the cries of a dying man. She quickly pushed open every door, without caring whether it disturbed someone inside. She stopped when the corridor branched off down two paths, each slanting back upward towards the surface. They broke from one another quickly, leaving enough room in the middle of the Y for a door, and behind that, a room. Of considerable size, she'd guess.

The wooden door stood apart from all the others she'd seen in this cavern from hell. There were no holes or splintered wood. It looked sturdy and strong, with intricately carved figures adorning its surface. Chief among them stood a coyote-human hybrid. Miriam quickly understood the depiction—a skinwalker.

She'd all but dismissed the notion that such creatures existed, but as the lump formed in her throat, she couldn't fully tamp down the feeling that one might lay beyond that door. But so might her father. She'd spent years, not necessarily wanting him dead, but certainly not caring whether he lived or died. But now.

Now she needed to save him.

No matter the odds.

She afforded a glance back to Tanner and Macy. Seeing the welts on their arms and faces reminded her that she had a few of her own. But the pain seemed distant. Manageable. Even her ankle seemed ready to ignore its limitations. For a little while, at least.

Hopefully, for long enough.

Though he still looked scared and confused, Tanner gave her a firm nod. Macy, who'd been by Miriam's side when she fought the kraken, looked ready for a fight. If not for Macy's eternal optimism, Miriam would have almost forgotten that the Macy she met in Rose Valley would have screamed, ran, and begged them to stop this advance.

Miriam had a good team. Good family. They could do this.

She took the last few steps forward, put her palm against the chest of the coyote-creature and pushed hard on the door. It flew open with a *thud*, slamming against the rock on the other side and leaving her staring into the biggest cavern she'd seen down here. In the middle stood a stone altar. Around it, she saw the goat. The deer. The coyote priestess. And a new figure. An old man in a hawk cloak.

She couldn't see the person on the altar, but it had to be her father. The hawk held a dagger above his head, ready to plunge it downward. Every one of them turned their heads towards her, but the adrenaline and the training that she'd learned to rely on started to kick in. It all seemed to slow down. She could see the path forward, knew she could move faster than they could react.

It all happened in a blur. She moved across the room with speed and grace. The deer and the goat reacted first, trying to intercept her, but she slipped past them just as Tanner came through the door and immediately engaged anyone he could reach. She wondered what he actually saw. If he could understand that they weren't skinwalkers.

As the path cleared, she didn't see her father on the altar.

Gabe.

Something in her heart screamed for her to save him. To reconsider all that she'd been told. All that she'd deduced. To trust that her doubts about him could all be traced back to paranoia. She shook off the feelings. The facts were ironclad. He'd betrayed her to this cult. He deserved what he got.

"Do it!" the priestess screamed at the hawk. "Now!"

Miriam saw doubt in that old man's eyes.

"Miriam," she heard from her right. The voice was faint, but unmistakable. A glance confirmed Skylar, sitting on the floor, leaning against the stone. One of his eyes had swollen. Blood caked his mustache and chin, mingled together so completely that Miriam couldn't tell where it had originated. This is who she came for. She could grab him and go.

"Mimi," Gabe said, drawing her attention back to the altar. "*¡Gracias a Dios!* Help me!"

The old man had dropped his arms to his side. He'd ignored the coyote priestess for now, and she didn't like it. Her mouth twisted up in a snarl and her eyes burned with anger. Miriam prepared for a fight, but the priestess instead crossed around the altar and snatched the dagger from the hawk before the old man could react.

Just a knife. Miriam could handle a knife.

Behind her, the struggle continued between Tanner, the deer, and the goat. Macy helped when she could, kicking shins and groins. Jumping on backs. They needed Miriam's help. Skylar needed her help. The hawk, the priestess, and Gabe could carry through with their little ritual.

Miriam rushed towards Skylar just as the priestess did the same. They met at the end of the altar, and

Miriam spun to protect herself. The priestess feinted, striking at Miriam with a half-hearted jab. The move was intended only to distract, though, as the priestess fell to the floor, crawled to Skylar, and put the knife up to his throat.

"Stop," she said. "Or I'll kill him."

Miriam froze.

Behind her, the deer fell against the altar, Tanner pummeling his face. The goat held Macy's arms, even as she struggled to break free.

"Tell your thug to back away," the priestess said, motioning with her head to the fight.

Miriam turned and placed a hand on Tanner's bicep. Not strongly enough to stop his fists from flying into the deer's mask, but enough to make him hesitate. He got in one more good punch before backing away. His chest heaved. His knuckles dripped blood. Miriam couldn't be sure whether it came from him or his opponent. Probably some mix of both. The mask that the deer wore had fractured, revealing a perfectly normal man behind.

Once Tanner stopped the assault, the deer restrained him and dragged him over next to the goat and Macy. Miriam didn't think for a second that the deer had any hope of actually keeping Tanner from breaking free, but it was Skylar's life that held them at bay now. Not the strength of a guy in a deer mask.

"You really have done me a great favor," the priestess said. "I didn't want to lose the young snake so soon." She turned towards Skylar and dug the blade into his chin. A tiny drop of blood formed near the end of the blade. "Up."

Skylar used the wall to push himself back to his feet, wobbling and unsteady as he went.

"Unshackle the snake," the priestess said to the old man.

The hawk complied, slowly fetching a set of keys hanging on the wall and then using them to release Gabe from the altar. Gabe stood up, rubbing his wrists. From the corner of her eye Miriam sensed his gaze, but she refused to look at him.

The priestess escorted Skylar to the altar and forced him to lay upon it. She didn't shackle him in like Gabe.

Miriam fumed. She didn't like this, and she refused to accept it. She just didn't have a way out yet. If she attacked, the priestess would be able to kill Skylar. The goat might be strong enough to break Macy's neck, or at the very least, choke the life out of her. The casualties would be too high.

From behind, she heard a sound of metal being removed from a leather sheath. A sound that no normal person would recognize. A glance back showed that the deer had removed a large bowie knife from a sheath on his thigh. That bastard had taken her knife. He drew it to Tanner's throat. Apparently, the deer also knew his strength wouldn't be able to hold his prey. Now she couldn't even count on Tanner getting away without possibly getting his throat slit.

"I don't envy your choice, girl," the priestess said. "But you can walk away from this."

As she spoke, the priestess glided around the room. She stopped in front of Macy, running her hand through Macy's red hair. She drew her hand back, lightly caressing her fingernails against Macy's dirty face. Next she moved to Tanner, eyeing him up and down as if she meant to eat him. She squeezed one of his biceps and smiled lasciviously.

"Your friends, too. As much as I'd like to keep this one for myself."

After admiring Tanner, the priestess crossed back to Miriam, bravely standing only inches away. Miriam considered a well-timed punch. She could surely take the bitch out in just one hit, but she couldn't be sure that doing so would cause the deer and the goat to stand down. Not to mention Gabe, who would be on her in a heartbeat. She wouldn't be able to overpower him.

The priestess expertly twirled the dagger in her hand, flipping it so that she held the blade, offering the hilt to Miriam. Was this lady offering Miriam a weapon?

Did she want to die?

The odds of escape seemed low, and if everyone she loved was going to die anyway, Miriam would certainly guarantee that the cult leader wouldn't make it out alive, either. She took the dagger quickly, before the priestess changed her mind. She couldn't use it yet, but better to have it than not.

"All you have to do is kill him," the priestess finished, motioning to Skylar.

In the back of her mind, Miriam knew that's where this conversation headed, but she'd remained so focused on possible escape that she hadn't confronted it.

She looked down at her father. He looked weak and old. The machismo and the arrogance had all disappeared. Her heart hurt for him, and while she hated the feeling, she also didn't shy away from it, as she had for the past few years. Now she felt it fully. He'd told her before, but now that he'd been stripped down to his barest form, she could actually see it in his eyes.

The love.

For her.

His voice was hoarse when he spoke. "Don't do it, Miriam. Don't let her win."

Miriam fought the urge to laugh, even as tears welled in her eyes. She thought maybe he'd tell her to end his life to save herself, but no. Of course he wouldn't do that. Not Skylar Brooks. Not her dad. Her dad was a survivor just like her.

She took his hand, holding the dagger loosely in her other, and squeezed. She took a deep breath. She didn't look forward to what she had to do.

Letting go of Skylar's hand, she brought the point of the dagger to her finger and pricked it against her skin. She watched the bead of blood form at the tip of the point. It was sharp. Deadly.

The priestess' face lit up with delight, full of certainty and surety that she'd win. Clearly confident that Miriam would do this to save her friends.

But the priestess was wrong. Win or lose — live or die — Miriam would take the hard road.

In one swift, graceful motion, she jabbed the dagger into the priestess' side. The priestess opened her mouth to speak, the anger of retribution threatening to unfurl from that silver tongue. Maybe to order Tanner or Macy's death.

But before any of that could happen, Miriam swung with all her strength, her fist connecting hard with the priestess' temple. Those wide, angry eyes snapped shut. The priestess' jaw went slack. She crumpled to the ground unconscious, and Miriam prepared for an attack.

Surprisingly, nothing happened. The room fell into shocked silence.

CHAPTER 30

Gabe could hardly believe it. He'd come to save her, but of course Miriam didn't need saving. Not from these kinds of threats, anyway.

With a disgusted face, Miriam threw the ceremonial dagger on the ground next to the priestess. Gabe watched carefully to see what the goat and the deer would do. They stood in shock at first, but when the deer turned towards the goat, Gabe knew that a fight would come. He'd never met Tanner or Macy, but he surmised who they were. The only two people Miriam trusted. Of course they had also come for her.

Tanner processed the situation much faster than Gabe, lowering an elbow into the deer's stomach while simultaneously reaching up and pushing away the knife. A quick spin, and Tanner was free, facing off against an armed foe with nothing but his wits. Macy on the other hand...

The goat gripped his own wrist, barring his forearm against her throat. Macy's face had turned completely red, straining and sputtering, her mouth trying to gasp for air. Gabe threw his snake cloak to the floor and rushed over to save her. Before he got there, he met his own foe — one he didn't even know he had.

A punch grazed his cheek, and when he turned to face his attacker, he got a knee to the stomach. At least she didn't go for the groin. He tried to process the situation. Was Miriam hallucinating now? Who did she think he was?

She stomped on his toe, causing him to stumble backwards, his heel catching on the uneven floor and sending him to the ground. Miriam hovered over him.

"Stay down," she spat. "I'll deal with you in a minute."

With that, she turned and grabbed the goat's forearm. "I got ya, Macy. Hold on."

She pulled and pulled, but the goat held firm. By the time Gabe got back to his feet, Miriam took a different tactic and kicked the goat in the shin. His grip let up enough for Macy to take a ragged breath, but he didn't let her go.

Miriam moved quickly, dodging to the side and pummeling the goat's torso but it only caused him to tighten back up. Macy clawed in vain at his arm. Though not large, the goat was clearly strong.

Tanner busied himself fighting with the deer, both locked in an evenly-matched brawl. Gabe worried that the knife's advantage would ultimately tip the balance, so he chose to help there instead. Maybe Tanner wouldn't attack him.

Gabe couldn't boast the fighting skills of Tanner, so he couldn't quite figure out how to help. He tried to circle around to the back but the deer caught him and kept his stance open enough to anticipate attacks from both of them. Every time Tanner went in for a hit, the deer forced him to recoil with a swipe of the knife, preventing Tanner from landing a meaningful blow. Fists up, Gabe didn't have the confidence that he could dodge the knife, so he circled and bobbed, hoping to distract the deer enough to create an opening.

"Tanner," Tanner said between gasps for air. "You Gabe?"

Hardly the time to talk. Gabe had his hands full just tracking the deer's movements. But he managed to eke out, "Yeah."

Miriam must have told Tanner about him. It warmed his heart to think so. When she came down from the hallucinogens, he looked forward to talking to her. Maybe asking her on a date. His vision blacked out on that thought, as a blinding pain shot up from his sternum. He'd lost focus too long, and the deer had come in for a swipe that Gabe never even saw coming.

He didn't go down, though. His vision came back almost immediately, his hand touching the wound on his chest. His shirt had been sliced open and he could feel the wet blood oozing out from the cut underneath, but it had only been a slash. Painful, but not deep.

At least he'd successfully created the distraction. Tanner hit the deer's hand hard, and the knife skittered across the stone floor. Now, it was a fair fight. Tanner tackled the deer, throwing him to the floor, straddling him and punching him repeatedly in the face. The already-damaged deer mask started to chip away more with every punch, until Tanner's fists started hitting skin. He didn't stop until the deer stopped fighting back.

Gabe checked in on Miriam's status and saw that she'd managed to get Macy away from the goat. Now the two faced off, alternating between trying to grapple each other to the floor and taking shots wherever they could get them. The whole thing played like a boxing match, and the fact that Miriam hadn't lost her balance on that bad ankle seemed impossible. She fought on, as if all of this was perfectly normal.

"You ok?" Tanner asked, motioning to Gabe's chest as he moved towards Macy.

"Y-yeah," Gabe said. "I think I'm ok."

As Tanner checked on Macy, Gabe moved to Miriam just as the goat managed to push her to the floor. Immediately he wrapped his hands around her throat and pressed hard. She bucked and kicked, but his weight held her in place. Gabe broke into a run, reared back one of his feet and kicked the goat in the head as hard as he could. The mask flew off, and Gabe drove a fist straight into the goat's now-bare nose. It must have loosened his grip, because Miriam managed to roll her attacker to the ground. Kneeling over him now, she pummeled him in the face until he threw his hands up.

"P-p-please! Stop!"

Miriam relented, shooting a hateful look towards Gabe before getting back to her feet. The goat stayed down as Tanner moved over to guard him.

Satisfied that Miriam was now safe and unsure whether she'd come down enough from the drugs to trust him, Gabe moved to Skylar who laid on the altar, looking up at the ceiling instead of the chaos surrounding him. He was awake but looked pretty bad, having taken quite a beating. On his lips, though, he wore an unexpected smile.

"We're gonna get help, boss. Don't worry."

Skylar nodded. "I know."

Behind him, Tanner and Miriam, now joined by Macy, shared a few hushed words that Gabe couldn't make out. When Tanner shot him a dangerous warning of a look, Gabe knew that there was something he didn't know. Or understand.

Miriam turned towards him and started her approach. He didn't flatter himself by thinking that she was coming for him. She wanted to see her dad, so Gabe stepped aside.

When she bent down and scooped up the deer's abandoned bowie knife, questions started to form. What did she need a knife for now? All threats had been accounted for. Macy and Tanner were safe. Hector leaned on his cane across the room, having largely avoided everything.

Miriam picked up her speed, crossing the distance between them and leaving Gabe to wonder what was going on. But he didn't have time think too long before he felt cold metal against his throat and the weight of Miriam pressing him against the altar. Not the way he hoped to get close to her. He raised his neck to try to get away from the sharp edge, but she didn't press hard enough to cut him. Not yet.

"Mimi! It's me!" he exclaimed, hoping to knock her out of whatever hallucination she saw.

"I know who you are, traitor."

Traitor? What? Because of the cloak? "No. My uncle. He got me in. So I could save you."

Gabe would have said that the knife couldn't get any closer to his skin without cutting it, but somehow it did. If he moved at all, he'd end up slicing his own throat, so he remained as still as he could.

"Liar," Miriam said, her voice filled with more conviction and emotion than he'd ever heard. "You orchestrated all of this. You brought my dad out here for this messed up ritual."

"No!" Gabe begged, immediately regretting raising his voice as his Adam's apple bobbed against the blade. "I didn't know about *any* of this."

Miriam's eyes narrowed. Was this the drugs, or had someone gotten to her? Convinced her of a lie. He would never betray her.

"Then why did you insist my dad investigate the skinwalkers?"

"What?" Gabe asked. "I mean. I suggested it, yeah. But I was only trying to help. *Tío* and I were talking about all the weird stuff, and he mentioned how he'd heard that they were back, and so..."

Gabe's heart fell to the pit of his stomach. His mouth went dry. Had his uncle set this up? No. Couldn't be. His uncle would never do that to anyone.

The goat suddenly said, "Y-yeah, old m-m-man. W-w-hy don't you tell them the t-t-truth?"

From across the room, Hector's aging voice carried from under his cloak. "I'm sorry, Gabriel."

The knife backed away from Gabe's throat. Just a little. Enough for him to relax some of his muscles without risking his own death.

Hector continued, "I didn't know that it would be like this. I didn't know that it would hurt you."

Miriam let her arm fall away from Gabe's throat and pushed on his bicep. He scrambled away from her before she changed her mind.

"You did this?" she asked the old hawk.

Before answering, the old man regarded Gabe carefully, as if his verbal apology could be strengthened by the conviction in his eyes. Gabe didn't know what to think. Or how to feel, but he knew that his relationship with his *tío* would never be the same.

"It's been a long time in the making," Hector said. "Somehow, over the years, I forgot that I had a choice."

There'd been no time for Gabe to fully process that this man might have killed his mom. He realized now that he'd chosen to believe that his uncle had just told him those things to appease the coyote priestess. That it was all some sort of hazing. He'd been unwilling to believe his uncle capable of that sort of violence. But now... now it seemed possible, and it caused his guts to wrench in on themselves.

"What? So you watched the house? Knew when I'd come?" Miriam seemed more clear-headed now. Some of the rage had dissipated.

"Not me. But them." The old man nodded towards the goat and the deer. "It's been twenty years. The ritual has to happen, or she'll die." He choked out the last few words, "And I love her. She's the only woman I've ever loved."

As Hector finished, Miriam looked down for the priestess and gasped. Gabe followed her gaze and saw only empty ground.

The priestess had vanished.

Miriam jumped back suddenly. "Wait. Where is she?"

Miriam searched the room before returning to the altar. Tanner stayed to guard the goat and the deer, but Macy made a quick sweep of the room herself before shaking her head towards Miriam. Gabe stayed put, unsure of how sudden movement might be punished. The door remained closed. Gabe had a hard time imagining that the priestess had opened it. Even with all the fighting, the door would have been heavy and loud. Impossible to ignore. Perhaps this stone hid a trap door or hidden entrance.

"Gone," Hector said. "Take heart. She won't last long now."

Gabe couldn't see his *tío's* face, but he detected a slight quiver in the voice that told him that his uncle had begun to cry. Gabe didn't know what to do. How to cope with this. His uncle was almost assuredly a murderer. It had been years since they'd lived together, and that distance made it seem a little easier. Gabe knew he could live on his own. But he didn't know if he could deal with the ramifications of this realization. He didn't feel sad or angry. He just felt numb.

"That's a load of bullshit," Miriam said. "How'd she get out of here?"

"Who knows," Hector said. "She can take many forms."

From the altar, Skylar pushed himself into a sitting position. He didn't look much stronger, but the sudden movement seemed odd. The man had been nearly comatose minutes before.

Many forms.

"Mimi," Gabe screamed. "Watch out!"

She turned towards Skylar as he got to his feet. Then there was movement from the other direction. The deer had made it back to his feet, past Tanner, and now rushed Miriam, the sacrificial dagger in his hand. How had he even gotten it?

With Miriam facing towards the altar, she didn't register the deer coming at her. Skylar moved towards her with a speed that Gabe would never have expected, as if he'd drawn on the very last of his reserves to make this move. A lump formed in Gabe's throat as he rushed forward to help. He wouldn't get there in time. Both men would get to her before he could.

The deer yelled an ominous battle cry, drawing back the dagger. Skylar got to Miriam just a few steps before, pulled on her shoulders, spun, and pushed her to the altar. Miriam stumbled backwards, catching herself on the stone.

The deer's trajectory couldn't be changed now. He rammed against Skylar's back, jabbing the dagger deep into his spine. Skylar screamed in pain, falling to his knees. The dagger wrenched itself from the deer's hand as he went down. The evil apparition stood face to face with Miriam.

Gabe stopped in his tracks. The paranoia had gotten to him. For a second, he'd believed that somehow the coyote priestess had taken the form of Skylar.

But no.

Skylar wasn't attacking Miriam.

He was saving her.

CHAPTER 31

"Dad!" Miriam reached out as he went down. He looked like he'd meant to say something, but his eyes went dark as he fell face first on the floor.

No.

No. No. No.

Across from her stood the deer, his human face half-exposed and smiling.

Eliminate the threats, then check the wounded. Skylar taught her that. He would understand.

Fury fueled her every step. If her ankle still hurt, she didn't know it. Not anymore. Now she felt invincible.

When she got to her father's limp body on the floor, she leapt into the air and crashed into the deer's chest. That didn't take him down, so she kneed him in the groin and grabbed his prosthetic arm, ripping it from the leather mount around his back and throwing it to the floor.

He didn't react. He couldn't. She didn't leave him time.

In her other hand, she still held the bowie knife. She could have used it to kill him, but that would be too kind. She'd kill this bastard with her own bare hands. She dropped the knife and continued her assault, driving him backwards. He put his hands up to try to defend his face, so she moved to his chest and his stomach instead. When he tried to fend off those blows, she moved back to his face. The clank of his jaw felt good against her fist.

Barely anything of his mask remained. The hollow eyes and jaw were gone. One of the antlers had broken off. Miriam saw blood on his face. On her fists. She didn't know if it came from him or her. Maybe both. But she didn't care.

Soon, she had him all the way against the cave wall. His arms covering his face, he slid down to the ground, curling himself up into a ball. Smart. This covered all the most important bits. But she didn't stop. She kicked him in the back of the head but her bad ankle didn't like it, robbing her of balance and sending her to the ground beside him. She didn't let the fall deter her, though, switching to her fists to pummel him wherever she could get a shot in. Each blow came with less force, until she knew she wasn't really hurting him anymore. But it felt good, so she kept going anyway.

When someone grabbed her by the arms, she fought the grip, desperate to dole out more punishment. But the force against her was strong. Stronger than she. It could only be Tanner. After failing to break free a few more times, she noticed the tears streaming out of her eyes.

Was... was her dad dead?

She couldn't believe it. Refused to believe it. Not now. Not when they were on the path to making things better. She wouldn't be able to handle this. Wouldn't be able to recover from it.

All at once, the rage gave way to fear and grief. She turned and buried her face into a warm, muscular embrace. She muffled her sobs, but couldn't hide them completely, her chest heaving up and down. Arms went around her back and rubbed, trying to offer support, but they wouldn't be able to. No amount of support would save her now.

"He's alive!" Tanner said from across the room.

Wait. If Tanner was across the room, then...

Miriam backed up and felt a shock of rage and embarrassment as she stared up into Gabe's chocolate eyes. She wanted to be mad. Wanted to hold on to the hatred she'd felt for him earlier, but she just didn't have the strength to sort out what she believed about him right now.

She fought through the pain, pushed herself up, and moved past Gabe to see Skylar sitting up, his back against the altar, slowly taking ragged breaths. Macy and Tanner knelt beside him.

Miriam laughed through the tears. Not out of humor, but out of relief. Of course, Skylar wouldn't die that easily. He never made anything easy.

She looked around the room to assess any more threats. The goat cowered in the corner, despite having lost his guard. The deer was alive, but in no condition to run. She didn't know what to do about Hector, but he didn't seem to present a threat.

Nor did Gabe. For the moment.

She looked at him standing back, his arms wrapped around himself as if to fend off frigid air. Lines of worry stretched across his face, and she realized in that moment that she'd been truly deceived by the coyote priestess. He'd saved her from the goat. Helped them quell this threat. Gabe never meant to hurt her. Or Skylar. She tried to remember him from before her capture, but it all seemed distant and vague now, with only the hint of something that might have been growing.

"Macy, Tanner. Get Skylar some help," Miriam said. "Gabe. We need to find that priestess."

"You won't find her," Hector said.

Though Miriam didn't want to believe it, she knew somehow that Hector spoke the truth. Too much time had passed, and the priestess would know these tunnels better than any of them could. Something warned her that it was more than that. That the priestess had shapeshifted into some animal, but that just couldn't be true. Miriam could believe that ancient animals had evaded detection for hundreds or even thousands of years, but she would not believe in magic. A girl had to draw a line somewhere.

"We should find Brynn, too," Macy said.

Tanner helped Skylar to his feet, but Miriam didn't like the way her dad's ankles turned in on each other. It was only temporarily, she told herself. They'd get him to a hospital and everything would be fine.

Yet when Tanner took the first step without any assistance from Skylar's own strength, she knew it wouldn't be. The knife-wound had gone too deep. In the wrong place. She shared a look of concern with Tanner before he scooped Skylar up into his arms, easily taking the weight of it.

Macy followed Tanner out of the chamber, leaving Miriam and Gabe to contend with the deer and the goat. And Hector. They had too many loose ends to tie up. They didn't have the luxury of launching a hunt for the priestess.

"Can you carry the deer?" Miriam asked Gabe.

"Yeah. I think so."

The strain looked harder for him than Tanner, but Gabe managed nonetheless. The deer's head lolled and bobbed, dropping in and out of consciousness. Briefly,

Miriam felt guilty for the damage she'd inflicted, but told herself it was necessary. The goat complied readily to Miriam's demands, though she kept the bowie knife just in case.

Hector followed. Quietly and easily. As if resigned to his fate.

For the first time, Miriam wondered how Gabe would take all of this. But there would be time for that soon. They would sort out this whole mess. Like reasonable adults. Part of her wanted to just send him back to Rose Valley with Skylar. It wouldn't be that hard to push him out of her life. She didn't need more friends. Worrying about Macy and Tanner was hard enough.

As they plodded slowly up the stony path, though, Miriam found the clarity to admit to herself that her life had become intertwined with Gabe's. He meant something to her. She just couldn't be sure what. Something different and new. Foreign and exciting.

And scary.

***

The wait seemed impossibly long, but now all of Gray's Point was bathed in flashing blue and red lights. Ambulances, fire trucks, police. The whole nine yards. They'd all come from a town over, given that the law enforcement in Gray's Point currently sat tied up in the desert sand. Not even Hector protested his bondage. Gabe sat with the old man now, having a conversation that Miriam felt sure was uncomfortable and painful. As curious as she was about the conversation, she gave them space to work it out on their own.

Before long, the "skinwalkers" had all been loaded up into squad cars. Skylar was whooshed away in an ambulance. They asked her if she wanted to go along, but the thought frightened her. He seemed so frail. The mature thing would have been to stick by his side. To be with him if he died en route, but she couldn't stomach the thought of that, so she stayed behind and let Tanner and Macy go instead.

They hadn't found Brynn yet, but the Jeep was gone, which meant she'd probably fled to safety. Once they got back to civilization, Miriam promised herself that she'd call the hospitals until she made sure.

Some of the police and rescue stayed behind to search the caves—just in case. No doubt, there'd be a ton of stuff to uncover down there. Hopefully a lot of evidence to make sure this cult had drawn its very last breath. Though the EMTs recommended she take an ambulance to the hospital, Miriam refused the help. She was okay. A few stings and bites. A busted ankle. Scrapes and bruises. Nothing compared to the beating she'd taken from the kraken.

One helpful officer gave them a ride back to the gas station, where they could find Macy's old beat up Sentra.

"You think they'll ever find her?" Gabe asked as they climbed inside.

"I don't know," Miriam said. "I hope so."

She didn't feel compelled to find the coyote priestess. Her job was to hunt monsters, not lunatics. She was happy to leave this one to the police. It bothered her, not understanding how the priestess had gotten away, but that cave was full of traps, twists, and turns. She didn't have to struggle very hard to think up ways to escape the place.

Miriam drove. Her and Gabe alone. In awkward silence. She didn't mind, though. She had grown quite accustomed to awkward silence.

"I'm sorry," Gabe said suddenly. "I never wanted any of this to happen."

"It's ok," she said, not really sure yet whether she meant it. It was just the easiest thing to say.

"My uncle found me when I was trying to find a way in. He offered a way to find you, and I took it."

Fat lot of good it did. In the end, Gabe hadn't saved her. But she was starting to accept that he'd tried, and maybe that meant something. Maybe for a girl like her, she couldn't hope for a guy to do anything but try. Miriam had begun to learn that she wasn't always an easy girl to save.

"Why?" she asked, surprising herself with the question.

"Why what?"

"Why work so hard to save me? I can handle myself."

"I know," he said with a chuckle. "Oh I know."

"Why then?"

It's almost as if he didn't want to answer the question. Certainly, the prospect of the answer frightened her, but at the same time, she needed to hear it. She didn't know what she'd do with the answer, but, like all unknown things, she'd figure that out when she got there.

"I guess I... I mean, I barely know you, but..."

Something foreign and warm filled up Miriam's chest. It felt strange, as if she should suppress it or rip it from her bosom. But she sat with it as they drove. She vaguely understood what it was, but it would take a while to fully process.

Gabe continued with a new thought: "After we get all this sorted out. Get everyone safe. Wanna, maybe, go out some time?"

"Like on a date?" she asked.

"Yeah. Like that," he said.

Miriam had never been on a date. She'd never had a boyfriend. Never held hands or kissed anyone. Never really even wanted to. Not because she never envisioned those things for herself, but because the emotional effort required felt so distant and impossible. It needed to be worth the potential pain when she decided to go down that path. She didn't know if Gabe would be worth it.

She tried to concoct some meaningful response that would somehow capture all the hope and trepidation, but instead just answered, "Ok."

CHAPTER 32

Miriam made the short drive across Rose Valley until she came upon the *Skylar Brooks Center for Cryptozoological Research*.

Such a mouthful.

Given her dad's predilection towards grandiosity, she expected a state-of-the-art complex. Instead she found a modest, wood-framed building, likely converted from an old ranch-style house. Still, he'd given it a solid once-over, with fresh paint, new windows, and a parking lot that surely hadn't been there before. And, what she assumed to be the newest addition of all—wheelchair access ramps.

The lot was empty except for a yellow van, so she parked the Sentra in the nearest legal spot to the entrance. She took a deep breath before flipping the visor down to look at herself in the mirror. Her makeup was understated. A faint hint of eyeliner. Some colored lip gloss. It took every ounce of her will to resist Macy's insistence that she go for bolder colors. But Miriam wasn't a bold-colored gal. He would just have to accept that about her if this thing had any hope of working out.

She stepped out of the car and surveyed the building. Other than the large sign at the entrance to the parking lot, one would be forgiven for thinking this might be someone's summer house. A small sign on the front door said "OPEN," with a placard underneath announcing the hours of operation. Miriam pushed her way through the door, only vaguely registering the bell that sounded, and stood at the entrance to take in the sights.

While the outside displayed a certain humble charm, the inside was anything but. Marble tile floors stretched across a large room with artifacts, newspaper clippings, and paintings of all sorts of cryptids. A quick scan showed space for Bigfoot, the Loch Ness Monster, and the locally famous Beast of Rose Valley. And in the center of the room stood what appeared to be a temporary exhibit, large and bold. When Miriam read the title, her heart stopped in her chest.

The Kraken.

As she shuffled over to it, she realized that the exhibit didn't pertain so much to the legend of the creature, but to her specific expedition in Cape Madre. Attached were articles about her encounter, some she'd never even seen. A photo from her news appearance accompanied a carefully-written bio outlining her many achievements and skills. She pumped her knuckles, attempting to expend the overwhelming rush of emotion. In the cave, she thought maybe her father had been so scared of death that he'd said the things he thought he should. But maybe he hadn't said those things out of desperation. Maybe, over all this time, he'd actually been... proud?

"One of the greatest cryptozoologists of our time," a voice came from behind.

Miriam spun, and smiled at her dad, her eyes moistening. She supposed a wheelchair gave him the element of surprise. She hadn't even heard him roll in. She tried to hide the sorrow she felt seeing him that way. He'd never walk again, and though he seemed resigned to it, she still wasn't sure she could handle the thought. In some ways, Skylar Brooks almost seemed gone forever, destined to do nothing but run a museum in a tiny Texas town.

"How long has this been up?" she asked, some part of her insisting that surely he'd done this after the run-in with the cult at Gray's Point.

"A while," he said, rolling closer to her. "As soon as we heard. Can't really have a cryptozoology museum without acknowledging one of the greatest finds of the day."

Sound logic, she supposed, but that didn't explain what seemed like an over-focus on her, specifically.

Eager not to let the moment get too sentimental, Miriam changed the subject. "Sorry to hear about Brynn."

Skylar frowned. "Yeah. I really had high hopes for her, but she says she's not interested in this line of work anymore."

When Miriam didn't have a response, he continued, "She's still in town. Got a job at the Rose Valley Reporter, if you can believe it."

"As a journalist?" Miriam asked.

"Not yet. I think they have her doing research."

"Makes sense. I still don't understand how she drove herself to the hospital after all that."

Skylar shrugged. "Me neither. She says she doesn't even remember doing it."

"Weird."

The conversation fell into silence. Miriam spent the time studying the exhibit. Skylar sat in his wheelchair nearby. Everything felt different now. With finals done and summer upon her, she finally had time to dedicate to building her cryptid hunting business with Macy and Tanner. She looked forward to it, but with her dad out of the game, she felt the weight of his legacy weighing heavily on her shoulders.

"You look nice," Skylar said, breaking the silence.

She looked down at her brand new blouse and well-fitting jeans. Macy helped her pick them out specifically for this. Not knowing any better, Miriam went along with it. She supposed such an occasion called for a little special attention, but being so deliberate about her preparations just made the whole idea even scarier.

"Thanks," Miriam said, feeling the heat in her cheeks. "Macy."

Skylar nodded, understanding. Just then, the front bell rang. Her heart fluttered, and a lump formed in her throat. For all the nerves and adrenaline she'd felt in her life, this surge of emotion felt new. Her dad's knowing smile didn't help.

"Hey, Mimi," Gabe said from across the room. "Long time."

Only a month, really. And they'd talked frequently over that period. She'd worried that when she saw him again, she wouldn't feel the same attraction. That maybe the stress of Gray's Point had caused her to see things that weren't there.

But the time hadn't taken that away. It had multiplied it. For the first time in her life, Miriam thought that maybe she might actually like someone. *Like*-like.

Ugggh. Now she was one of those girls.

"You kids have fun," Skylar said. "I'd tell you to have her home by ten, but something tells me I don't get to tell her what to do."

Maybe it was the fear of the impending date. Maybe it was the exceptionally flattering exhibit all about her, centered in the museum. Or maybe even the overwhelming mix of emotions that she couldn't handle. But, without a thought, Miriam bent over and hugged her dad. He seemed surprised at first, taking a moment before wrapping his arms around her in return. It had been a lot of years since... well, that.

Maybe, this is what it felt like to be happy.

Embarrassed, she backed away and gave Skylar a half-smile. "Umm. I'll stop back by before I leave town."

"Promise?" he asked.

"Promise."

By the time she turned, Gabe had crossed the distance between them and stood only inches away, his welcoming smile and warm presence filling her every sense. He smelled good; a far cry from their days sweating in the desert together.

In an old-fashioned move, he offered an elbow. "Shall we?"

She only nodded and curled her hand around his strong bicep. She'd work up the courage to say something to him eventually, but she needed to process it all first. What it meant for her. For her life. For her job. Though people went on dates every day, to Miriam this step felt incredibly abnormal.

But the abnormal was beginning to feel normal. The constant of change followed her. Every unbelievable encounter made her think that maybe she'd be able to relax, but Miriam finally realized that it was time to stop trying. Her life would be hectic. Dangerous. Frightening and death-defying sometimes. She'd never be normal, like Macy. Or naturally chill, like Tanner. Or even big-hearted, like Gabe.

She was just Miriam Brooks. A quirky girl with a need to hunt monsters.

And, for once, she felt totally okay with that.

EPILOGUE

She looked horrible. The mirror reflected a shadow of someone she barely remembered. Sometimes, she felt a glimmer of hope. A light at the end of the tunnel. But then she'd sink again. She didn't eat much. Slept even less. Somehow, she managed to hold down her new job at the Rose Valley Reporter as a staff researcher. Truth was, she didn't have much to research in the sleepy little town.

Brynn splashed some water on her face and patted it dry with a scratchy paper towel. Today, she had hope. A little bit. She knew she needed help, but she didn't have the money to procure it, until she found out about this place from a flier in the mail. A new clinic. An unproven therapist. But they offered her a free session.

This was her lifeline.

Convinced that she looked as good as possible in her current state, Brynn made her way back to the empty waiting room and collapsed into one of the two chairs. The walls were stark. The lighting was dim. Calming music echoed in the small space, agitating Brynn more than relaxing her.

Fragments of memory had started coming back to her, but she still didn't have the whole picture. She'd been sure she'd die up there, but someone had helped her up.

Or something.

In her broken memory, she pictured a dog lifting her to her feet, but that didn't make any sense. Whatever—or whoever—it was got her down the path and back to the Jeep. Had Brynn driven herself to the hospital? She couldn't really remember, but it's what she'd told everyone. The mysterious Samaritan had disappeared.

This therapist would help her piece it all back together.

Brynn haphazardly reached down to her purse on the floor and slid her hand into the pocket reserved for Gabe's mother's journal. She should have turned it over. Admitted that she'd found it. But she didn't. She kept it with her. Always. Sometimes, she thumbed through it. It held a power over her that she couldn't justify. There was more to it than just the last words of a poor immigrant. A puzzle, of sorts. But Brynn hadn't cracked it yet.

It comforted her to touch it. Gabe didn't really deserve to have it anyway. He hadn't called even once since she'd quit working for Skylar. If he knew how far she'd fallen, though... Would he call her then?

Fresher air *whooshed* into the room as the door across from her parted to reveal the therapist standing in the doorway. A woman. Neither short, nor tall, with dark, inky eyes and raven hair. Though they fit the woman well, her clothes looked like they'd come from another century. Brynn tried to assess the therapist's age, but came up empty. She seemed almost ageless, though the makeup slathered on her face surely hid some of the years.

"Brynn!" The woman's eyes turned up when she smiled.

This was Brynn's way out of this hole. Her savior.

"Come in, my child," the woman said. "Let me ease your pain."

Brynn walked through the doorway, past a rack with a strange-looking fur coat, and sat primly on the couch across from a wing-backed chair. The therapist closed the door softly, sat in the chair, and trained her vacuous eyes on Brynn's. Brynn tried to hold the gaze, but ultimately turned her hazel eyes to the floor.

The silence hung, urging Brynn to look back up. When she did, she met the smiling face of her new therapist. Brynn returned the smile. It had been a while since she'd done that. It felt good.

"Now," the therapist said. "Tell me about your family."

ACKNOWLEDGEMENTS

We've got a well-oiled "Lorestalker" machine going on here! Three books in one year seems crazy (and probably unsustainable), but it wouldn't have been possible without a great team behind me that's responsive, professional, and just plain good at what they do. Evolved Publishing is such a great partner in bringing these books to life, specifically Mike Robinson, Richard Tran, and Dave Lane (aka Lane Diamond). I know they've been the first tip of the hat at the end of every book, but it's with good reason.

I'd also like to thank love. Well, actually, I'd like to thank my critique partner's insistence on it. The fact that romance didn't really make it into *The Kraken of Cape Madre* hurt Mistie's soul, so she was ready and on point with all of her critiques of this one. As always, Mistie took the time to really understand my characters, gently helping to perfect them. I think she may have a crush on Gabe, actually, now that I think about it. She also seemed to take way too much fiendish delight in pointing out that I have no idea how twenty-somethings talk. Yes. I'm old.

And then my beta readers... always willing and ready. I didn't get this book done as early as I would have liked, but they came through and read it almost immediately so that I could get my schedule back on track. Rachael's innate ability to spot typos and inconsistencies was of utmost value. Amanda, while always providing actionable feedback, took on an extra role this time as my Spanish expert. If the Spanish is wrong in this book, you should probably still blame me, but I might secretly blame her. And

Steve. He's been my best friend for thirty plus years now, so he pulls no punches and is nerdy enough to know mundane details that make the book better (like schooling me on what ranch fences are actually made of).

Then there's my wife. Beta readers and critique partners may eventually move on, but Akaemi (hopefully) never will. She acts as cheerleader, champion, saleswoman, and beta reader. It's a lot of hats, and every one of them helps to fill in the gaps of what I'm capable of.

I set out to write three books as quickly as I could, and I did it thanks to everyone above and the encouragement of countless family and friends. The "Lorestalker" fan base may be small for now, but it is mighty. Thank you to everyone who's ever taken the time to really learn about my books. I'm looking forward to what we can all accomplish together in the future.

ABOUT THE AUTHOR

J.P. Barnett grew up in a tiny Texas town where the list of possible vocations failed to include published author. In second grade, he worked harder than any other student to deliver a story about a tiger cub who singlehandedly saved the U.S. Military, earning him a shiny gold star and a lifelong appreciation of telling a good story.

Fast forwarding through decades of schooling and a career as a software engineer, J.P. Barnett stepped away from it all to get back to his first real passion. Years of sitting at a keyboard gifted him with some benefit, though, including blazing fast typing hands and a full tank of creativity.

As a child, J.P. consumed any book he could get his hands on. The likes of Stephen King, Michael Crichton, and Dean Koontz paved the bookshelves of his childhood, providing a plethora of fantastical and terrifying tales that he read way too early in life. Though the effect these books had on his psyche could be called into question, these masters of storytelling managed to warp his mind in just the perfect way to spin a fun yarn or two.

J.P. currently resides in San Antonio with his wife and hellion of a cat, both of whom look at him dubiously with some frequency.

For more, please visit J.P. Barnett online at:
Website: www.JPBarnett.com
Twitter: @JPBarnett
Facebook: JPBarnett.Author
Instagram: JPBarnett.Author

WHAT'S NEXT?

J.P. Barnett always has at least one book in the works, including the fourth book in the "Lorestalker" series. Please stay tuned to developments and plans by subscribing to his newsletter at the link below.

www.JPBarnett.com/Newsletter/

MORE FROM EVOLVED PUBLISHING

We offer great books across multiple genres, featuring hiqh-quality editing (which we believe is second-to-none) and fantastic covers.

As a hybrid small press, your support as loyal readers is so important to us, and we have strived, with tireless dedication and sheer determination, to deliver on the promise of our motto:
QUALITY IS PRIORITY #1!

Please check out all of our great books, which you can find at this link:
www.EvolvedPub.com/Catalog/

Thank you!

CPSIA information can be obtained
at www.ICGtesting.com
Printed in the USA
BVHW041432230323
661010BV00005B/202